Ma
Call of the Elements
Book One

Yvette Bostic

Acknowledgement

I'd like to start by saying, while there are some references to places and events, any similarities to specific people are purely coincidental.

I hope you enjoy the beginning of the *Call of the Elements Series*. I had a blast writing this tale and allowing the characters to run wild with their own stories.

Book 2 - *Vampire's Crucible,* and Book 3 - *Elemental's Domain* are both live on Amazon.

I want to say thank you to the people who've helped me throughout this process. My husband has been my encouragement, as well as the perfect sounding board and first-draft proof reader. I could not have done it without his positive attitude and patience. Thank you to my wonderful editor, Hannah at Between the Lines Editorial (www.btleditorial.com). She is an extremely talented young woman who's also a joy to work with.

Also, a huge shout out to my proofreader, Aryl Shanti (https://www.facebook.com/ArylsAuthorServices)

And thank you to Aleksandra Klepacka (https://www.facebook.com/AlissandraArt/), the very gifted young artist who created my cover art.

Thank you to my very gracious beta readers. Your comments and opinions about the characters, events and time lines make all the difference!

And last but not least, thank you to my readers! You're the reason I continue to write.

Books in the *Light in the Darkness Series*:
Light's Dawn: A Novella
Light's Rise-Book 1
Light's Eyes-Book 2
Light's Fall-Book 3

Chapter 1

I shuffled up the last flight of steps to my fourth-floor apartment, exhausted from the hours of endless walking through the streets of Vegas. The apartment complex had an elevator, but I'd already been stuck in it twice and had no desire to experience it again. Reaching my oh-so-cheap paradise, I slid the backpack from my shoulder, digging around until I found my keys.

Locking the door was truly pointless. The flimsy thing wouldn't keep out a determined burglar and my building had several, but the false sense of security was born of habit. I kicked the door closed with my foot and tossed my keys on the counter in the small kitchen.

Two rooms defined my apartment: the living room and the bathroom. A second-hand day bed filled the far wall, serving as both a bed and sofa. The building's maintenance guy who lived next door surprised me one day with four old crates and a wooden door that he fashioned into a desk. It was also dual-purpose, masquerading as a dining table. My budget didn't include money for cable or internet, so the old tube-style television, also supplied by my friendly neighbor, sat silent on one corner.

The only extravagance I allowed myself was my trac-phone. I'd upgraded it to a smartphone from the old flip-style I'd kept for the last four years, not caring that the model was already three years old. It was cheap and a smartphone. It was also before I lost my most recent job.

One of the customers caught a glimpse of me when my scarf slipped off my head. His look of revulsion sealed my fate. Ten minutes later, my boss' voice boomed from the walkie-talkie hanging on my belt, telling me to meet her in the office. I knew what was coming. As long as the customers didn't see me, I could keep my job. But when the first one complained about the ugly, deformed girl touching their precious stuff, it was over.

That was a week ago. Today, I spent five hours applying for every open position that didn't require face-to-face interaction with Vegas' massive tourist population.

My favorite artist's song startled me from my self-pity, until I remembered it was my new ringtone. I didn't recognize the number on the screen, but I answered it anyway figuring what the hell. If it was an answer to one of my applications, I'd be cheery and agreeable. If it was a telemarketer, I'd invite them into a dark ennui to leave them wishing for death. I was nothing if not adaptable.

"Hello?" I asked tentatively.

"Ms. Johnson?" The man's voice was strong and confident, unlike my own.

"Yes."

"This is Jack, from The Sanguis Casino. We'd like you to come in for an interview."

I could barely contain my excitement. I'd never got a call the same day.

"Of course," I squeaked, then cleared my throat. "When do you want me to come in?"

"Can you be here in an hour?"

"Absolutely!"

"One of the girls will meet you at the employee entrance."

"Thank you, very much!"

A soft click ended the call without the traditional, 'You're welcome' or 'Good bye', but I didn't care. It was an interview. My rent was due next week, and my empty bank account screamed to be fed.

I immediately called my only friend.

"AJ, I can't really talk right now."

"Guess what, Sharon?" I said, not allowing her to stifle my enthusiasm. I knew she was at work, but her job revolved around being on the phone. One more call wouldn't really matter.

"The maintenance guy brought you a working TV?" Sharon asked.

"I have an interview at The Sanguis," I replied, ignoring her question.

"Oh my God, AJ! That's great!" Sharon squealed. "You can do this, girl. Don't let them talk down to you. Stand your ground and tell them how hard a worker you are."

Tears pooled my eyes and threatened to spill.

"Thanks," I replied. "You always know what I need."

"Call me as soon as you're done, girl."

"I will."

"Good luck!"

"Thanks."

I dropped my phone on the counter next to my keys. I had half an hour to try to make myself into something I wasn't. My enthusiasm disappeared completely.

I pulled down the large piece of cardboard covering my bathroom mirror, my hand shaking wildly.

"Don't be stupid. It's the same image you've lived with your entire life."

I snorted at my fears and snatched the cardboard from the mirror. Small, icy blue eyes stared back at me, peeking out from behind the multicolored scarf wound around my head. I pulled the corner of the colorful fabric, revealing my bulbous jawline and features that were so close together they could fit inside a coffee cup. My large nose sat on top of lips so thin they were barely there. My long, pale forehead ended in pure white hair that I cut short every few weeks. I didn't bother trying to style it when my scarves always covered the tangled mess.

"There's no point. I'll just keep the scarf."

Tears pooled in my eyes again as I replaced the cardboard, hiding the monster in the mirror. I hated that even I couldn't see the person behind my scarf.

~~~~~~~~~~~~~~~~~~~~~~

I tentatively knocked on the door to the employee entrance of the Sanguis Casino, waiting several moments before it silently swung open. A tall, thin woman with dark, loose curls and deep brown eyes stood in the open space. I cleared my throat and straightened my shoulders, trying not to feel inferior to the tall beauty looking down at me.

"I'm here for an interview," I stated, my voice quivering with uncertainty.

The woman looked down her pointed nose but didn't move.

"You're rather short for an entertainer," she said in a high-pitched tone. "I didn't know we had any other positions open."

"I applied for housekeeping assistant," I explained, craning my neck to look up. I was used to it, but it was never comfortable. The only reason I reached five feet tall was because of my shoes. "Jack called and said he wanted to meet with me." I realized Jack never gave his full name; just Jack. I should have been addressing him as 'Mr. So and So.'

"I see." The woman turned and disappeared into the darkened hallway.

I wasn't sure if I was supposed to follow her or not. She seemed to dismiss me, almost immediately, leaving that all-too-familiar sense of rejection hanging between us. I threw back my shoulders in defiance. I wouldn't be rejected today,
~~~~~~~~~~~~~~~~~~~~~~

so I followed her, pulling the door closed behind me. Soft lights lined the floor, illuminating the plush carpet beneath my feet, but not providing enough light to see the art on the walls as I passed by. Who would hang pictures on the wall that no one could see? Maybe the same person who went out of their way to elaborately decorate the employee entrance.

My escort stopped at a large, wooden door and tapped lightly. Without waiting for a reply, she pushed it open and stood back.

"Enjoy your interview," she said, baring her bright, white teeth.

"Thank you."

I slid past her and into the room, and my mouth dropped open. I was immediately grateful for the scarf that covered it. Low lighting circled the room but didn't hide its extravagance. The same thick carpet from the hall covered the floor. Small groupings of artwork decorated the walls, and every surface supported an intricately designed sculpture. I felt like I'd stepped back in time a hundred years. Everything had to be a priceless antique or an expensive replica.

My gaze finally settled on a large, ornate desk occupying the center of the room. My face flushed with embarrassment as the man behind the desk stared at me. He was incredibly handsome with carefully combed, dark brown hair and equally proportioned features, so unlike my own.

"Sorry," I stammered. "Your office is beautiful."

"Yes," his low voice drifted across the space between us, drawing me towards him. "Everything I keep is beautiful."

His rich, hypnotic voice pulled me forward. I stopped at the low-backed chair in front of his desk, not realizing I'd even moved. But I hadn't lost all my senses. I knew what I was, and he said he wanted beauty. "Then I should leave," I mumbled.

"No, you are exactly where you're supposed to be Ms. Johnson," he replied, indicating the chair. "Please, sit down."

I watched him warily as I sat on the edge of the flowered fabric covering the seat, uncomfortable under his gaze.

"You've applied for the housekeeping assistant position," he continued. "Do you have any training or experience?"

I looked down at my shaking fingers and took a deep breath. Had he not read my employment history? "Yes, I've worked in several of the hotels here in Vegas."

"And why are you not still with them?" His tone didn't carry an accusation, just curiosity.

I heard him shift in his chair, and I looked up. Eyes the same color as the woman who escorted me held mine for several long moments. I tugged at the scarf that concealed all but my own eyes.

"My appearance upsets the guests," I replied reluctantly, knowing I couldn't avoid it. "But as long as I remain out of sight..."

He held up one finger, and I snapped my lips shut. "Can you start tomorrow?" he asked.

This was too good to be true. Was he really offering me a job without calling references or a background check?

"Of course. Just tell me what time to be here," I responded before he changed his mind.

He raised an eyebrow as he pulled a folder from the drawer to his left. He pushed it across the desk and leaned back. "Fill out these forms. Be back at six tomorrow evening. I'll tell the staff to be expecting you."

"Thank you very much," I said, reaching for the manila folder.

Jack's hand was on mine before I realized what happened. A jolt of electricity sparked between us, and I snatched my hand back. A smile spread across his handsome face as he stood.

"Sorry," I whispered. "Too much static buildup from the carpet, I guess." I stood, grabbing the folder. I sounded so stupid.

"Yes, it happens frequently." He moved from around his side of the desk and towards the door. "Let me see you out."

As soon as I emerged onto the sidewalk out front, I called my bestie.

"Sharon, you won't believe it!" I yelled into my phone as I walked towards the nearest bus stop. "I start tomorrow!"

"AJ, I'm so happy for you," my friend replied. "We should celebrate. I'm on my way home now, let's meet at Sandy's in half an hour for dinner. My treat."

I could almost hear the smile in her voice.

"See you there."

I looked at my ten-dollar wrist watch. Six thirty. Instead of getting on the bus, I decided to walk the few blocks over to Sandy's Diner. It was a small, local shop, not normally frequented by tourists. Its location on the northwest side of Vegas made it inconvenient for people who wanted to experience the more luxurious hotels and shows.

It was perfect for me. Cheap. The owner knew my foster parents before they left me and Vegas behind. Sandy's pity was irritating, but it kept me fed.

"Hi, AJ," Sandy's voice greeted in a croak earned from decades of smoking. "Is Sharon joining you this evening?"

"Hi, Sandy. Yes, I'll have the usual."

Her bleach blond ponytail bobbed up and down as she wrote a ticket and hung on it on a peg behind her.

I made my way to the smallest table at the far end of the bar, the one I felt most comfortable at, hidden from the rest of the customers. I dropped the folder on the wobbly table and hung my bag on the back of the chair. The waitress rounded the corner a few moments later.

"So, what's got you smiling today?" she asked, placing a glass of water in front of me.

"Is it that obvious?" I asked, my hand instinctively checking to make sure the scarf was still in place; it was.

She winked. "Only to those who look."

"I start a new job tomorrow," I said, excitement bubbling in my core.

"Good for you! Where at?"

"The Sanguis," I replied, watching her expression. It was one of the oldest casinos but still in good condition. "In housekeeping."

"I'm happy for you," she responded, placing a hand on her hip. "Dinner's on me tonight. I'll bring you the special: chicken fried steak and mashed potatoes. You need more than two eggs and toast."

She walked away before I could answer, but I smiled. I might not have much in life, but I was grateful for both Sandy and Sharon. I turned back to the stack of papers and focused my attention on filling out the direct deposit form.

"The most important one," I mumbled.

"I agree."

I jumped and looked up to find a man standing next to me. My small eyes widened as I took in his tall frame covered in black, skinny-jeans and a black t-shirt. The corded muscles in his arms flexed despite his relaxed posture. The stranger's long, black hair fell to the left, revealing shaved sides beneath. He looked good in Goth, but what was he doing standing in front of my table? His thick, dark eyebrows shadowed the brown eyes watching me with curiosity.

"May I join you?" he asked quietly.

I shook my head, grateful for the scarf covering my reddening face. No one ever joined me except Sharon. "I'm expecting a friend."

"I'll make room for her when she arrives." He sat down in the chair across from me, uninvited.

My discomfort turned to anger. How did he know I was waiting for a girlfriend and not a boyfriend? Did he just assume from my appearance that no man in his right mind would join me? I frowned and tugged at my scarf, making sure it was still in place. Why wouldn't he?

"I'm not really interested in company right now," I said, shifting under his intense gaze.

"I'll wait for you to finish your paperwork," he replied, leaning back in the old metal chair.

I closed the folder and rested my pen on top of it. "What do you want?"

"You, of course," he replied candidly.

I was speechless. It was obviously a lie, no one wanted me for anything, not even a bad thing. I shook my head. "Nice try. What do you really want? I have no money or anything of value."

"You have no idea how much you're worth, princess." He leaned towards me, resting his elbows on the table and intertwining his fingers. "My informant was fairly descriptive, but seeing you in person..."

"I'm not..." I snapped my mouth closed when Sandy rounded the corner with a tray balanced on the palm of her hand.

"Here you go," she said, arranging the plates on the small table. "I swear, Sharon'll be late for her own funeral." She chuckled. "Do you think she'll want the special?"

I looked from Sandy to the man across from me, who was no longer there. An empty chair occupied the space. Had

I imagined the conversation? How did he leave without Sandy noticing?

"AJ, are you okay?"

I swallowed hard. "Yeah, just overwhelmed and maybe a little nervous."

"You'll do great." Sandy's genuine smile eased my anxiety a little. I rubbed my eyes with the back of my hand and adjusted my scarf.

"Thanks, Sandy. You should probably wait until Sharon arrives to find out what she wants. She changes her mind too much for me to keep up."

"Ain't that the truth." Sandy tucked the empty tray under her arm and walked away.

I lowered the edge of the scarf covering my nose and mouth, then picked up my fork. I glanced nervously at the empty chair, waiting for my imagination to conjure up another strange man. When it didn't, I turned to my dinner. The chicken cut easily, and a smile spread across my face. I couldn't remember the last time I had anything other than eggs or cereal. The first bite was heavenly. I closed my eyes and chewed as slow as I could, relishing the tender chicken, crispy breading, and creamy gravy.

When I opened my eyes, I nearly choked. The stranger sat across from me once again, an irritating grin turning up his too-perfect lips.

"What the hell?" I grabbed my scarf, trying to cover my features.

"Don't stop eating because of me," he replied. "You need some weight on your bones."

"Get away from me," I demanded, "before I scream."

"And I would be gone before you opened your mouth."

I glared at him, trying to tamp down my fear. Most people went out of their way to ignore me, and I did my best accommodate them.

"What do I have to do to make you go away?" I asked.

"Nothing," he replied, his grin growing wider. "I'll be in touch." He winked at me, pushed himself to his full height and walked away.

I turned in my chair and watched him until he disappeared around the corner, then let out the breath I didn't realize I'd been holding. My heart thudded against my ribs, and my hands shook. What did he mean about my worth? I was nothing. Did he intend to pawn me off as some freak in a creepy side show? Did he plan to kidnap me? With the way he disappeared, would I be able to avoid him? And how did he even do that?

Sharon's bubbly voice interrupted my dark thoughts. "Hey, girl! You didn't order for me?"

I looked up at my friend and couldn't stop my tears. Sharon dropped into the chair across from me.

"What's wrong, AJ?" She reached across the table and took my hands, squeezing them gently, her happiness instantly replaced by worry.

"I don't know," I replied. "This strange man just left. He said..." I forced myself to take another breath. "He said he was watching me and would be back."

"What do you mean?" Sharon asked, eyebrows knitting together.

I repeated the conversation, the whole event sounding even more bizarre as I described it.

"You need to report him to the police, AJ," she said urgently. "They need to know someone's stalking you."

"Why would they care, Sharon?" I pulled my hands away from hers. "They'll agree I belong in one of the freak shows. They'd tell me to embrace it and take the money they offered."

"If you don't go to the police, I will. You are not a freak. And who says this guy is offering you money to join one of those shows? I mean it. Go to the police, or I will." She folded her arms across her chest. "Now, tell me about your new job."

I shook my head, grateful for my friend's loyalty. "It's just another housekeeping position, but the manager didn't seem put out by my appearance. I'll do my best to stay out of sight and work hard. I really need the money."

"Well, they'll be convinced of your talents after the first day, if the stupid bastards can look past their own prejudices."

I chuckled, but there was no joy in it. "It's not that easy to look past, and you know it."

"That's because they don't give you a chance." Sharon uncrossed her arms and leaned forward. "You're the most beautiful person I know."

"Liar." I smiled and picked up my fork. A congealed pool of gravy floated on top of my cooling chicken, but I dug into it anyway, not willing to waste the meal.

Chapter 2

The next day, I found myself tapping lightly on the employee entrance of The Sanguis Casino. I hadn't gone to the police. They had more important things to worry about than some deformed girl being bullied by a man who never touched her. They'd just take my name and statement and throw on it on the pile with the rest of the non-urgent reports.

I pulled at my scarf and waited. After a few minutes, I knocked again. The door swung open, and I back-peddled away from the man who greeted me.

"Good evening, princess." It was the same man as the day before, and he flashed me the same mischievous grin. "Please, come in."

"I think I've changed my mind," I replied, continuing to backpedal.

"Then I need to work on my first impressions," he responded with a bow. "My name is Logan. It's my job to give you a tour of the facility and introduce you to your new boss. Please, come in."

"And yesterday?" I asked warily. "What was all that about?"

"I was merely confirming your identity and rumors of your unique appearance." He took a step back into the dark hallway. "I meant no harm. I'm sorry if I upset you."

Anger flared through my chest. He was making fun of my appearance, just like everyone else. I bit my tongue and tried to ignore the instincts telling me to run away and never look back. Visions of my empty bank account made me hesitate. I was running out of employment options. Could I really afford to walk away because one more dumbass decided to make a mockery of me? I took a deep breath and straightened my shoulders, then passed through the open door.

"Impressive," Logan whispered as I brushed by him.

More like stupid or desperate or both. Rather than going to the end of hall, he opened the first door on my right and ushered me inside. A narrow staircase wound upwards and out of sight.

"Shall we?" He didn't wait for a reply as he started up the steps.

I looked back at the door automatically closing behind me, and apprehension rolled over me in waves. Nothing about this felt right. I'd worked at dozens of the hotels and casinos in town. None of them treated my first day with such obscurity, but again, I was running out of options. I followed Logan up the steps.

Deep, gasping breaths escaped my lips when we finally stopped. The winding staircase made it impossible to tell how many floors we traversed. I would've guessed five or six, but there was only one landing and one destination.

My guide pushed the door open, motioning for me to go inside. I peered around the thick, wooden frame only to find another hallway with six or seven doors on each side.

"I don't think so," I said, backing away from the door. "I accepted a position in housekeeping. I have yet to see the lead housekeeper, laundry room, or cleaning supply room." I looked up at my escort and took several more steps back. His friendly expression changed to a scowl.

"There is no choice here, for either of us," he said in a low voice. "Don't fight me. I have no desire to hurt you."

My thoughts moved into overdrive. Could I outrun him? I certainly couldn't fight him; he'd toss my ninety-five pounds to the ground within seconds.

"Please," he said through clenched teeth and motioned towards the doorway again.

I turned and ran down the steps. I didn't make it five feet before his strong arm wrapped around my tiny waist and lifted me off the ground. I kicked and screamed my way back up the steps and through the door. It thudded closed behind me, echoing down the hall. He carried me all the way to the end and opened the last door, then tossed me in and slammed it shut.

Tears swelled in my eyes as I planted my forehead against the hardwood floor. Why didn't I listen to my instincts? I knew I should've walked away. The pay wasn't even that good. Why did I allow myself to be led into this obvious trap? Who would possibly want me? No one good, that's for sure.

"Come on, girlfriend." A soft voice caught my attention. "You don't want to be lying there when they toss in the next one."

I raised my head and pulled at my scarf, immediately panicking. It was in complete disarray, and I knew my short, white hair and deformed head were showing. I frantically wound it around my skull and face, then turned to my roommate.

A young woman, likely close to my own twenty-five years, sat on one of two narrow cots on each side of the small room. She wore blue jeans, a snug t-shirt, and white sneakers. Her dark skin, high cheek bones, and pointed nose were smooth and perfect. Her straight, black hair hung to her shoulders, and I wondered if it was natural. I self-consciously pulled my scarf tighter around my face.

"Have you already eaten?" the woman asked.

"Yes."

"Good, they brought dinner an hour ago," she replied.

I sat on the edge of the cot opposite her and stared at the floor. "Do you know why we're here?" I asked, not sure if I really wanted to know the answer.

"Yes, don't you?"

I blinked. "No, I have no idea why they took me. I'm not exactly, well, no one would want me."

My roommate chuckled. "I don't know. Some men like really thin women."

I snorted and watched a nervous smile cross her face.

"I'm Kate."

"AJ," I replied. "Is that why I'm here?"

"I wish. We might survive a whorehouse. You really don't know?" Kate asked, raising both eyebrows.

"No, what am I missing?"

Kate rubbed her hands together and closed her eyes. A tingle ran across my skin, making the hairs on my arms stand on end. I frantically rubbed at them wondering what just happened.

"Have they questioned you yet?" Kate asked, opening her eyes.

"I'm guessing the fake interview for housekeeping doesn't count."

"No." A look of regret and pity shadowed her features. "Then I won't tell you. Your ignorance might save you." Kate's full lips turned into a deep frown. "Don't lie to them. They'll know if you do."

"Who are they?" I asked, a twinge of apprehensive poking at me. "What do they want with me?"

Kate shook her head and looked at the door. I followed her gaze, and fear surged through me as it swung open. Logan filled the space.

"Let's go, princess," he said, his expression unreadable.

This was not happening. Not to me. "No," I replied, balling my hands into fists to keep them from shaking.

"And what will you do to stop me from dragging you from this room?" His lips twitched. Was he suppressing that irritating grin?

"Nothing, but I'll force you to drag me," I replied defiantly. "I will not cooperate with you. People have gone out of their way to make me feel less than human for as long as I can remember. Your threats mean nothing to me." That was a complete lie. I was terrified, but I learned early in life that being a victim was worse.

Before I could take a breath, Logan draped me over his shoulder and left the room. I bounced up and down, watching his feet *not* leave indentations in the carpet. How could his two-hundred plus pounds not leave a dent in the carpet? My scarf slipped from my head, and I gasped in horror. I reached for it, but my fingers merely grazed the edge as it fluttered to the floor.

I pounded on his back as he wound his way down the stairs. When my arms wore out, I kicked his chest. He chuckled as he pulled my legs into his abdomen, restricting my movement. I screamed in frustration and pushed away from his back, rising into a semi-standing position. He stopped and looked up at me with that stupid grin spread across his face.

"They have no idea what they're getting," he said in a low voice.

Fear and anger surged through my veins. I brought my hand back to hit him, but he loosened his grip and let me drop to the floor. My knees buckled with the sudden impact, and I fell on my butt. My face burned hot with embarrassment as he stared down at me.

He knelt in front of me and pressed his hands against the sides of my face. "I wish there was a way to strengthen this so they could not see what I see."

A tingling sensation raced across my skin, giving me chills. I watched his deep brown eyes delve into my own pale blue orbs. I sat there, frozen in his grasp as my heart rate increased and stars blinked in and out of my vision. Pain flared in my chest for several moments, then subsided. I still stared into his brown eyes, noticing the small flecks of green scattered in the background. What did he just do?

"Get up," Logan commanded, the harshness returning to his voice. "Do not fight me in front of the Council."

He grabbed me beneath my arm and jerked me off the floor. I glared at him but didn't resist as he pulled me down the dark hallway, stopping in front of Jack's office. Logan tapped once on the door, then pushed it open. The room looked the same as last time, with the exception of six new people. They sat in large, wing-backed chairs, flanking each side of the dark, mahogany desk. Each man varied in appearance, but they were all stunningly handsome.

Self-consciousness assaulted me, and I looked at the floor, knowing my ugliness was on display for all of them to see.

"What is your name?" a deep voice asked from the left side of the room. He sounded Russian. Was that possible?

"AJ," I replied, staring at the carpet fibers.

"What is your real name?" he asked again.

I heard the impatience in his voice and swallowed the lump in my throat. Like they didn't already know. They had my application for the job that apparently didn't exist.

"Alisandra Johnson."

"What is your talent?" another deep voice asked from the right with a distinct Spanish accent.

"I have none," I replied, suspecting they didn't want to hear about my ability to clean up after nasty tourists.

"Look at me when I'm speaking to you," the man on the right demanded.

I snapped my head up and looked in that direction, unsure which one spoke. The man farthest on the right leaned back in his chair, one arm slung over the back. An amused smile spread across his smooth features. I'd give anything for his beautiful, blonde hair. An Asian man next to him appeared distracted by his cell phone, steadily tapping at its surface. The man sitting right next to Jack's desk stared at me with contempt, his dark eyes roaming up and down my body.

"You have been bound," he said. "Why?"

And there was the Spanish accent.

"I don't know what you mean by bound," I replied, my voice catching. So much for hiding my fear and confusion.

A voice from the left side drew my attention. "You've been disconnected from your magic."

"Magic? Really?" I said, then snapped my mouth closed.

The man on the right, with the sly smile, laughed. "She's either a really good liar, or someone bound her as a babe. She has no idea what we're talking about." Was that a British accent? Who were these people?

"There is no record of Alisandra Johnson being born in Vegas twenty-five years ago," the man with the phone interjected.

"Johnson is my foster parents' name," I explained. "My birth certificate just says Alisandra, no last name."

I watched each of the men exchange glances, then all of them turned to Jack. I withered under his dark gaze and returned my focus to the floor. Surely they didn't expect me to believe anything they just said.

"Take her back upstairs, Logan," Jack commanded.

I allowed my escort to lead me from the room and down the hall, following quietly behind him as he strolled up the steps. What did these people want with me? Did they truly believe magic existed? And I thought I was a freak.

When we reached the top landing, he stopped with his hand on the knob.

"Trust no one, except for Kate and her brother," he said.

His icy stare stopped me from asking the hundreds of questions running through my mind.

Chapter 3

I lay on my narrow cot in the dark. The lights automatically went out at eight. Logan let me pick up my scarf on the way back to the room, and its concealment was comforting, even in the dark. I closed my eyes and tried to calm my wild thoughts, but they insisted on running circles around the day's events. I couldn't believe anyone would want to take me. It wasn't like I had money, and I definitely wasn't prostitute material. So, what could they possibly want? Maybe running drugs, but it's not like I would do it willingly.

"How well do you know the man that brought me in here?" I asked, breaking the silence.

"Not at all, why?" Kate answered.

"I'm not sure. He said some things that don't make sense to me." He'd done a few things, too.

Kate's cot squeaked as she shifted. "Like what?"

"He said I should only trust you and your brother," I replied, rolling to my side even though I couldn't see her.

"Really?" The surprise in Kate's voice seemed sincere. "I've never met him until today."

"They took you today too?" I asked, not hiding my own astonishment. I don't know why I assumed she'd been here longer.

"Yep, as soon as the sun set, they snatched me from the sidewalk."

"Who are they?"

Silence filled the room, and I worried she wouldn't answer.

"How much do you know about the supernatural?" Kate finally asked.

"I like to read fantasy books," I replied. "But I'm guessing that's not what you mean."

Kate chuckled. "No, not at all. I enjoy a good paranormal romance myself, but they're definitely fantasy."

"Then I guess I know nothing."

"The council you met with earlier are vampires," Kate said, lowering her voice. "I assume Logan is too."

"Really? Like blood-sucking vampires?" I asked, knowing my voice sounded harsh and judgmental. Were all these people off their rockers?

"Yep, really. They're collecting mages," Kate continued. "Our members have been disappearing over the last year or so, despite our Magister's claims that they haven't."

"Why would vampires want mages? And who is the Magister?" I questioned, my disbelief still obvious.

"That's the question of the day," Kate replied. "For your second question, the Magister is the leader of the North American mages."

"They think I'm a mage?"

"They know you are."

"But I'm not," I argued. "Have you seen me? If I could do magic, I wouldn't look like this."

Kate shifted on her cot again, the springs squeaking in protest. Her voice was barely a whisper when she spoke. "AJ, for some reason, your magic has been bound. Even I can see that."

I rolled my eyes. "You can't really expect me to believe vampires and magic are real."

"Believe what you wish. The facts remain the same."

Was this all a joke? Some ridiculous prank? If so, who even knew me well enough to do it? No one cared about me except for Sharon, and she'd never do this. How could I even consider that Kate was telling the truth? There was no way I believed in the supernatural. Sure, people did some really weird stuff, especially in Vegas, but she was talking about vampires and mages. I refused to believe it, but I needed a friend right now, so playing along seemed like a good idea.

"Can we unbind this magic?" I asked.

"I can't," Kate responded, "but my brother could."

"Any chance he'd be looking for you?" I questioned hopefully, grateful I didn't insult my fellow captive earlier.

"I'm certain he is, but it won't be easy to get us out of here."

"Wait, if you can do magic, why can't you do some spell to blast our way out?"

Kate's laughter filled the room, but I couldn't see the humor in our situation. Okay, maybe I could. Magic wasn't real, so of course she couldn't blast her way out. Joke's on me. Way to go.

"Do you think I'd still be here if I could get out?" Kate asked.

I sighed, not even really knowing how to respond. Did I keep playing along with the obvious joke? I had no idea. "No, I suppose not."

"There's a magical buffer on this entire floor," she explained. "As soon as you enter the door at the end of the hall, you're separated from your magic."

So, she was still insisting I believe her story. My frustration level ratcheted another notch.

"Then, what did I feel earlier, when I first got here?" I asked, glad she couldn't see my raised eyebrow and deepening frown. "You did something that made my skin crawl when you rubbed your hands together."

"That was just me feeling your magic."

"But how could you feel it if I'm separated from it, twice even, if I've also got this binding thing?" I challenged.

"I can't explain it," Kate replied, her own frustration made clear in her voice. There was no way she couldn't hear my disbelief.

I let it go. None of it made sense to me, and I wasn't trying to make enemies. They'd either let me out or not. I rolled onto my back and stared into the darkness. My logic warred with everything else. Regardless how stupid it all sounded, I'd felt *something* from her. Logan tried to make my heart stop with whatever he'd done. The really creepy 'vampires' downstairs insisted magic was real.

"Tell me more about the vampires," I said. When my request was met with silence, I took a deep breath to calm my voice. "Are they like Hollywood portrays them?"

"Sort of," Kate replied. "They need blood to survive, but they aren't affected by garlic or holy water. You have to remove their head to kill them, but their speed makes it very difficult to do so."

"Does the sunlight kill them?" I asked, not wanting to sit in silence.

"It weakens them, but they don't explode into a pile of ash," Kate replied.

"You think Logan's a vampire?"

"Yep," she replied nonchalantly.

"He met me at Sandy's Diner last night," I continued, thinking of how he disappeared without anyone seeing him. "I thought he disappeared, but he probably just moved really fast."

"He met you at the diner and didn't take you?" Disbelief colored her voice; it was her turn to question my tale.

"Why would he when I'd already been hired?" I asked in response. "I delivered myself to them."

"Yeah, that sucks," Kate replied. "Does anyone know you're here?"

"My friend Sharon."

"Will she be worried when she doesn't hear from you?" Kate asked cautiously. "Would she come here looking for you?"

"Oh, I hope not!" I replied, sitting up in my bed. "What would they do to her if she showed up looking for me?"

"Probably just send her away, saying you showed up for work and did great, then went home. They wouldn't keep her unless they thought she was a mage," Kate replied. "They don't want to draw attention to themselves."

"As long as they don't hurt her," I mumbled. "She's the only friend I have."

Chapter 4

At some point, I fell into a fitful sleep. I dreamt of vampires drinking blood from stone gargoyles and Gandalf in a wizard's dual with Wonder Woman. Typical dream style – none of it made sense. Kind of like my life at the moment.

A violent shaking woke me with a start. I sat up abruptly and smashed my forehead into Kate's. We both yelped and rubbed our brows. The lights were back on, and I noticed my scarf in a crumpled pile on my lap. I quickly picked it up and started wrapping my head.

"What the hell, Kate?"

"Shh, someone's in the hall," she said in a loud whisper, still rubbing her forehead. If she noticed my appearance, she hid it well. "Get dressed, quick."

I didn't have an extra change of clothes, so it only took a few minutes to pull on my blue jeans and sneakers. I regretted sleeping in my t-shirt but couldn't bring myself to take it off.

We crept to the door and pressed our ears against it. Muffled shouts and the sound of slamming doors reached us just as our door pushed inward, throwing us backwards.

Two men burst into the room. From my seated position on the floor, I gawked at the blood dripping from their long swords. *Who the hell carries swords?* They both wore dark pants and black t-shirts that hugged their muscular frames. Blood coated the front of their shirts and a long gash ran down the shorter one's arm.

"Chica!"

"Raul, thank God you're here!" Kate jumped to her feet and wrapped her arms around his neck.

The other man frowned. "Seriously, he's the only one worthy of hugs from our favorite mage?"

"Sammy, you know better." Kate released Raul and hugged Sammy, but with less enthusiasm. "You guys ok?"

"I'll fix him up when we're done," Sammy replied.

"I bet you will." Kate grinned. "Just make sure I get to help. Now, tell me how many were here?"

"Fifteen, besides you two," Raul replied, and both men turned to face me, sliding their swords into leather sheaths on their backs.

I remained sprawled out on the ground gaping at their exchange. These two men clearly killed or wounded someone to rescue us, and no one felt bad about it.

"This is AJ," Kate said, waving a hand at me. "Looks like she's bound."

"Not very well," Sammy stated. "I can still feel her magic."

"Yeah, I want to see my brother before we go back to the Magister," Kate stated, leading the way out of the room.

"Kellen said the same," Raul replied. "Come on, little mage." He held his hand out to me. I looked at him skeptically. "I promise I won't bite," he said with a smile.

"I bet she does," Kate called over her shoulder from several feet down the hall.

"I will not," I retorted and grasped his hand.

A jolt of electricity burst through me as soon as our fingers touched, sending us crashing into opposite walls. What the hell?

"I told you so," Kate's voice sang from the stairwell. "Her binding is falling apart."

Raul pushed himself to his feet, leaving a smear of blood on the wall behind him, then looked at me. "Damn girl," he said, eyes wide. "You need to see the man now."

I stood and rubbed my shoulder. I didn't know what to say. What the hell was that? No amount of static build-up would knock me on my butt. I'd never reacted to anyone's touch before, including Logan and Kate just yesterday. But that wasn't true. Jack shocked me, though not as severely as just now. I followed our rescuers down the stairs, through the hall, and into the back alley. I considered leaving them here and running back to my apartment, but Jack had my address from my application. Would he just send Logan to come get me? If he did, there was nothing I could do to stop him.

"Why weren't we stopped?" I asked as fifteen other people piled into a waiting van.

"The new girl should get shotgun," Raul suggested. "So, she ain't touchin' no one."

"I've never had issues with touching before," I said defensively. "Have you considered it's just you?"

"Definitely not me." He raised his eyebrows suggestively at Kate who blushed.

"It's cool, AJ," Sammy said. "You can sit up front with me. I won't bite ya."

I hesitated for a moment, then climbed into the front passenger seat and readjusted my scarf. Listening to the soft chatter in the space behind me, it sounded like everyone except me believed in magic and the vampires that took them.

"Sammy, why didn't they try to stop us?" I asked again, watching the man's profile as he drove.

"They did. Raul didn't cut himself," he replied, not drawing his focus from the road. "We killed one and wounded the other. They only have two guards during the day."

"Shouldn't we be taking care of your friend's arm?" I asked.

"Nah, it isn't that deep." He glanced in the rearview mirror. "Besides, Kate's already on it."

I twisted in my seat and noticed Kate wrapping a length of gauze around his arm. A first aid kit lay open on her lap.

"Why do they want them?" I asked, nodding towards the back of the van.

"Mages? We're not sure," he replied, glancing at me. "You're one too, ya know."

I shook my head. "Everyone keeps saying that, but I've always just been me. I don't even believe in magic."

"There's something more than *just you* hiding behind your veil."

"Just a really ugly face," I mumbled.

"I wasn't talking about the pretty scarf," he said, the corners of his mouth twitching. "Kellen'll set you straight, don't worry."

Chapter 5

We drove for over two hours before rolling to a stop in front of a set of wrought iron gates. I looked out the passenger window at the tall stone wall that seemed to go on forever.

A man's voice crackled through the speaker at Sammy's window. "Report."

"Got 'em boss," Sammy replied.

The gate rolled open, and Sammy drove through, parking the van in front of a sprawling hacienda-style home. Three sides of the house wrapped around a large patio garden. Red tiles covered the roof and contrasted beautifully with the sand-colored stucco on the walls.

Everyone spilled from the van with moans and groans, stretching out their cramped joints. I felt a little guilty for taking up the front seat, but then I remembered the way Raul zapped me at the hotel. Maybe it *was* better if I didn't touch anyone until I figured out what was going on.

"Let's get to the bathroom before everyone else does," Kate said.

I nodded in agreement and followed her into the lush garden. Tall palm trees lined each side, swaying gently in the breeze. Flowering bushes surrounded by colorful stones filled the space beneath them. Mid-day approached quickly, but the shaded garden felt wonderful.

"This is amazing, Kate," I murmured. "How do you get all this to grow in the desert?"

"Um, magic," she said with a grin. "Come on. Everyone else will be rushing to the bathroom in the main house. We'll use mine. I have a thing about germs."

I smiled beneath my scarf, grateful for the inclusion, and followed Kate. I briefly let myself believe she was looking out for me, knowing I wouldn't want to be gawked at. Several sets of glass doors faced the garden, but she headed for one on the right arm of the house. The door slid open and she walked in, leaving me to follow. The cool rush of air conditioner greeted me, and I quickly closed the door.

A modest size bedroom surrounded me with chocolate-colored walls and white furniture. A queen-sized bed rested against the far side with a wall of mirrors on the opposite end. One of the mirrors glided open, and Kate emerged.

"Your turn," she said with a smile.

I hesitated even though my bladder screamed for relief. There was a really good reason I had no mirrors in my small apartment. I didn't need reminders of what I looked like. If Kate noticed my hesitation, she ignored it.

"I'm going to find Kellen. Be right back." She moved to the interior door and stopped at the last second. "We really need to remove your binding. If we can't do it now, that damn veil has to go at a minimum."

"I like my scarf," I argued, offended that she would want to remove it.

"Not your scarf. The veil that covers your true appearance." Kate came back into the room and stood in front of me. She was taller by several inches, but everyone was. "I don't know who would do this to you, but this is not who you are. I can't see past the veil, but it's definitely hiding something."

Kate turned and walked out, leaving me in a state of shock. Was she saying my appearance was false? I couldn't wrap my brain around magic, let alone the concept of someone hiding my appearance. Stuff like that just wasn't possible. Maybe I should've stayed at the casino. These people were clearly off their rockers. I needed to ask Sammy to take me back to Vegas.

My bladder reminded me that I had urgent matters to take care of. The bathroom was just as elegant as the bedroom, with the same chocolate color covering the walls, except for a panel of mirrors over the double sink. I avoided looking in them and took care of business.

When I slid open the mirrored door a new face greeted me. His resemblance to Kate was uncanny. He had the same dark skin and smooth features. He kept his straight, black hair short around his ears, but still long enough to fall across his forehead. His brown eyes traced my body from head to toe, making me blush.

He turned to Kate, who was standing next to him. "Take the others to the Magister."

"Can you remove her binding?" Kate asked.

"Possibly," he replied. His unreadable expression bore into me as he continued to study me.

"Do you need my help?" Kate continued. "Or should I just run along with the other kids?"

He turned to her and smiled, his stony façade changing completely. "I do not need your help, sister," he replied, kissing her forehead. "Take the other kids back to school. I'll be there shortly."

She turned towards the garden door but stopped short. "If you're going to do something destructive, do it in your room, not mine." She didn't wait for a reply as she skipped out the door.

I smiled as I watched her disappear into the garden. What I wouldn't give to have that relationship.

"Follow me," Kate's brother said and turned to the interior door.

"I assume you're Kellen," I said. "Glad to meet you."

He continued walking, seeming to ignore me.

"It's nice to meet you too, AJ," I said in a deep voice, trying to mimic his. "I hope you enjoyed the ride from your vampire prison."

I felt like a juvenile as I followed him down the hall and into another part of the home, but I couldn't help it. Everyone expected me to accept this bizarre reality. And vampires, really? The mind could only take so much.

He opened a door at the end of the next hall and went inside, obviously expecting me to follow. I took a deep breath and walked through the door. A pair of large hands gripped my shoulders and a wave a nausea assaulted me. My world spun as those same hands guided me to the floor. I rolled back onto my butt and rested my head between my knees. It took several deep breaths to push back the bile that rose in my throat.

A few moments later, a cool towel draped across the back of my neck, and a small trash can appeared at my side.

"Take the time you need," Kellen said.

"Thank you," I replied. "What was that?"

"I removed the veil."

I lifted my head to find him sitting on the floor across from me. I glared at him, but his expression remained impassive. Had he used magic on me without permission? I didn't feel any different beyond the nausea that threatened to empty my stomach on his floor.

"You couldn't have told me first?" I asked. "Maybe I didn't want it removed."

"You wanted to keep your previous appearance?" he asked. "Kate described it to me. I can't imagine you being happy with it."

Tears welled in my eyes at his dispassionate remark. "You have no idea what I lived through with that appearance."

"Then why would you want to keep it?"

I choked on the lump in my throat. His harsh opinion hurt. I knew what I looked like and certainly didn't need him to remind me. "I don't want it, but you have no right to do stuff without my permission."

He raised his eyebrows at me. "Fair enough." He rose from the floor in one smooth motion and held his hand out to me.

"I got it," I said, ignoring his hand and pushing myself off the floor. "The last person who touched me didn't like it very much." I swayed, still feeling the effects of his stupid 'magic.'

"We'll see if we can fix that too," he replied, standing in front of me. He had to be at least five foot ten, maybe taller.

I craned my neck back to look at him and frowned. "You'll tell me what you're doing before you do it so I can be prepared."

"Of course." His eyes softened with his voice. "Can you remove the scarf? I need to be able touch your face to remove the binding."

My thoughts immediately went to the vampire. He'd done the same just before my meeting with the council. I reached for my scarf but couldn't move my hand to unwrap it. It was my security, my safe space against the looks of disgust and rejection I'd faced my entire life. I wasn't ready to reveal my ugliness to someone else. While a small part of me wanted to believe it was just a mask, I couldn't.

"Can I do it for you?" Kellen asked gently, no hint of malice or disgust in his voice.

"You might have to," I replied. "I don't think I can."

He reached out and tugged the edge of the nylon fabric at my chin. It loosened, and he pulled it from my head. His eyes widened and his mouth hung open for a second, before he snapped it shut. He draped my scarf over my shoulder and turned his back to me.

I hung my head and tears welled in my eyes. Why did I let this handsome man see me? I should've run as fast as my legs could carry me. "Can I go home?" I asked, wrapping my scarf back over my head, leaving my eyes and nose visible.

"It's better if you didn't, especially now," he said, but didn't turn to face me.

I watched him stroll to a nearby sofa and fall into it, with his head in his hands. I looked around and realized we were in a small sitting room. A matching sofa faced the one Kellen sat in. A large, flat-screen TV hung from the far wall and glass doors opened onto the desert. Rather than the stark contrasts in Kate's room, this one was filled with muted shades of tan and white.

I started to speak and stopped several times, uncertain what to say. Had I just traded one prison for another? This one was certainly nicer, but that didn't mean he'd keep me here. I could run, but where? Several hours of desert separated me from home. Did I have any options?

"Come here and sit. We have a lot to discuss," he said, lifting his head from his hands.

I moved to the sofa across from him and sat down. He looked at me and shook his head.

"This cannot be possible," he said, staring at my face. "What did Logan say to you while you were at the Casino?"

His abrupt change in topic startled me, along with his knowledge of the so-called vampire. "Nothing really, but now I realize it might have been a lot," I replied. "How do you know him?"

"Explain what he said."

I sighed. "Some people are so demanding. He acted a lot like you. Cool, impartial, bossy." I watched him raise an eyebrow, but he remained silent. I leaned back and sunk into the soft fabric on the sofa, unable to contain my unwillingness to cooperate. "Wow, this is nice."

"Continue, please." His scowl sent a jolt of fear up my spine.

I pulled my scarf around my neck. "Just before my meeting with the council, he said he wished he could prevent them from seeing what *he* saw." I held my hands out, as if I were cradling his face. "He placed his hands on my head and did something weird. I thought my heart would explode."

I dropped my hands into my lap and looked at Kellen.

"Anything else?" he asked.

"He told me to trust no one but you and your sister," I replied.

"So, did he see the real you?" Kellen asked. "Or did he only suspect the veil hid your true identity without being able to see it?"

What did he mean? His reaction to seeing me could only mean I was still the same person. There was no stupid mask waiting to reveal a secret identity. Should I confront him with it or play along? I was tired of playing along, but maybe it was the best way to get a ride back to Vegas. I didn't know the answer, so I asked another question. "Logan let Raul and Sammy in this morning, didn't he?"

He gave me a surprised look. "What makes you think he would?"

"Because I'm not stupid. For obvious reasons, I have no social life, which made me an excellent student and avid reader," I retorted. "Logan also said neither of us had choices, which means he was being forced to play his part." I settled deeper in the soft material and sighed. "Besides, I know there were seven high profile men there last night. In every movie I've ever watched, powerful people have an entourage that travels with them, which means several more vampires," I air quoted to show my disbelief, "for each council member. Where were they when our rescuers showed up?"

He rubbed his chin and looked out the window behind me. A deep scowl replaced his thoughtful expression.

"What now?" he asked as the door swung open and Kate darted into the room.

"Kellen, the Magister..." She stopped mid-sentence and mid-stride, staring at me. "Holy shit."

Chapter 6

"What do we do, Kellen?" Kate asked as she closed the door and moved into the room. She dropped down next to her brother, still staring at me. What were they gawking at? The only things showing were my eyes and maybe my nose. Had something really changed? I reached beneath the scarf at my neck and traced my fingers along my chin. My eyes widened to find a smooth transition from my face to my neck, not the bulbous deformation I'd lived with all my life. My fingers trembled as I pushed them through my hair, forcing my scarf to fall from my head. A smooth scalp caressed my hands, not the bumpy ridges from my deformed skull.

"I assume the Magister wants to see her," he said, also staring at me.

"Yep."

"Where can I find a mirror?" I asked, my whole body now trembling.

Kellen rose, strolled across the room and disappeared through a door next to the TV that I hadn't noticed. He re-emerged with a square, hand-held mirror. When he reached the sofa, he held it out to me.

"It won't explain anything for you," he said. "But I understand your need to know."

I tentatively reached for the mirror and held it in front of my face. A stranger stared back at me. I had the same pale skin and white hair, but my icy blue eyes were no longer hiding behind abnormally large eyebrows. Thin lips sat perfectly beneath my tiny upturned nose and a round, smooth chin replaced my deformed jaw. I was no longer a monster. My fingers continued to tremble as I touched the perfect skin on my cheek. Tears rolled down my face, and I lowered the mirror. Could I continue to deny the magic they claimed to possess?

"Is this me or another veil?" I asked in a small voice. Even if I wasn't convinced about the vampires or magic, I couldn't deny that Kellen had somehow changed my entire face.

"It's you," Kate replied gently.

"Who would do that to me?" I asked, looking at my reflection once more. "Who would hate me enough to put me through a lifetime of that torture?"

The siblings looked at one another in silence.

"We can't keep it from her," Kellen finally said.

"But it changes everything, Kellen," Kate argued. "How could she do this? She can't deny that AJ is her blood. They're mirror images of one another." She clapped her hand over her mouth and twisted on the sofa to face her brother. "I have to bring her back to the palace," she said between her fingers. "but I can't."

"I know, Kate." He looked from me to Kate and back again.

"We could disguise her," Kate suggested, waving her hands in the air. "She's small enough. We could dress her up as a boy. Put a hat on her head to cover her hair."

"It might work," Kellen agreed, "But, I think our best option is to take her to the Magister's Palace just as she is." He held up his hand to interrupt his sister's protests. "We make sure as many people as possible see her and recognize her. If we disguise her, only the Magister will recognize her true identity. She would be free to make AJ disappear with the next group of mages." His gaze landed on me and softened. "But if we parade AJ through the palace, the Magister cannot harm a daughter she just found."

My mouth hung open as I tried to process what they were saying. Did they just say daughter?

"My mother is alive? Surely she didn't do this to me?" I asked. "You guys make her sound evil."

"We don't know if she did or not," Kellen replied, regaining his place on the sofa. "We're jumping to conclusions, for which we have no proof. I'm not sure I would call her evil, but some of her actions of late have been questionable at best." His gaze swept over my features again. "You never knew your parents?"

"No," I replied, looking away from his intense gaze. "I grew up in foster care. I hoped my parents would come back for me, despite everyone's cruel comments. But they were right, who would want me?" Tears threatened to spill over again. "She's been alive all this time and never came for me."

"There may be reasons that just aren't obvious, AJ," Kellen said. "Let's take one step at a time."

I looked back at him through my tears. Was that compassion from him or pity? I wiped my face with the back of my hand, refusing to cry for a woman who didn't want me. "Explain this binding thing Kate talked about. Is it real? Will you remove it before we go?"

He shook his head. "A binding is a spell that confines your magic, making it unusable by you and hidden from others. I think it's best I don't remove it. There are very few people who can remove a binding." He looked at his sister. "The one who placed it is the obvious choice, as they know what they did. I'm the only one I know of in several hundred miles who can remove it, but it will be difficult because I don't know the caster's intent."

"You think the Magister would offer to remove it herself?" Kate asked, curling her lip. "She's not stupid."

"We don't know that she did it. But no, I'm certain she'll make me remove it. Which is fine, I want to witness her reaction to seeing her daughter bound."

"My mother," I whispered, laying the mirror on the sofa beside me. I couldn't stop the tears spilling down my cheeks. "All this time I assumed I didn't have one. My foster parents couldn't wait to leave me when I turned eighteen, and they certainly never loved me." I looked up at the siblings across from me and tamped down my jealousy. I'd never known love from anyone. "I don't think I can face her."

"I think you're much stronger than you give yourself credit for," Kellen replied. "You survived a childhood most people would have abandoned before the age of ten." His gaze swept to his sister, then back to me. "We will not abandon you, no matter what occurs with the Magister. There's more happening here than you realize, and I think you're the catalyst for it all."

"Do you mind explaining that?" I asked.

"Let's see the Magister's reaction first," he replied.

Kate leaned forward to embrace me, and I shifted away. "No touching, remember?"

"How could I forget?" She grinned. "I owe you a hug when he's done."

The corners of my mouth twitched up, but worry and sorrow washed away my smile.

"We'll use the portal to get back," Kellen said, rising from his seat.

"Can I go to my apartment first? I've been wearing the same set of clothes for two days. I also need a shower, especially if I'm going to be paraded through a palace."

"I might have something small enough for her," Kate offered, glancing at me. "Maybe."

"You've got twenty minutes," Kellen replied. "The Magister will already be unpleasant to deal with. Forcing her to wait will only make it worse."

Chapter 7

I stared at the stranger in the mirror while Kate cursed over how small I was, and how she would never find clothes in her closet to fit me. The skirt she gave me hung just below my knees even though it was meant to be above them. Kate also loaned me a white tank top with adjustable straps and a light blue button-up shirt that I wore over the top. None of her shoes were small enough, so I kept my own well-worn sneakers.

Twenty minutes later, I stood in front of a shimmering portal framed in dark wood with strange patterns engraved along the edges. Its inky surface distorted the image beyond. I couldn't imagine going through it. Kellen insisted it was the only way to get to the Magister's Palace, but I didn't want to go. Why did I care if a bunch of weirdos knew who I was? I reached for the scarf that Kellen said I couldn't wear. Why was I listening to him? I never went anywhere without it.

My fingers grazed the smooth skin on my cheek, and a shiver ran down my spine. They said it was my true appearance, and while I marveled at how lovely it was, I wanted to know who would do this to me and why. Which meant going through this damn portal.

"What if only half of me makes it through?" I asked.

Kellen rolled his dark eyes, and Kate giggled.

"I promise it will not hurt you," he said. "I'll throw you through myself if you don't do it on your own."

"No touching, remember?" I fired back.

"Your magic will not hurt me, little girl."

I looked at the portal once again and swallowed loudly.

"Alright, I'll see you two on the other side," Kate said before disappearing through the shimmering light.

I tried to make out Kate's form through the portal, but the inky haze blurred everything.

"On your own, or am I tossing you?" Kellen looked down at me with narrowed eyes.

"If you can touch me without either of us getting hurt, then why can't you hold my arm as we walk through?" I was pretty sure I couldn't do it on my own, and tumbling out on my ass wasn't the best first impression.

He held out his hand to me, and I placed my palm in his. The size difference was astounding, but the contrast between his dark skin and my paleness was even more so. He wrapped his fingers around mine and pulled me through.

The world lurched, and my stomach rose to my throat. I squeezed my eyes shut and held my breath until I slammed into Kellen's solid form. He released my hand, and I dropped to my knees.

"That was rather unpleasant," I mumbled, pushing myself up onto my wobbly legs.

"Let's go," Kellen said, strolling across a large, paved courtyard.

I cursed and jogged to catch up, stumbling as I reached him. He grabbed my elbow to keep me from falling. I looked up to thank him, but my words died with his scowl. I jerked my arm away and smoothed the skirt Kate gave me. Unconsciously, I reached for a scarf that wasn't there. Damn him for not letting me wear it.

Kellen regarded me for several seconds before starting off again. The courtyard ended at a set of wide, sweeping steps leading up to a genuine castle. At the top of the stairs, I stopped and gawked at the beautifully carved wooden doors set in white stone walls.

A large hand on my back reminded me I had someplace to be. The doors swung open, and I was awed once again. Black and white tiles lined the entryway, and the buzz of low conversation drifted around me. My gaze rose to the high ceilings and dark, stained rafters. On a second-floor balcony, people stopped what they were doing and stared back at me. Again, I reached for a scarf that wasn't there. My already fragile insecurity threatened to crumble beneath the weight of their scrutiny.

Kellen pushed me forward, and silence fell over the enormous space. His frustrated huff echoed against the stone, and he grabbed my hand, dragging me towards another set of ornately carved wooden doors. Low mumblings followed us, a large crowd gathering in our wake.

My escort stopped at the doors and looked down at me. Uncertainty flashed in his eyes for a moment, increasing my own apprehension, before he pushed open one of the doors. It moved silently, and he dropped my hand as he entered what I assumed was the Magister's Hall.

Low whispers followed us into the room, followed by several gasps. Dozens of people were already present, some of whom I recognized from our long van ride out of Vegas. I took a deep breath and followed Kellen through the crowd. They parted for me with looks of shock, suspicion, and hope. The latter confused me. What could they possibly hope for from me? I still struggled to believe any of this was real, and I knew nothing of the people around me.

Kellen stopped before a dais covered in fresh cut flowers. Sitting on the top step was a tall, slender woman with white hair, icy blue eyes, and a small, round face much like my own. A long, black dress clung to her slender frame, making her pale complexion appear sallow. I stared at her with mixed emotions. This was the woman who gave birth to me, then threw me away. Anger and hatred won out over my curiosity, and I struggled to keep my face passive. It would be difficult to deny my relation to her, but instead of joy or surprise, she held a dismissive look, as if someone presented her a puppy she didn't want.

"My goodness, Kellen. What have you brought me?" The woman said, her voice a slightly deeper version of my own.

"She was with the others that were rescued this morning," he replied, looking past the Magister. "A veil covered her appearance, and I thought it wise to remove it before introducing her to our palace."

"My palace," she corrected.

"Of course, Magister."

He continued to avoid her gaze as her eyes drifted over him. She didn't even try to hide her desire, allowing a small smile to grace her lips. Did they have a history, or was this woman pining after a man young enough to be her son?

"It's known by very few that I bore a child. I was told she died just after birth, but there is no denying her, is there?" The woman transferred her icy gaze to me, and I struggled to keep my trembling fingers from reaching towards my face. I missed my scarf and the security it gave me, no matter how false it was.

She rose from her perch and stepped down the stairs, crushing the flowers beneath her sandaled feet. Low mumbling drifted up from the crowd of people behind me, but the Magister ignored them. She stopped in front of me and looked down her nose, then reached out a finger to touch my chin. I turned away.

"It's not a good idea to touch me," I said in a low voice.

"Why is that child?" the woman asked, tilting her head.

"I might bite," I replied with a growl.

The Magister dropped her hand, her eyes narrowing into slits. "She is still bound."

She turned to Kellen, and I noticed his lips draw into a thin line. I didn't miss the fact that she said 'still.' She knew I was bound before I got here.

"Why have you not released her?" the woman asked.

"I was not certain what the binding intended," he replied, almost casually. "I was hoping you would be able to see something I could not."

The Magister glared at him. "Of course I cannot see any more than you," she hissed.

"I hoped your parentage would reveal a link between you," he said, shrugging. "The binding is intricate. I was concerned for her safety."

"Of course you were." The crease between her brows deepened. "Undo it now."

"With everyone here?" he asked. "I would prefer it be done in a controlled environment in the event that her suppressed power needs to release unexpectedly." His gaze deliberately drifted over the Magister's head and landed on me. "It seems she has been bound since birth. It takes a powerful mage to create such a binding, or someone must have renewed it every four or five years."

"You're right, of course," she said, waving her hand in the air, as if the matter were settled. "Take her to one of the training rooms and see it done."

She turned her back to the room and strolled up the steps, disappearing behind a curtained partition. Just like that. I stood there gaping at the fluttering curtain, expecting her to come back and say something to me.

Kellen snatched my arm and pulled me from the chamber. I could almost feel his anger as we stormed down the hall. The woman never even acknowledged an ounce of emotion for her long lost daughter. No remorse, no relief for finally finding me, nothing. Tears streamed down my face as Kellen led me away.

A trail of people followed us, adding to my anxiety. I was still a freak show, a spectacle for everyone to stare at. I was grateful for Kellen's hand tightening around mine as he pulled me through a stone doorway into a cold, dark room.

The sound of grinding rock drowned out the murmured protests behind us until nothing but silence and darkness surrounded me. Anxiety crept along my skin as I stood motionless in the complete blackness.

Kellen's large hand still gripped my small fingers. His labored breaths mirrored my own, but the darkness only added to my raging emotions.

"Sit," he commanded, pulling me to the ground.

I folded my legs beneath me, and he released my hand. Panic replaced my anger, and my heartrate soared once again. I blinked several times, foolishly thinking it would help ease my panic. I didn't think I was afraid of the dark, but the total lack of light was unnerving.

"Kellen?" My voice quivered uncontrollably.

"I'm still here," he replied.

As his hand settled on my knee, my fears retreated.

"Are there no lights in here?" I asked, reaching for his hand and lacing my fingers in his. He didn't pull away.

"I need a moment of silence." His voice was low and harsh, so I refrained from speaking. I wasn't sure what triggered his anger, but he obviously needed to calm down. Several minutes later, he inhaled deeply, then exhaled. He repeated the process six more times. I counted, using his methodical breath to sooth my own fears.

"I'm going to attempt to remove the binding," he said quietly, "but I fear it will be painful for us both."

"Should we just leave it then?" I asked. "I don't really care if I can do magic or not. I've spent my whole life without it. It's not like I'll miss it."

He didn't reply right away, and I wondered if he would.

"Bindings do not last forever, AJ," he finally said. "Someone has been entrancing you every five years or so. The fact that we can see it means it's weak. It needs to be redone or removed."

"What do you mean by entrance?" I asked, suspecting I knew the answer. I'd read enough books to recognize the term.

"The mage would cast a spell that numbed your mind and allowed him or her to do as they wished," he replied, his voice still harsh. "Most of the time, the victim remembers nothing."

I gasped. "Can any mage do that? Have I endured all kinds of abuses without even knowing it?" A new reason for my abduction slipped into my mind. Had I been a victim of some sadistic bastard, and he decided to keep me for his own? "Can vampires entrance people? Was Logan doing it all this time?"

"No, not all mages can perform that spell. It's actually extremely rare." Kellen took a deep breath. "Vampires can entrance humans in a different way, but I don't believe it was Logan," Kellen replied. "Creating a veil like the one you had is also very rare. I believe the same person renewed the veil and the binding."

"My mother?" I spat the name from my lips.

"No, she can't create a veil. At least, not that I'm aware of." Kellen's displeasure was obvious. "There is so much you need to know."

"Then tell me."

"We'll release your magic first," he said, lifting my hand with his. "I need to feel your mind. Place my hands on the sides of your face."

I guided his hand to my face. "Why don't we turn on the lights?"

"Because then everyone will see."

"That's a bad thing?"

"Yes, they should not know your strengths or weaknesses, not yet. Now, be silent."

A wave of energy washed over me, raising the hairs on my arms. Kellen drew a deep breath and placed his forehead against mine. I fidgeted with the hem of my skirt, unsure where to put my hands.

A light, prickly sensation started at the base of my skull and traveled down my spine. I arched my back as it plunged into my lower back and through my abdomen. A small cry escaped my lips as it crawled towards my heart. I tried to push away from Kellen, but he leaned closer to me and held onto my face.

"Relax," Kellen whispered.

"That isn't exactly pleasant."

"I warned you it might be painful." A slow hiss escaped his lips as the sensation delved back into my mid-section. "Put your hands on my face," he instructed.

I lifted my hands to where I thought his face was. My fingers grazed his neck, and I followed the corded muscle to his square jawline.

"What can I do to help?" I asked.

He didn't reply. The little spark danced around inside my core, the constant movement making me nauseous. I tried to ignore it, but sweat broke out across my brow, and saliva filled my mouth.

"I think I'm going to be sick," I whispered.

Kellen leaned back away from me, removing his hands and forehead from mine. I scooted back and tucked my head between my knees, taking long slow breaths.

"I don't think I can remove it," Kellen said. "At least not here."

"Is that normal?" I mumbled from my crouched position.

"No," he replied. "We'll do this in my home, where I have resources available to help."

~~~~~~~~~~~~~~~~

"What do mean you could not remove it?" the Magister demanded.

She wasn't waiting at the door with the dozens of other mages, but she met Kellen and me in the hall before we reached the courtyard.

I noticed Kellen looking past the Magister once again and wondered why he wouldn't meet her gaze. There had to be a history between them.

"The binding's intent is complicated," he replied, his tone cold and harsh.

"Isn't it always." She took a step closer to him and placed her finger on his chest. "What makes this one so difficult?"

"This one was meant to kill her," he replied, still looking over her head.

I watched the Magister's lips turn up. "I'm sure you'll not allow that to happen."

She brushed by him, trailing her hand over his chest, then glanced at me before disappearing into the crowd. A lump formed in my throat as I watched the woman who gave birth to me walk away. The Magister showed no emotion
~~~~~~~~~~~~~~~~

towards me at all. Nothing. All my life, I dreamt of a mother's unconditional love. Maybe it didn't exist, at least not for me.

Kellen's hand on my shoulder distracted my thoughts. I wiped my face and looked up at him.

"Let's go."

Chapter 8

I followed Kellen through the patio garden and towards the opposite side of the house that I visited earlier that day. The setting sun cast long shadows across the flowering bushes I didn't have names for. He pushed open the sliding glass door and waited for to me to enter.

"So, he does have manners," I said as I walked by, hating that I used sarcasm as a reflex. I wanted to ask about what had just happened. I needed him to explain his comments about the binding being designed to kill me. Of course, I didn't ask any of that, choosing a snide remark instead.

The door slid closed, and he brushed past me through a hallway that followed the garden. Halfway down, he stopped in front of a large wooden door and looked back at me with a strange expression before shaking his head.

I followed him inside and gasped. The lack of air conditioning hit me first, but the dirt beneath my feet distracted me from the change in temperature. The room was a perfect circle with long, narrow windows cut into the stone walls and skirting the ceiling. I took a step forward, but Kellen's iron grip stopped my progress.

"Remove your shoes."

I looked at my worn sneakers. They were ugly, but they were cleaner than the dirt floor.

"Just take them off," Kellen said more gently. "I'll explain in a minute."

He sat on a low, wooden bench removing his own shoes and socks. I shrugged and sat next to him, kicking my sneakers off my feet and peeling away my socks.

Kellen rolled up the ends of his jeans, exposing his well-toned calves. I looked down at the skirt I still wore and the boney legs connected to my small feet. A childish giggle escaped my lips before I could stop it.

"How ridiculous do we look?" I asked, pointing at the difference between us.

"You need to eat," he said, pushing himself from the bench, and seeming to ignore my absurdity.

"Yet we haven't had a meal all day," I retorted, my humor quickly fading. "And here comes the witching hour."

He stopped and looked at me, his lips turned down in a frown. "I'm sorry. You're right. Let's get some food before we do this."

"As hard as it is to believe, my body is used to one meal a day," I replied. "I haven't died of starvation yet. I'm sure a few more hours will hardly matter."

He continued to stare at me, then mumbled to himself and moved to the middle of the room. When I didn't immediately follow him, he rolled his eyes and pointed at the ground next to his feet.

"Stand next to me," he said with barely controlled patience.

I strolled towards him, enjoying the cool soil beneath my toes, and stopped at his side. He turned me around and pointed me at the door.

"A mage's magic comes from the four elements," he began. "The earth beneath our feet, the air around us, the water that gives us life, and fire."

Water cascaded into a large fountain covering several feet of wall on the right side of the door, and an open fireplace took up the left side, a small fire flickering at its base.

My heart jumped. I looked up at Kellen and smiled. "You're going teach me magic?"

"I'm going to explain the fundamentals so that when your binding is removed, you'll understand what I ask you to do." He stepped around in front of me and looked down. "I need you to be cooperative."

"I was cooperative earlier, wasn't I?"

"Yes, but you were trapped in complete darkness." He swept his arm wide. "Here, you will be distracted."

"These things were in the other room?" I asked.

"No, that was the fire room," he replied. "I need more than that to undo what has been done without killing you."

"There is so much I don't understand. Will this binding thing really kill me? Why would someone do this to me?" I frowned at him, wanting to ask a dozen more questions. I refrained, suspecting his demonstration would explain some of it.

"Yes, if the binding is not removed or renewed, it will kill you," he replied. His expression softened for a moment before returning to his impassive stare. "Mages typically attune to one element, and most of the time, that's dictated by their heritage." He sat down in the dirt, folding his legs. "Your mother is attuned to air, hence the color of her eyes. I suspect you are as well." He looked up at me with a scowl. "Sit down in front of me as we were earlier."

My face flushed with embarrassment, which only worsened when I tried to sit. I was still wearing a skirt. I couldn't possibly sit cross-legged in front of him in a skirt. I knelt on my knees with my feet tucked under my butt and tugged at the edge of the skirt as it rode up my thighs.

"Don't roll your eyes at me," I warned. He did anyway, and my ears grew hot.

"I assure you that your scrawny legs will neither offend nor entice me," he said. "The longer you delay, the longer it will take to do this."

Anger quickly replaced my embarrassment. How dare he? I repositioned myself in front of him, giving him a defiant stare. He returned it with a look of amusement.

"I'm attuned to earth and fire," he said when I finally settled. "I'll need to draw from both to untangle the spell keeping you from your magic."

"You knew you couldn't do it earlier, didn't you?" I asked. "Even before we went to the palace."

"I suspected as much," he replied, "which is why I didn't put much effort into making it happen, nor did I protest."

I looked at him skeptically. That was not much effort? "Then why were you so mad when we arrived in that fire room?"

He stared back at me in silence, then exhaled deeply. "Mothers are supposed to be better than that."

I dropped my gaze and forced back the tears that immediately swelled in my eyes. "Oh."

"Are you ready to do this?" he asked.

"I don't really have a choice, do I?"

"No, not really."

His fingers brushed beneath my chin, and I allowed him to push it up.

"The spell is wrapped around your heart," he said, the softness in his eyes returning. "I know this will be uncomfortable for you, but I need to have my hands in places they should not be."

My eyes widened. I'd never been touched by anyone. I'd never even been to the doctor. My pulse raced at the thought, and I wasn't sure if it was apprehension, fear, or something else.

"I will have one here." He placed his right hand over his stomach. "And the other here." He placed his left hand on his chest over his heart. "The easiest and most comfortable thing for you is to sit in front of me with your back against my chest."

"Have you done this before?" I asked, my voice cracking as I looked at the placement of his hands.

"I've removed dozens of bindings, but none like yours," he replied, lowering his hands into the dirt. "A typical binding can be undone with my hands on the person's face."

I raised my eyes to meet his and was met with a kindness I had not seen there before. Why was he doing this for me? Did he really care whether I lived or died? Or was it because of my mother?

"Maybe we should leave it there," I said.

"If we leave it, and the mage that did this doesn't come back to renew it, you will die."

"Now that my identity is revealed, they won't come back, will they?" I asked with resignation.

"Not likely. It appears he or she was tasked with keeping you hidden."

As much as I hated my life, I didn't want to die. I took a deep breath and let it out slowly, then crawled into his lap. I felt small and insignificant as I folded my thin legs over top of his strong thighs. The heat from his chest radiated through the back of my shirt as I leaned into him.

"I'm sorry," he whispered as his hand snaked beneath my shirt and wrapped around my stomach, pulling me closer.

I flinched and closed my eyes as his other hand pulled the tank top down and settled between my small breasts.

"This will hurt," he said when his hands quit moving. "There is nothing I can do to ease that. Feel free to react however you like, but don't move my hands."

I nodded, afraid to speak or open my eyes. The same tingling sensation ran across my skin, but this time it originated from my stomach, beneath his hand. I tracked the tiny spark as it raced towards my heart and giggled as it danced in circles beneath my sternum.

"Does that tickle?" Kellen asked.

"Yes, is it not supposed to?"

He didn't reply. I opened my eyes and gasped. A ring of flames circled us about ten feet away. I didn't notice the heat until I saw them. I also hadn't noticed the soil bubbling beneath the flames.

"Kellen, that is so cool!" I blurted out. "Tell me what you're doing."

"Be silent."

"Oh, right, distractions," I whispered, putting my hands on his knees. I watched the dark earth move in waves beneath the fire. Its constant motion mesmerized me, and my head leaned back against his collar as I relaxed. Wasn't this supposed to hurt?

His fingers started a light drumming against my chest. With each tap, the tingle grew sharper until it felt like needles piercing through my ribs. I gritted my teeth as it turned into a wrenching pain, as if someone played tug of war with my heart. My pulse pounded in my ears, and I squeezed my eyes shut trying not to cry out.

Kellen's embrace tightened, and I struggled to breathe, but it was nothing compared to the pressure beneath my ribs. A loud snap, immediately followed by more pain, radiated from my sternum, and I ignored my foolish need to be stoic. I slammed my fists against his knees and screamed, but his grasp remained firm.

When I thought I could endure no more, a blinding light erupted around me, throwing both of us backwards. I inhaled deeply, but it was cut short by the pain shooting through my side. I switched to short, gasping breaths, each one excruciating.

Kellen sat up with me still in his lap and held tight against him.

"Relax," he said quietly. "One of your ribs is broken. Take short, shallow breaths and calm your mind."

Yeah, right. I tried to do as he asked, but it didn't work out so well. I couldn't force myself to think of anything but the pain.

"Can you let go," I asked between gasps.

"Not yet," he replied. "Open your eyes."

I forced my eyes open and nearly choked. Coin-sized droplets of water floated in the air around me. That wasn't exactly right either. They floated on small, wispy clouds.

"What is that?" I asked, reaching out with my hand. Pain surged through my middle, and I dropped my arm.

"That is you," Kellen replied.

He removed his left hand from my chest and rested it beside my arm. His right hand remained wrapped around my aching ribs.

"I thought you said I would have air," I whispered.

"You do," he insisted.

"But that's water."

"Yes."

I could almost hear him smile. My doubts about magic being real vanished. No one could stage something like this.

"Are you saying I have both?"

"Water gives us life, AJ. Your first lesson will be to heal your broken rib."

"Have you lost your mind?" I asked, shifting on Kellen's legs and regretting it as a new wave of pain surged through my left side. "I need to go to the hospital."

"If you cannot do it on your own, we will," he responded.

"You've got to be kidding me," I mumbled. "What do I need to do?"

"I have no idea," he replied coolly.

"You're impossible." I leaned my head forward, and another stab of pain assaulted me. "This is unbearable. I can't even think."

"Then don't. Reach out to the water around you, and tell it what you need."

My eyes narrowed at the ridiculousness of his statement. Had I been able to turn around, I would've slapped him. "Just wait until I feel better."

Still, I turned my attention to the droplets of water that now danced on their cloud pillows. Their actions almost seemed playful as the clouds wove around each other, and the droplets bounced from one to the other. I forced my hand towards the nearest one with a grunt of pain. Four of the playmates stopped near my fingers. My arm grew weary, and the pain in my side thumped with my heart beat.

"Please," I whispered, feeling silly for talking to a drop of water.

All four bounced from their pillows into my hand, then merged together into one about the size of large marble. It rolled around my palm as I lowered it to my knee.

"It's kind of cute," I said. "Why did the rain never respond this way?"

"How often does it rain in Vegas?" Kellen asked in return.

"Not very, but enough that I would have noticed this."

"Your binding was strong, AJ."

I nodded and continued to watch the water roll around. "How do I make it do what I need?"

"Each element is different," Kellen replied, shifting slightly beneath me. "The earth is solid, strong, resilient, but also nurturing. It listens well but is slow to act. Fire, on the other hand, is volatile, arrogant, fiercely rebellious, and quite intolerable. It requires authority mixed with bribery."

A small laugh rumbled through me, and I moaned with the pain that followed.

"Okay, so water is?"

"I don't know. I would guess it's reclusive, but it could also be demanding and forceful like the ocean." He held his palm next to mine, and the marble stopped rolling. "But I also know that it heals, so it must have compassion."

I watched it inch towards the edge of my palm and stop. A tiny tentacle-like strand stretched towards Kellen's palm. As soon as it touched, steam rose into the air, and the marble rolled away.

"I don't think it likes you very much," I said, with a weak grin. Exhaustion washed over my pain. I'd never been able to ask for help. Not that I didn't want to, but no one was ever there to offer it. Everything I had, as little as it was, came from my own hard work and sacrifice. Now, I had to ask a sentient puddle of water to heal my broken body. A nervous laugh escaped my lips. I must be losing my mind. "Little one, I really need your help."

It started spinning in place, faster and faster, with small drops shooting from its sides. Then, as suddenly as it started, it stopped. The air became thick with moisture, and I looked around me. Kellen's fire smoldered, and the droplets had vanished.

"I think we're about to get wet," Kellen whispered in my ear. "Look up."

I tilted my head back with effort and gasped. An enormous rain cloud hovered above us. Before I could react, a deluge of water fell on us both.

I expected it to be cold, but sighed with relief as a warming sensation washed over me and settled into my side. Much like Kellen's tingling spark, I felt the water's smooth motion as it moved towards my tender ribs. A dull ache followed its path until it wrapped around the broken bone. A loud pop preempted the surge of pain, forcing a scream from my lips.

Kellen held me tight as I pushed against him and clawed at his hand.

"Get it out!" I yelled.

"No," Kellen said, "let it fix what is broken."

He grabbed my free hand in his and wrapped me in a fierce embrace. My ribs moved, the muscles knitting back together. I squeezed my eyes shut, and flashes of my horrid childhood blinked between my hopes of a loving mother and a normal life. They died quickly as another spike of pain tore through my chest, and visions of my new reflection intermingled with Kellen, Kate, and Logan. I pushed the thoughts away, knowing I couldn't deal with my emotions and the pain at the same time.

Tiny pinpricks swept across my stomach, and the tearing pain subsided. I opened my eyes in time to see the water bleed away into the dark soil beneath me. Kellen loosened his grip, and I rolled to my side and folded into him like a child.

I was grateful when he didn't hesitate to just hold me and let me cry. The reality of the last twenty-four hours came crashing down with long, shuddering sobs.

Chapter 9

I woke with a start in a soft bed, covered by a thin quilt. Moonlight filtered through the sheers hanging on the window across the room. A long dresser covered the space below the window. A soft light outlined a partially closed door on the wall adjacent to my bed.

"Where am I?" I whispered. "Please tell me that was a dream."

I pulled the covers back and gingerly placed my hand on my ribs, only to find a huge t-shirt covering me. Nope, not a dream. I pushed past the fabric and reached my stomach, flinching. My ribs were still tender and probably bruised, but at least they weren't broken.

"Because the water healed me. How does that even happen?" I whispered to myself.

I slid off the bed and felt a cool floor beneath my bare feet. I looked down at the enormous t-shirt hanging to my knees. The neckline fell over my bony shoulder, and I tugged it back in place.

"I really hope Kate is responsible for this," I said, shaking my head.

I padded across the room and started opening the dresser drawers. They were all empty. Cursing quietly, I pushed open the door next to me, revealing a bathroom similar to Kate's but with another door on the far end. I took care of the necessities and went in search of my new friend.

I poked my head out the bedroom door and into the dark hallway. Small nightlights lit the corners, but I wasn't sure which way to go. My temporary room didn't open onto the patio garden, so I assumed I was in the center of the house.

To the right, then. I tip-toed down the hall and stopped at the first corner. I peered around the edge and noticed a soft glow coming from the last door. Could that be Kate's room? Or maybe the sitting room Kellen took me to?

I wasn't sure why I felt the need to sneak down the hall, but I didn't want to be the only one making any sound. Voices from the room forced me to stop just outside the door. I didn't want Kellen to see me in the stupid t-shirt that I assumed was his.

"You were not followed?" Kellen asked, his voice drifting into the hall.

"Of course not."

The second voice sounded familiar, and I tried to place it.

"Have they already found more?" Kellen continued.

"I don't think so, but they suspect my involvement. My usefulness to you may be at an end."

An uneasy silence followed. I felt a little guilty for eavesdropping and decided to go back to my room or maybe investigate the hall in the opposite direction. I turned and ran into a solid wall of muscle.

"Hello, princess," Logan whispered.

I clasped my hand over my mouth, stifling my scream.

"Come. It's more civilized to be part of the conversation." He gestured towards the door with his hand.

My face flushed, but I didn't move. "What are you doing here?" I asked in a low voice.

Logan chuckled, his gaze dropping down my body to my bare toes and back to my face. "You look marvelous, now come on. Everyone already knows you're here."

Where did that statement come from? I was positive I hadn't voiced my concerns out loud. "Don't avoid the question," I demanded.

He folded his arms across his chest. "You can walk in with me and act natural or walk in by yourself. It matters not to me." He stepped around me and towards the door.

I took a deep breath, trying to make a decision. I wasn't getting answers from him, and I cringed at the thought of anyone else seeing me like this. Kate was one thing, but having a conversation with two men was something else entirely. "Never mind, I'm going back to bed."

I rushed back down the hall, expecting him to stop me, but I made it all the way to my bedroom without interruption. I closed the door and leaned against it. What was I thinking? I found a small lamp on the bedside table and turned it on, then hopped back onto the soft mattress.

Kellen did mention that they knew each other, but why was Logan here? I didn't trust him, but I wasn't sure I trusted Kellen either. He had removed the binding that would've killed me, but could he have been lying? He wasn't the friendliest, but he did treat me with compassion and respect when he removed the binding. I sighed. Having both of them together had to mean trouble. What were their plans for me? Obviously, there had to be one. Logan lured me into that damn casino in the first place.

I thought about his conversation with me before meeting with the so-called Council. He had to have seen past the veil. He knew who I was, but he obviously didn't share it with Kellen. Why not? Were they just manipulating me or each other as well? What did it mean for me, now that my identity was revealed?

I needed to get back to my apartment. I also needed to find my bag and phone. I looked at the door and sighed. Logan was the last one to have them. How did I get thrown into this mess? More importantly, how did I get out?

I pulled the quilt up to my chin and wrapped my arms around my knees. I wasn't hideous anymore. Could I actually get a real job? I wasn't stupid, but I didn't go to college either. I might be able to apply at one of the dozens of timeshare groups or possibly a realtor. An involuntary shudder ran through me as I thought of the many casinos who kicked me out. I wouldn't be able to look at them without seeing vampires in every dark corner, anyway.

I certainly wouldn't find anything sitting in a borrowed t-shirt, hours away from civilization. I needed to talk to Kate. I looked at the bedroom door, debating if I should follow the hall in the opposite direction of Kellen and Logan. No. I'd find her in the morning.

Three quick knocks startled me, and a small yelp escaped my lips.

"Can I come in?" Kellen's muffled voice asked.

"It's not locked."

The door swung open, and he stepped inside. He was wearing baggy, gray sweatpants that hung low on his hips and a light-colored t-shirt.

"It's not polite to walk in uninvited," he stated, his impassive expression boring into me. "How are you?"

"Fine," I replied curtly.

He shifted his weight and dropped his gaze. "Kate is washing your clothes. They should be ready for you in the morning."

"Thanks."

"I promised to answer your questions," he began. I noticed an uneasiness that hadn't been there before. "We can do that now... or in the morning if you're still tired."

"What time is it?" I asked, watching him closely.

He shifted his weight again, and my suspicions started running wild. Why was he so nervous?

"Eleven," he replied.

I tossed the cover aside and slid from the bed. The neck of my too-large shirt fell over my shoulder again, and I grabbed it. "I don't suppose there's anything else for me to wear."

The corners of his mouth twitched, but he didn't smile. "Kate's sleepwear is even more revealing and would never fit you."

"Fine." I huffed and pulled the neck closed with one hand and stomped towards him. I was getting answers and food from him. "I'm hungry."

"Then let's feed you." He pulled the door open and led me down the hall to the right, the same direction I went before.

"You know, smiling isn't painful," I said to his wide shoulders.

"It might be," he replied, not turning around.

I quickened my step to catch up and walk by his side. He looked down at me and shook his head, but I didn't miss the softening in his eyes.

"So, what's on the menu?" I asked.

"Whatever you're cooking."

"You might be disappointed then. My specialties are eggs and cereal."

He pushed open the door I'd hidden behind and motioned for me to go in. It took a few moments for my eyes to adjust to the light, but I smiled when they did. I walked into a large open space with the same slate flooring as the hallway and my bedroom. Several small groupings of chairs filled one side of the room, while an open kitchen with a long bar filled the other.

"Is that really all you eat?" Kellen asked, interrupting my gaping.

"Just about," I replied, "except when Sandy takes pity on me and gives me fried chicken."

"Sandy?"

"Yeah, the owner of Sandy's Diner." I strolled towards the kitchen and ran my free hand along the black, granite countertop. "I'm afraid all this high-end stuff is wasted on me," I said. "Point me towards the cereal."

"I don't think so," Kellen replied. "You need real food, little girl."

"Some of us can't afford real food," I snapped back and immediately regretted it. Despite my suspicions, he'd been kind to me, mostly. "I'm sorry. That was rude." I pushed myself into one of the bar stools at the counter and studied the chips of rock in the polished granite, feeling foolish for bringing up my financial status. It wasn't his problem.

He leaned on the counter across from me, and I could feel his stare.

"What?" I asked, still focusing on a chip of gray stone.

"We have some leftover pasta and grilled chicken breast in the fridge." He reached over and pushed my chin up with his fingers. "You'll eat, then we'll talk."

Chapter 10

Kellen moved efficiently through the kitchen, placing a large portion of food on a plate for me. He popped it in the microwave and resumed his lean on the counter.

"My parents left this place to us when they passed away," he said. "My sister and I were taught to manage their holdings and, so far, haven't screwed it up."

The microwave dinged, and he removed my plate, setting it in front of me.

I didn't know how to reply to his statement, so I changed the subject. His financial status and upbringing were clearly the exact opposite of mine. "Why aren't you eating?" I asked, eyeing the pasta in front of me.

"I already did, while you slept," he replied.

My faced flushed. I'd cried like a baby in his arms, and he let me. So much for my accusations. "Sorry about that," I said, twisting my fork between my fingers. "I can't believe I cried myself to sleep."

"It was what you needed. You had a rough day."

"Yeah, just a little."

He pushed off the counter and started cleaning up the mess he made, and I delved into my pasta. It was amazing, but everything tasted amazing to me. Disappointment filled me a few minutes later as I stared at an empty plate.

"You can have more," Kellen said.

I looked up to find him watching me.

"Nope, I'm good." I hopped off the stool and took my plate to the sink, pulling on the neckline of my shirt as I went. I already felt trapped between his kindness and my inability to leave. Accepting anything else from him would come with a price. "Can we go back to my apartment? I really need some clothes."

When he didn't respond, I turned to look at him. He was still leaning against the counter, with his arms folded across his chest.

"Logan will be packing up your apartment," he replied.

"What? He can't be there, nor can he touch my stuff!" I wrinkled my nose and bit my bottom lip. I didn't have much, but it was mine. I didn't want a complete stranger going through my things, especially one I didn't trust. My cage shrunk with each second that ticked by. "Why is he doing that?"

"You can't go back, AJ," Kellen said. "The vampires know who you are. One of them saw past your veil."

I narrowed my eyes at him. Of course one of them did. Had Logan passed the news to his buddies? Was the vampire playing both sides? I didn't know whose side he was on.

"Why does that matter? Who cares if your Magister is my mother? She certainly doesn't," I snapped.

"Let's sit down and talk about this."

I stomped across the room to a trio of over-stuffed chairs. Sinking into the nearest one, I folded my legs beneath me, and pulled the t-shirt over my knees. I looked down and gasped. The neckline stretched farther than it should be. Kellen chuckled as I struggled with the ridiculous wardrobe.

"This is not funny," I hissed.

"It really is," he countered, "at least from my perspective." He leaned back and grabbed a dark gray throw from the chair behind him. "Take this. It might help."

I snatched it from his outstretched hand and wrapped the small blanket over me. It felt great, and I pulled it around my neck, nestling my chin into the thick, fuzzy fabric. It swallowed my entire body.

"Why can't I go home?"

His smile faded, and he looked toward the door.

"It starts with your family. The Magister's line has been in the same family for generations," he began. "Your mother is an only child despite her parents' efforts to have more. When they passed away, your mother inherited the mantle. For the first couple of decades, she worked relentlessly to uphold our ways. No one minded that she refused to marry or have children, as all her time and efforts were devoted to making our lives better." He paused and looked at the door again. Was he expecting someone? "But the pressures for an heir became overwhelming. She hid her pregnancy well, but there were still rumors. When the baby never came, it was assumed she couldn't carry one to term." He turned and his expression confused me. "No one knows who your father is except your mother."

I picked at the threads on the throw in my lap, my mind whirling with the new information.

"Why wouldn't she want a child?" I asked.

"She doesn't want to give up her throne." Logan's voice startled me. He stood at the door, watching us. Had he been there the entire time?

"That doesn't make sense," I argued. "She'll have to eventually."

The vampire strolled into the room, pulling his fingers through his dark hair. "That depends," he replied, leaning against the chair next to me. "Water mages live a very long time, longer than other mages."

My gaze bounced between the two men. "But I thought she had air, not water."

"You are correct, princess, but her partner was a water mage. It's how she's lived as long as she has."

"I thought she didn't get married." My confusion quickly turned to frustration. "What are you trying to say?"

"You haven't told her?" Logan said to Kellen, who glared at him.

So, he hadn't been there the whole time.

"We just started this conversation," Kellen retorted. "I haven't made it that far, but since you brought it up, you can explain."

Logan returned the glare and dropped into the chair between us. "As you know, most mages attune to one element, which by itself is not balanced." He pointed one long finger in the air. "For instance, fire is very destructive on its own." He raised another finger and brought them together. "But if you pair it with earth or water, it becomes stable and more easily controlled."

"Yes, Kellen sort of explained their dynamic," I agreed cautiously, not sure if Logan knew of Kellen's dual talents.

"Exactly! Kellen is a perfect example." He dropped his fingers and motioned towards Kellen. "He doesn't require a partner because his elements balance each other. Mages with only one element need a partner to balance them, or the mage becomes unstable, along with their element."

"Oh, that makes sense." I thought about my own elements and wondered what that meant for me. Did Logan know I also had two?

"The Magister's partner was a water mage. He agreed to slow her aging as long as she pursued a family. It's the Magister's duty to her people to ensure the line is not broken." He folded his hands in his lap and avoided my rapt attention. "She played along for a while, but it became evident that she had other ideas. I... her partner discovered her making plans with one of the vampire council."

"You were her partner?" I asked in a soft voice, not missing his correction. "You're a mage?"

"Yes and no. I'm a vampire," he replied, still not looking at me. "My element considers me dead, which is technically true."

I scooted to the edge of my seat and placed my hand on his knee, suddenly feeling sorry for the man I didn't trust. "But why?"

He looked up at me, pain clouding his eyes. "I was her first experiment with immortality. She paid the vampire council a very large sum of money to change me, against my will." He gently removed my hand and held it in his own. The gesture was tender and personal. "She thought I could be a mage and a vampire. She assumed my element would heal whatever damage the vampire venom did, and I would be an immortal mage. I tried to tell her that my element would not tolerate the curse of death, but she wouldn't listen. She insisted I could call it back." He shook his head and rubbed his thumb across my palm. "Don't let her take it from you."

"Can she really take it?"

"If you go back to Vegas, the vampires will find you," he replied, dropping my hand and leaning back in the chair.

I looked over at Kellen, then back to Logan. So, I really was trapped here. According to these two, it was just to ensure my safety. I gathered the blanket around myself again and folded my hands in my lap. Logan's gentle touch seemed just as sincere as his sadness for being forced into a vampire. Something my mother did to him.

"How old are you?" I asked, a theory swirling around my thoughts.

The two men looked at each other and shrugged.

"Does it matter?" Kellen asked.

"Yes, well, no, but kind of," I replied. They both gave me a skeptical look. "I have a lot of questions, and you two keep adding more than you're answering. First question is for

Logan: was I born before or after..." I paused, uncertain how to say his change to a vampire.

"I became this long before you were born, princess," he replied.

"Okay, so that eliminates you as my father," I said, eliciting surprised looks from both of them. "Second, Kate said she never met Logan, but obviously you two know each other very well."

"We've kept Kate out of this," Kellen replied. "The less she knows of my traitorous plans, the safer she is."

"So, she isn't here right now?" I asked, pushing down my panic. He told me Kate changed my clothes.

"It would seem counter-productive to have her here, wouldn't it?" Logan responded.

"Then who changed my clothes?" I could hear my voice rising quickly. "You said that Kate did." I pointed at Kellen accusingly.

He leaned back in his chair and laughed.

"How dare you think this is funny!" I yelled at him.

"It's hilarious, little girl," he said, still grinning. "We've dumped a lot of really bad news on you in the last few minutes, and you get pissed because you think I saw you naked."

A burning heat rose from my neck and across my face. I turned my glare on Logan who threw his hands in the air.

"Don't look at me. Kate wasn't here when I arrived."

"Settle down," Kellen said with a chuckle. "Kate found us in the practice room. She took care of all your needs before she left."

"You're an ass," I said, drawing my knees to my chest and pulling the blanket tighter.

"Probably," he replied, shrugging. "What's your next question?"

"I don't know. You distracted me." I continued to glare at him as I tried to bring my brain back on track. "Alright, what happens when a mage's partner is gone?"

Kellen's smile vanished. "Eventually, the mage and their element will become unstable."

"How long has your Magister been without a partner? And what does unstable mean?"

"About forty years," Logan replied. "Air is not as volatile as fire, but she's declined rapidly in the last five years. She will eventually go insane."

"That explains the looks of hope I saw at the palace," I said. "They don't expect me to fight her, do they?"

The two men exchanged glances.

"No!" I leapt to my feet, letting the throw fall to the floor. "Look at me! Do I look like a fighter to you?"

"Yep." Logan smiled and draped an arm over the back of the chair. "I've had firsthand experience with your viciousness."

"You are not funny," I hissed. "There is no way she feels even a little threatened by me."

"You're right," Kellen agreed. "And I'd like to keep it that way."

"How dare you call me weak!" I heard the absurdity in my words as they flew from my lips, but I couldn't stop them.

A burst of laughter erupted from Logan. He leaned forward with his elbows on his knees and hid his face in his hands. His wide shoulders shuddered with his muffled amusement.

"You two are unbelievable," I said, picking up the throw and wrapping it around my shoulders. "I'm going back to bed."

"AJ, wait," Kellen said, holding a hand towards me.

I saw his lips twitching, and it infuriated me even more. I knew I was being childish, but how was I supposed to cope with everything they told me?

"There's more you need to know that can't wait," Kellen continued, smoothing the smile from his face. "I told Kate you were attuned to air and asked that she report it to the Magister. I also told her not to come back because the portal was acting glitchy."

"Why would you do that?" I stopped just outside the small circle of chairs.

"If the Magister knows you have water, she will try to force a partnership," Kellen explained. "But if you have the same element as her, she won't consider you a threat *or* an asset."

"What does it mean to force a partnership?" I asked, sitting on the arm of my chair. "Can't mages decide on their own?"

"The element decides, not the mage," Logan replied, his previous humor at my expense now gone. "Mages have been trying for years to choose their own, for all kinds of reasons, but it never ends well."

"But the Magister is desperate," Kellen added, my gaze snapping to him. "She hasn't found what she wanted with the vampires, and she knows she's losing her mind."

My brow furrowed as I absorbed all the information. The concept of balancing the elements made sense, but the rest of it didn't. "So, why lie about the portal? Or is it broken?" I asked, moving to the next question on my mental list.

"It's glitchy because a vampire has tampered with it," Kellen replied. "We'll be attacked tonight, and the vampire horde will destroy our portal in their attempt to reach the palace."

"What?" I looked at Kellen with panic rising in my chest. "You're not serious, are you?"

"Yes and no," Kellen replied. "Logan will destroy the portal. I'll call Kate and let her know that you and I went to town to shop for clothes for you. When we returned, we found the portal shattered."

"She'll believe that? How many people shop in the middle of the night? And wouldn't the 'vampires' just use the portal?"

"They can't. The portal is designed for the living, not the dead," Kellen explained. "The group that invaded my home were young and didn't realize the limitation." He crossed one leg over the other and continued. "It's Vegas. When don't people shop?"

"Oh." Once again, my gaze danced between the two men. They had this all figured out. How long had this plan been in place? "Where is the Magister's palace? I assumed it was nearby since the others used the van to get there yesterday."

"They didn't use the van," Kellen replied. "They used the portal, which is why they arrived at the palace before we did. The location of the palace is a closely guarded secret. The only way to get there is through a portal."

"And yours is not the only one, right?" I asked. "Wait a minute. Why would you have one? It seems like you'd have to be pretty important to be allowed that access. And shouldn't there be tons of guards at the house protecting it?"

"So inquisitive," Logan interjected, "and a little too observant. This conversation could last for hours. The more you tell her, the more she wants to know."

"You thought I would just sit back and listen to your tale without questions?" I argued. "Until yesterday, my biggest concern was my next meal and my next extremely temporary job."

Kellen stood and looked down at me. "Just know this estate is well protected by many things. Having a retinue of armed guards would draw attention, which we don't want."

I realized that was the only answer I was getting, but it didn't satisfy my need to know.

"So why have you isolated us from them?" I asked.

"To train you."

Chapter 11

"What do you mean I have to share my space with him?" My outrage escalated when Kellen informed me that Logan would be staying at the estate. "He's a vampire, and I'm dinner."

"There isn't enough of you to be more than a snack, princess," Logan quipped, smiling at me. I glared at him and turned back to Kellen.

"This." I pointed at the vampire but didn't look at him, keeping my scowl targeted at Kellen.

"The house only has so many rooms, AJ," Kellen replied. "You aren't sharing a room, only the bathroom that connects your rooms. Logan will not bite you, and I don't imagine he'll use the bathroom for more than the occasional shower."

"The keyword there is 'connects.'" I deflated, sinking into the deep cushion. I couldn't really argue. He was giving me a free place to stay so I could learn how to overthrow my mother, the ruler of the mages. I wasn't doing this. "I can't do this. I'd rather go back to hiding in my apartment, thinking I was the monster."

"You can do this," Kellen replied, kneeling in front of me.

"No, I can't. I'm going back to bed." I pushed his shoulder. "I want you to take me home tomorrow."

Kellen stood and backed away, allowing me to stand and leave the room. I wanted nothing more than to crawl beneath the covers and hide from everything I just learned.

~~~~~~~~~~~~~~~~~
~~~~~~~~~~~~~~~~~

Sunlight streaming in the window woke me several hours later. I stretched on the soft mattress and wound my fingers around the quilt. My mind didn't wait for me to wake up before it started cataloguing everything that happened in the last thirty hours or so.

Could I really stay there with two complete strangers, one of them being a vampire? Was he really a vampire, or were they just trying to scare me? He didn't behave as I expected, and I didn't see any fangs hanging from his mouth. I knew he was really fast, but did that make him a vampire?

I pushed myself into a sitting position, pulling my knees to my chest.

Why would I stay? They clearly expected me to fight. My ninety-five pounds wasn't fighting anything, let alone a powerful mage. And what was I fighting for? I owed these people nothing; I didn't even know they existed until a day ago. My mother clearly didn't want me, so why did I care what happened to her?

Then, there was this whole magic thing. How was it real? I had to admit it was. I'd seen it with my own two eyes. I wondered if the magic was mine or if Kellen was just trying to make me believe I was a mage. Did I care either way? Did I really want to be part of whatever drama was brewing in their palace?

My thoughts drifted to the Magister. I didn't even know the woman's real name, but I couldn't deny we were related. Was she really my mother? The Magister didn't deny it, but she didn't act like the mother I expected. Then again, neither did my foster-mom. At least my foster parents did the best they could to raise a child everyone shunned.

I sighed, my mind overflowing with contradictory questions and answers. Thinking in circles wouldn't solve anything. I pushed the blankets aside and remembered I was still wearing that ridiculous t-shirt. I mumbled complaints all the way to the bathroom, but I paused when I grabbed the door handle. What if Logan was in there? I didn't want to barge in if he was in the shower. I put my ear to the door and listened but didn't hear anything. I tapped lightly, and when no one responded, I went in.

"There better be a lock on the door," I mumbled.

I looked across the room to the door on the other side. The plain, brass knob was missing the little locking mechanism. Oh, hell no! I pulled a towel from the rack next to the shower and wrapped one end around the doorknob. Regardless of my efforts, the thick towel wouldn't stay tied around the knob. My face flushed at the thought of Logan walking in while I was peeing.

I looked down at the t-shirt I wore, smiled, and pulled it over my head. I tied one end around the doorknob and wrapped the other end around the towel bar. Confident that I wouldn't be interrupted, I finally looked in the mirror that covered the wall above the double sinks.

A younger version of the Magister stared back at me. Well, sort of. My poorly cut hair stood out on one side, but it didn't detract from the beauty that was now mine. I tentatively touched my face with shaking fingers, trailing the perfectly curved chin that hadn't been there the day before. My wide eyes were flawlessly spaced above my small nose. Why did someone make me suffer a lifetime with that monstrous appearance? Didn't they realize how hard it would be?

I shook my head and got in the shower.

When finished, I untied the shirt, pulled it back over my head and returned to the bedroom. My clothes sat on the dresser in a neatly folded pile. Grateful to have something of my own, I didn't hesitate to get dressed.

The smell of freshly brewed coffee met me half way down the hall, and the thought of breakfast quickened my steps. Maybe I could try to make pancakes or waffles—anything but eggs.

When I opened the door, Kellen was sitting at the kitchen bar.

"Good morning," he said, watching me walk across the room.

"Morning."

"There's coffee if you want."

I went to the kitchen and started opening cabinets, looking for the one with coffee cups.

"Two more over to the right," Kellen suggested.

"Thanks." I rifled through the collection of cups and found one emblazoned with 'I Love NY.' I filled it to the brim and sat down next to Kellen.

"Black coffee?" he asked, raising an eyebrow at me.

"Yep." I almost mentioned my lack of funds to buy fancy creamer or sugar, but I held my tongue.

"Do I get more than one word at a time this morning?"

I rolled my eyes. "Thank you."

"What did I do to deserve thanks?" he asked, turning on his stool to face me.

I rubbed my finger around the top of the cup, recognizing the loaded question. "I don't know," I replied, uncertain how to explain my emotions. He revealed a part of my life that had been hidden from me. I wasn't sure if I should be grateful or not, but he went through a lot of trouble to make it happen.

"I see. Well, we're going to Vegas today to take care of your apartment and buy you some clothes." He slid off the stool and stood next to me.

"I have clothes at my apartment," I replied, watching his expression, which remained impassive.

"Of course. I'll be getting the car ready. Meet me out front when you're done."

I watched him walk across the room, pull open the glass door and disappear into the gardens. "Damn."

"That's a rather unpleasant word from such a pretty face." Logan's voice startled me, and I nearly spilled my coffee.

"Stop doing that! I could've been taking a drink and choked to death," I snapped, waving my hand at him dismissively.

"Not likely," he replied with a grin, taking the seat Kellen had just vacated. "So, what did you decide?"

"What are you talking about?"

"Are you going to stay here or force Kellen to leave you in Vegas?"

I rolled my eyes at him. "Like I could force Kellen to do anything."

"He won't make you stay here, princess."

I looked up into his brown eyes and noticed the tiny green flecks I'd seen earlier. "Why do you call me princess?"

"Because it's who you are," he replied. "Your mother calls herself Magister, but your family was much more."

"I really can't do this, Logan," I said. "I'm not that person."

"I hope you change your mind." He rubbed my chin with his thumb, making me shiver. "At least let us train you."

I leaned into his touch and he cradled my face in his palm. "Are you trying to entrance me?" I asked, feeling a compulsion to be near him and thinking of my conversation with Kellen about my veil and binding.

"Nope, I just don't want you to have any reason to fear me," he replied. "I'm your protector, nothing more and nothing less."

I lifted my head away from his hand and stared at him.

"No, I won't explain. You've had enough thrown at you in the last day. We can talk more later." He stood and held out his hand to me. "Are you going to run from Kellen?"

I looked at his hand as if it would have the answers we both wanted. I didn't know what to do. "I'll try not to," I replied, taking his hand and allowing him to guide me from the tall stool.

"Good, because I need some sleep. I didn't want to have to follow you around Vegas and make sure you behaved." He winked, then turned around and left the room, leaving me to finish my coffee and follow Kellen outside.

Chapter 12

I was surprised I slept for most of the ride back to Vegas. The cool, leather seats in Kellen's SUV cradled me perfectly, and his silence encouraged my sleepiness. I pushed the button on the automatic seat, and it raised me to a sitting position. A large, green interstate sign passed over my head, making me blink several times.

"Did that sign just say, 'Reno - Next Exit?'" I asked.

"Yes, it did," Kellen replied.

"What the hell?" I rubbed my hands across my face and took a deep breath.

"I received a message shortly after we left that it was not safe to go back to Vegas," he replied. "For either of us."

"What is that supposed to mean?"

"If they were only looking for you, we might have been able to avoid notice," he explained. "But it looks like the Magister didn't buy my story."

"So, why didn't you just go back home?"

"When they don't find us in Vegas, that's the first place they'll look," he replied, not taking his eyes from the road.

"But what about Logan? He said he was going to bed."

Kellen glanced at me, then turned back to the road. "Why are you now suddenly worried about Logan? Last night you were ready to throw him to the wolves."

"That's irrelevant," I retorted, not wanting him to distract me from an answer. I was beginning to notice that pattern with him, always changing the subject when I asked too many questions. "I got the impression he was your friend. I can't believe you'd leave him there by himself, knowing that someone, possibly many someones, would show up with ill intent."

"First, he's not alone." Kellen removed his right hand from the steering wheel and held up his index finger, then added his middle finger. "Second, he's perfectly capable of taking care of himself. And third..." He raised his ring finger. "I'm not explaining the estate's defenses."

I huffed and looked out the passenger window. I'd hoped to go back home and possibly even escape from my newest capturer. I wasn't a hideous monster any more. I could get a real job and have a future. But I was beginning to think it wasn't going to be an option. Was Kellen just being nice to try to fool me into thinking I wasn't a prisoner? Was the threat to our safety a convenient way for him to keep me in his grasp? It was beginning to look that way.

We exited the interstate on the outskirts of town. Numerous signs lined the road for hotels, food, and shopping.

"So, why are we in Reno?" I asked grudgingly.

"You need clothes, and I need supplies," he replied, turning into a fast food restaurant. "The small towns surrounding my house don't provide either. According to Kate, the clothing options are worthless, and I need a specialty shop for the items I require."

I huffed again and continued to look out the window as he found a parking place. "I don't have any money, and I'm not taking yours. If you would've taken me back to my apartment, I could've picked up my things."

"Logan emptied your apartment last night," he said, turning off the engine. "All of your belongings are in a trunk at the end of your bed."

I thought about all the furniture in my borrowed room. I hadn't seen a chest at the end of the bed, but I hadn't really looked, either. It still irritated me that these two men now dictated every part of my life. The thought of Logan packing all my stuff made me cringe. I didn't have much, but it was mine.

"My rent is due next week," I mumbled, already feeling the lack of air conditioning inside the vehicle.

"Your landlord is not expecting you to return," Kellen replied.

"How dare you!" I turned sideways in my seat and glared at him. "This is my life, not yours! You have no right to turn it upside down and take my choices from me."

He sighed and turned the engine back on. The cool breeze from the AC felt great, but I wasn't telling him that. He twisted in his seat to face me with barely subdued patience.

"Everything I have done was to keep you alive," he began from between clinched teeth. "I could've left that veil and your binding, which would've killed you. I could've left you at the palace with the Magister, which also would've seen you dead. And I could've left you at the estate this morning and took care of my errands on my own, which would've been much easier." His voice rose as he spoke, and I noticed his brown eyes shifting to a lighter shade. "Logan may have been able to protect you, but it wasn't guaranteed. So, I brought your ungrateful ass with me."

I didn't feel like I'd been ungrateful, but when he said it that way, it made me sound petty. Regardless, he still had no right to make those decisions for me. I stared at him for several seconds, before dragging my eyes away. I heard him take a deep breath.

"I'm hungry, and you're eating whether you want to or not." He tossed a ball cap at me. "You should cover your very memorable hair." He turned off the SUV again and got out. I watched him storm towards the entrance to the restaurant and stop at the door. He turned around and glared at me.

I pulled the cap over my head, opened the door, and hopped out. He was infuriating, even more so because he might be right about my pettiness, but he was wrong about my personal choices. I pursed my lips together as I approached him and let him open the door for me.

We ordered food, and I went in search of the bathroom. I shuddered when I found it. Why did they always have to be nasty? Two stalls and a cracked sink filled the tiny space. One of the stalls was occupied, so I used the other, doing everything I could not to touch anything. I wasn't even sure I wanted to use the sink to wash my hands.

The other occupant exited her stall the same time I did. She was several inches taller with wide shoulders and a muscular frame, almost like a woman body-builder. She stood in front of the sink, facing me with her thick arms hanging loose at her sides. Her full lips spread into a wide grin, revealing extremely white teeth.

A strange tingle raced across my skin, and I wondered if this woman was a mage.

"My, my," the woman drawled. "Today's my lucky day."

The simple words made my pulse race. Her smile was anything but kind. I squeezed by the woman, rushing out the door into the restaurant. I reached the counter where Kellen waited and discreetly stepped behind him.

"What happened?" he whispered.

The woman exited the bathroom, and I ducked behind Kellen's large frame again, feeling foolish and terrified at the same time. I didn't move for several moments, thinking I gave her plenty of time to leave. I took a step forward just as my admirer walked up to the counter. She winked at me, and I tried not to react. A weird glow emanated from her wide shoulders and down her thick arms. My eyes widened as one of the woman's fingers elongated into a single claw.

"I'll wait in the car," I whispered harshly, pulling on Kellen's arm.

He grabbed my shaking hand as the teenage worker behind the counter handed him our bag of food. "Come on," he said.

I didn't resist as he led me out the door and through the parking lot. Kellen waited until we were back on the road before he assaulted me with questions.

"What did she say to you?" he asked, constantly glancing at me.

"She said it was her lucky day," I responded. "But her tone implied I wouldn't like it. What was she?"

"What did you see when you looked at her?" he countered.

"I don't know," I squeaked. "One of her hands started to turn into a claw, right there in line!"

"You saw that?" His voice raised in disbelief.

"Well, I didn't just make it up."

He clamped his mouth shut, and a deep furrow formed between his eyes. A few minutes later, he turned into the only open spot in the sprawling parking lot of a large shopping plaza. He slammed the car in park and turned towards me.

"We're going to make this really quick," he said. "We're walking into the specialty shop at the end of the plaza, picking up my stuff and leaving. We'll buy your clothes online."

"Kellen, what was that?"

His hand rested on the key that was still in the ignition. "That was a bear," he replied, "which means every other shifter in town will know you're here. Let's go, before they find us again."

He turned off the SUV and exited the vehicle. I met him at the front of the car. Did he really mean a bear? I'd read enough urban fantasy to recognize the term 'shifter,' but surely that's not what he meant. People couldn't really turn into animals, could they?

"Don't leave my side," he whispered harshly.

I had to jog to keep up with his long, hurried strides and was out of breath by time we reached the last shop in the end of the plaza. News articles depicting historical events from the last few decades covered the windows, making it impossible to see inside the store. Kellen pushed open the door, eliciting the familiar ring of a bell attached to the handle.

The dim lighting inside the store forced me to stop and let my eyes adjust.

"We're not stopping," Kellen whispered and grabbed my hand, dragging me down the center aisle.

My eyes finally adjusted when we reached a glass display case that also acted as the cashier's counter. Kellen pushed me in front of him and sandwiched me between the case and his body. He wrapped his arm around my waist and tapped the shell-shaped bell next to the old-style cash register with his free hand.

"Yeah, yeah, just a sec," a man's voice called out from behind a row of shelves, covered in comic books.

"I'm in a hurry, Ray," Kellen yelled back.

"Kellen, my man." Ray emerged carrying a cardboard box, which he dropped on the counter in front of us. "I just finished packing these up for you."

Ray looked down at me and smiled. The familiar feel of magic raced across my skin, and I looked into his hazel eyes. They seemed to change color from brown to green as his gaze roamed over me.

"Who do we have here?" Ray asked.

"AJ, this is Ray," Kellen said, handing Ray a roll of twenty-dollar bills.

My eyes widened as Ray counted out five hundred dollars. Who carried around that much cash? Kellen, obviously.

"Always a pleasure doing business, my man," Ray said with a smile.

Kellen nodded, tucked the box under his free arm and pulled me away from the counter. The sound of the bell jingling on the door brought him to a halt.

"Damn," he whispered and turned to face me. "This could be unpleasant, AJ. I need you to stay calm no matter what they say. It would be best if you didn't speak." He tugged at the hat on my head, pulled me to the side, then faced the newcomers.

Chapter 13

Two men and a woman stood in front of us.

"Kellen," the man on the left said, nodding once and making his sand-colored hair fall across his forehead. He wore faded jeans and a gray t-shirt, just like the man next to him. I assumed they were brothers, their resemblance strong enough that it couldn't be coincidental. In total contrast, the woman wore short-shorts and a pink tank top that matched the color of her hair.

"Matt. Mike." Kellen nodded back but didn't move.

"Is that really her?" Matt asked, glancing at me.

"Depends on who you think she is," Kellen replied.

"It's been a long time since I seen you out with a girl tied to your hip," Mike chided. "So, she's either a cute lay or the Magister's whelp."

"I'm betting the latter," Matt concluded. "We all know you're waiting for your partner." His harsh laughter only lasted for a few seconds but added to the already tense room. "Like a dual mage will ever have one."

I looked up at Kellen. He glared at Matt and gently put the box on a shelf next to him, pushing me behind him.

"Is that how it's gonna be man?" Mike asked. "It'd be easier for all of us if you just handed her over."

"Really? And what are your plans for her?" Kellen argued. "Does her bounty include a live body?"

Tension rolled off Kellen in waves. I placed my palm against his lower back and felt him flinch. The small spark I recognized as him rushed through my fingers, then back to its owner. The feeling made me giddy, and I suppressed a smile as I hid behind him. I had a sudden urge to wrap my arms around his waist, and it took a huge amount of restraint to remain still.

"The Magister's bounty wants a dead body, but the boss wants her alive," Matt replied.

"She wants me dead?" I asked in surprise, stepping out from behind my protector. "That bitch! We spoke for, what, five minutes, and she decides she hates me?"

"Oh, I like her," the woman chimed in. The smile spreading across her face made her deep blue eyes shine. "Definitely taking her to the boss."

Kellen's hand ran down my back, and I looked up at him. His narrowed eyes and pronounced frown said it all. I was supposed to remain silent.

"Sorry," I whispered.

"What does Victor want with her?" Kellen asked, dragging his eyes from me.

"You'll have to ask him yourself, man," Mike replied. "He said 'bring the girl,' but since you're attached at the hip..."

Kellen let the comment slide and glared at the trio. Would Kellen fight them? One against three only worked in the movies.

"None of you are driving my car, but Matt can ride shotgun to make sure we get there," Kellen conceded.

The brothers looked at each other, and Matt nodded.

"We'll be right behind ya," Mike said, then turned and walked out the door.

The woman winked at me before following him out. Why did everyone wink at me? They obviously knew something I didn't, or I had a booger on my face.

Kellen retrieved his box and held out his free hand. He would tell me if I had something on my face, right? I took his hand and felt that little spark jump once again. I looked up at him, confused. He shook his head and moved towards the door. We were definitely talking about it later even if he didn't want to.

"Thanks for not tearing up the place," Ray called from the back.

No one responded to him, so I smiled and waved as Kellen pulled me out the door.

I sat in the back seat of Kellen's SUV, watching the two men in front toss glares at one another. It appeared Kellen didn't need directions to 'the boss' place,' which meant he'd been there before. But that only made sense. He obviously knew who these people were. They rode in silence for fifteen minutes along the west side of Reno, then turned onto a narrow road that wound into the foothills of the Sierra Nevada mountains.

I'd never been into the mountains and was awed by the beauty that surrounded me. Tall, narrow pines dotted the landscape, and the mountains set an amazing backdrop, with their snow-capped peaks. I momentarily forgot the oppressive heat of the late Nevada summer.

"Can you hand me that bag of food?" I asked, my growling stomach interrupting my sightseeing.

Matt twisted in his seat and looked at me. His face almost looked kind. Bushy eyebrows shaded his hazel eyes and his light, brown hair was a little long, making him appear younger than I suspected he was. The familiar buzz of magic flowed over my skin as he handed me the bag.

"Could you not do that?" I asked, not hiding my irritation. "Didn't anyone ever teach you guys that it's rude to touch others with your magic?"

Matt threw his head back and laughed. "No, no one's ever mentioned it," he replied, grinning.

I fished a hamburger out of the bag and glared at him. "If there's something you want to know, you could just ask me, rather than poking at me."

"Okay then. What's your talent?" he asked.

I now understood the meaning of that question. Should I tell him? It's not like he wouldn't find out later.

"Air," I replied.

"I suspected as much. It usually runs in the family."

"What about you?" I asked. "What's your talent?"

"I have many talents, pretty lady," he replied, winking at me. "I'll be happy to show you later."

"He's a wolf," Kellen answered with his own growl.

"Kellen would make an amazing wolf," Matt continued, glancing at Kellen. "He's fierce, loyal, and has a better growl than half our pack."

My mouth dropped open. He couldn't possibly be serious. Matt acted as if he liked Kellen, or at least respected him. Had I judged him wrong? And I really didn't want to hear I was sitting in the car with a man who could turn into a wolf.

"Kellen didn't tell you?" he asked. "I'm wounded." He placed his hand on his heart and feigned an agonizing death. I laughed at his antics, making his smile widen.

"No, he didn't tell me," I replied. "But in his defense, we've been a little busy."

"Damn, I was hoping to show you my talents later, but Kellen doesn't share." He wagged his eyebrows at me, and my ears grew hot with embarrassment.

"That's not what I meant," I said defensively. "Kellen and I just met the day before yesterday. A lot's happened since then."

"Then maybe..." Matt winked at me again, and my entire face flushed. I'd never had anyone flirt with me, even if it was feigned. I took a bite of my burger trying to hide my embarrassment.

"When we get to their lodge, stay with me, and try not to speak, AJ," Kellen said, interrupting Matt's ogling. "The mutts are easily distracted."

"He's testy today," Matt stated, turning back around in his seat.

Kellen turned onto a dirt road that wound its way through the trees and ended at a large, two-story lodge with a covered porch lining the entire front of the building. Tall pines surrounded the house, nearly blocking out the blue sky. I stuffed the rest of the sandwich in my mouth and washed it down with water.

Kellen parked his SUV and jumped out, then opened my door on the driver's side. "Stay with me, AJ," he said, his eyes almost pleading. "Don't let them separate us."

"Okay," I replied, confused by his expression. I didn't feel threatened by Matt, not like I did with the bear we met earlier.

He once again held his hand out to me. I looked down at his large palm and long fingers, placing my own small hand in his. I smiled at the contrast between them, suppressing a giggle. We probably looked ridiculous. He laced his fingers in mine, and we walked towards the wooden steps leading up to the large home.

Matt opened the door for us, and I gasped. Six leather sofas and three low tables filled the left side. Windows stretched towards the ceiling with nothing covering them, providing a stunning view of the forest beyond. An enormous stone fireplace took up the center of the room, and I realized I could see through it to the other side. Two sweeping staircases flanked each side of the hearth, disappearing behind the stacked stones.

On the right side was the largest dining table I'd ever seen. Dozens of chairs lined the solid wood table, half of them occupied by men, women and several children. They stopped eating and looked at the new arrivals. Snarls and growls erupted immediately. I involuntarily stepped back, but Kellen released my hand and wrapped his arm around my waist, holding me in place.

Matt waved his hand at the group and the growls subsided, but the hostile looks did not.

"Come on, Victor will be in his study."

I followed Kellen and Matt through a wooden pocket door that disappeared into the wall. I almost turned around and pulled it back out of the wall but thought better of it. I shouldn't behave as if I'd grown up dirt poor and unrefined, even if that was my reality. The transition from wood floors to thick carpet surprised me. A deep brown, area rug covered the wooden planks and ran beneath a large, light oak desk. It reminded me of another lavish room with a desk as the centerpiece. An involuntary shiver ran through me, and Kellen rubbed my back, easing my tension. Did he know about Jack's office, or was he just trying to calm my nerves? Probably the latter.

The leather office chair at the desk was empty, but the largest man I'd ever seen stood at a dry bar just behind it. His wide shoulders and thick torso supported an equally broad neck. His light brown hair hugged his scalp, and a well-groomed beard covered his square chin. He stared back at me, ignoring Kellen and Matt. His deep brown eyes seemed to search my soul, but I didn't feel the familiar buzz of magic that usually accompanied that gaze. He inhaled deeply and closed his eyes, holding his breath for several seconds.

"She has more of her grandfather than her mother." His deep voice reverberated through the room.

He crossed the space between us quickly and stood in front of me. I craned my neck back to look up at him and wrinkled my nose. He had to be six and half feet tall, at least. I was used to feeling small around everyone, because I was, but his size was overwhelming.

"Sit and talk to me," he commanded and turned towards a grouping of chairs to the left that I hadn't seen when I came in. "Matt, tell Glen that the bounty is paid. Make sure he spreads the word quickly."

"Yes, boss." Matt snapped his heels together, then left.

"I'd tell you to leave as well, Kellen, but I can see that you won't." He lowered himself into a large wooden chair with an upholstered seat and motioned for us to do the same. "My name is Victor. I apologize for the unfortunate means for bringing you here."

"I'm AJ," I responded, not sure how to reply to his apology.

"And what does that stand for, AJ?" he asked.

"Alisandra Johnson," I replied.

"Hmmm. Why would you hide such a beautiful name?" He leaned his head to the side and raised his eyebrows. I tried not to think of my neighbor's German Shepard that did the same thing.

"I had a difficult childhood," I replied, my thoughts sobering quickly. "Kids are cruel."

"That, they are." He glanced at Kellen, then back to me. "How did you end up with our favorite mage?"

I also looked at Kellen, who stared back at me. I didn't know if I should tell Victor the truth, part of the truth, or make something up.

"She was with a group of mages we rescued from the vampires," Kellen answered.

Victor scowled at Kellen, his eyebrows joining in the middle. "She is more than capable of speaking for herself."

"I know more of her capabilities than either of you, Victor," Kellen said in a low voice. "She was bound until yesterday. She knows nothing of our world."

Victor's eyebrows shot towards his hairline as he turned back to me. "Is this true?"

I nodded.

"That is fortunate for us," he said, leaning back in his chair. "We have the opportunity to train her and teach her the history of our people. You will leave her with me."

"I will not," Kellen stated.

Victor's eyebrows made the trip back together, and a low growl rumbled in his throat. I was enthralled with the animation in his face. "You don't have a choice, mage."

"She is my partner," Kellen stated. "She will stay with me and *I* will train her. Her elements will respond quicker when paired with mine."

"Prove it," Victor commanded. "Prove it, and I'll allow her to leave."

"She is not trained," Kellen argued. "Our elements have not even been introduced to each other. If she tries to command one now, you'll be left with a pile of logs in place of your home."

"Then she doesn't leave."

Both men leaned forward in their chairs, and the hair on my neck rose with the tension. Why did men always feel the need to thump their chests at one another? I rose from my chair and stood between them, facing off Victor first.

"You will not dictate my life," I stated, pointing my bony finger at his face. "I've spent the last twenty years a victim of bullies who thought they could do whatever they wanted with me. I will choose my fate, not you."

His eyebrows once again receded to his hairline.

I turned on Kellen and frowned. "You and I will have a private conversation about the information you have chosen not to share with me." I shoved my hand at him. "Give me your hand."

He tentatively reached for me, guilt etched on his face. "You don't have to prove anything to him, AJ," Kellen said.

"Apparently I do," I retorted.

I turned my body so Victor could see our hands. I flipped Kellen's over so his palm faced the ceiling, then hovered mine over the top of his. I closed my eyes and thought of the little spark that raced through me the day before, then again only an hour ago. A warm glow beneath my fingers forced my eyes open. A tiny flame danced in Kellen's hand. I rested my fingers near his, and the flame skipped towards me. I felt it hesitate and looked up at Kellen's face.

"It will burn you," he said, meeting my gaze.

"Not on purpose," I replied. "I can feel its intent."

"Pull the humidity from the air and give it a buffer against your skin."

"I can do that?" I asked, my eyes widening in surprise.

He rolled his eyes at me, and I stuck out my tongue.

"Remember what we talked about when we removed your binding. It's the same principle. Just make sure you don't call on the wind." The corners of his mouth turned up. "Victor won't like the results."

I smiled with him, then thought of the little droplet that rolled around in my hand. The air grew thick around me, and Victor gasped. Moisture clung to my skin, then ran down my arm, filling my cupped palm and running over onto the rug beneath my feet.

"Not all of it, AJ," Kellen said, presenting his empty hand.

"Sorry. I didn't put out the fire, did I?"

"Yes, you did." He chuckled. "But I can bring it back."

A smaller version of the flame flickered to life once again. I lowered my hand full of water next to Kellen's. The flame tentatively moved towards me, then jumped the space between us, landing in my palm. The water steamed but remained in place. The flame flickered but didn't run away.

I lowered myself to the floor and smiled. I was holding a little flame in a puddle of water. *Magic was awesome.*

"Impressive." Victor's voice startled me, and I dropped my hand. The pool of water consumed the flame, and I yelped.

"Oh God! Did I kill it?"

"No, it takes more than that to extinguish my fire, little girl."

I heard the humor in his voice and flushed with embarrassment.

"You will ally with us?" Victor asked, drawing my attention.

"As long as our goals align, we will fight by your side," Kellen replied. He took my hand and pulled me to my feet.

"Will there be a time when they don't align?"

"I hope not," Kellen answered. "You know my intentions and motivations. I believe I know yours. So long as that doesn't change, we're allies."

Chapter 14

"You have a lot of explaining to do," I said as we drove away from Victor's lodge.

"You do realize we have only known each other for less than forty-eight hours, right?"

"Of course, I do," I replied. "But you've left out some very important details. Like being partners."

"I wanted you to be familiar with your elements before we tried to do anything else," he argued.

"And you thought that was an excuse to not tell me about this partner thing," I retorted. "I don't even know what it means."

"Logan explained it last night." He flipped his visor down to block the setting sun. "It's important for mages with a single element."

"And what about mages with two?" I pressed. "What does that mean for us?"

I watched his profile, perfectly outlined by the sunset. It reminded me of the paintings of the Egyptian Pharaohs. Was his family from the mid-east or northern Africa? My mind continued to wander until I realized he'd stopped the car.

He turned in his seat to face me, and a strange expression crossed his features. He pulled his lips into a tight line and narrowed his eyes, but it wasn't his normal, foreboding look. This was something else. I waited and watched as he struggled to pull his thoughts together.

"As Logan explained," he began, looking out the windshield, "dual mages don't need a partner to balance their elements. They automatically balance each other. Opposing elements would never choose to be together." He bit his lower lip and turned to me. "Unless the elements chose another dual mage, but even then, it would have to be a mage with the opposing elements. Mine would never choose another mage with fire or earth."

"That seems a little complicated, doesn't it?" I asked.

"Any more so than everything else that's happened to you in the last two days?" he countered.

"I suppose not." I looked out the window at the pinks and golds stretching across the sky. "So, I'm stuck with you forever?"

"We are mage partners, not lovers," Kellen replied. "Our magic is strongest when we work together."

I thought I saw sadness, or disappointment, flicker across his face. I hadn't forgotten Mike's comment about Kellen waiting for his partner, so why did he look upset if he found... me?

"And this alliance with Victor?" I asked, moving away from the subject that made him uncomfortable.

"The Magister turned to the vampires to find her immortality. What she got was a ramped-up vampire." He shook his head. "Logan is one of the few who opposes the vampire council's plans. The others are being used as weapons against the other supernatural families."

"Why do the vampires want a war?"

"It's complicated," he replied, turning in his seat and putting the SUV back into drive. "Not all of them do. Most are happy to leave everything the way it is, but others are tired of hiding in the dark. Several times throughout history, one or more of the supernatural families decided it was a good idea to reveal themselves to humans. It never works out well. We all know what happens when humans discover something they don't understand." He paused, and his frown deepened. "Some of our mages are willingly going to the vampires to become weapons for them."

I thought of the Salem witch trials, the tales of vampires and werewolves, ogres and Bigfoot. Humans always hunted and killed what they didn't understand. "Why would our mages want to be a vampire? Doesn't their element abandon them?"

"Yes, it does," he replied. "Single mages who don't find their partner are destined to lose their element and their sanity. I'm not sure what choice I would make if I faced that. Becoming a vampire ensures they keep some magic and their lives."

"But what about the whole blood-sucking thing? How could they be okay with killing humans to survive?"

"And here I thought you were an avid paranormal romance reader," he replied, glancing towards me for a second. "Vampires don't have to kill their victim. Many even have human slaves solely for feeding purposes, so they don't have to go out into the population and risk exposure."

"But that doesn't change my argument," I said. "How can they be okay with that?"

He stared in silence at the oncoming highlights, and I wondered if he would answer. "Kate hasn't found her partner," he finally said. "I can't stand the thought of losing her. She's my only family."

Sadness and understanding washed over me. I didn't even have a family, but could still imagine losing the one person who mattered most. I didn't know what to say, so I remained silent.

~~~~~~~~~~~~~~~~

When we arrived back at Kellen's estate, three black sedans blocked the front gate. Kellen pulled up next to the lead car and rolled down his window. I leaned across the
~~~~~~~~~~~~~~~~

center console to see who was in the car, but Kellen's hand pushed me back.

I was tempted to stick my tongue out at him, but he was probably right, again. I pulled my ball cap lower on my head and slouched in the seat.

"Can I help you?" Kellen asked.

"We're looking for Kellen Jaber," a woman's voice stated from the other car.

"If I see him, who should I say is inquiring?" Kellen asked.

"Commander Smith would like to speak with him about The Sanguis Casino," she replied.

Kellen leaned out the window for a few seconds. "I'll be sure to let him know," he rolled his window half way up, then back down again. "By the way, camping at his gate will not likely get you an audience."

Kellen drove away, and I turned to watch the cars dropping into line behind us.

"Well, that doesn't look good," I muttered.

"Nope."

"Were they normal humans?"

"The ones I could see, but sometimes it's hard to tell." He glanced in the rearview mirror, then handed me a business card. A name and phone number were the only things printed on the plain, white paper.

"Commander Jonathan Smith," I read out loud. "Do you know who he is?"

"No, which worries me. I thought I knew all the players." He leaned forward and pulled his cellphone from the dashboard. "I want you to dial that number," he said handing me the phone. "It's imperative that you do not speak."

"Seriously? Why are you always telling me to be quiet?" I asked, taking the phone from his hand.

"I need to know what he wants," Kellen replied, tersely. "If he knows you're here, he won't give me the answers I'm looking for."

I scowled at him, knowing he was right, *again*. I tapped the number into his phone and pressed call. The SUV's Bluetooth picked up a few seconds later, and we listened to four rings before a woman's voice answered.

"How can I help you?" she asked without announcing a company name or her own.

"I need to speak with Commander Smith," Kellen replied.

"May I tell him who's calling?"

"No."

Light static filled the vehicle for several seconds. Kellen tapped the steering wheel impatiently.

"He may not accept the call if I cannot tell him who it is," she finally responded.

"I'll take that chance."

"Hold please."

A bad rendition of Mozart's Symphony Number 39 replaced the woman's voice, and I cringed.

"They need to pick a better artist for their music. This guy's destroying a classic," I mumbled as the artist missed another note.

We listened to the hold music for a few minutes before the man finally picked up the phone.

"I assume this is Mr. Jaber," a harsh voice said, reminding me of the old cook at one of my recent jobs.

"You assume correctly," Kellen replied. "What do you want?"

"I don't appreciate your tone, boy," Smith retorted.

"I don't appreciate three obviously federal vehicles parked outside my home." Kellen paused. "Now, what do you want?"

Silence filled the vehicle for several moments before Mr. Smith replied.

"You have something of great value to me."

"I have many things that are worth a lot of money," Kellen responded.

"I have no use for any of your antiques or artwork, and you know it." The man's harsh voice crackled with irritation. "I will give you five hundred thousand for the girl."

My eyes grew wide, and I clamped my hand over my mouth. Kellen looked at me with raised eyebrows.

"I've already had better offers," he replied. "Try again."

"If you've had a better offer, you would've taken it," Mr. Smith retorted.

Kellen smiled at me and looked in the rearview mirror. I turned around to see the black sedans still following us.

"That's your problem, Commander," Kellen replied. "You're like all the rest. You value money over everything else, and you truly believe it will solve all your problems. I don't need money."

Mr. Smith grunted, followed by muffled voices, as if he held his hand over the mouthpiece to talk to someone else. "What can I give you for the girl?" Smith asked after his muffled conversation.

"What do you want with her?" Kellen didn't hesitate to ask. "The others want her dead. What are your intentions?"

Another muffled conversation ensued and Kellen rolled his eyes. "We want her alive," Smith replied. "But I won't discuss our plans over the phone."

Kellen's eyes narrowed, and I recognized the expression. He was deep in thought. "I want three days to consider whether or not I'll cooperate," he stated. "And I trust you're intelligent enough to know that I will not hand her over. If your intelligence has failed you, then I suggest you take the next three days to figure it out." Kellen ended the call as the Smith started to argue.

"Wow," I said, letting out a long breath. "Five hundred thousand is a lot of money. Have you really had better offers?"

"No, only death threats," he replied, glancing in the rearview once more.

I swallowed hard. He could've given me up, but he didn't. Why? Was I really that important?

"We need to lose the idiots behind us," he continued. "Take the wheel for a minute." He looked over at me and tilted his head to the side. "On second thought, you're small enough for us to just trade places." He pushed the driver's seat all the way back and held his right arm towards me.

"I can't drive," I said, looking at the floor. It wasn't something I wanted to admit.

"Really?"

I heard the surprise in his voice, and my embarrassment deepened.

"I can't afford a car," I replied defensively, "so I didn't see any point in getting a license."

"Alright, I just need you to steer," he said, but he didn't move the seat forward.

He looked in the rearview again, then back towards the road. Without warning, he cut the wheel to the left and plowed across the desert. The SUV bumped across the rocky ground and Kellen cursed.

"There's the road," he mumbled and jerked the wheel to the right.

The jarring motion subsided, but only slightly. I turned around to see the three sedans react to the sudden turn, dust billowing out behind the trail of vehicles.

"Get over here," Kellen demanded.

"But." I snapped my mouth shut as his eyes met mine. We needed to lose our pursuers, and I suspected he would use the miles of sand and rock around us to make it happen. I crawled over the center console and onto his lap, gripping the steering wheel with both hands.

"I should be able to regulate our speed, so just keep us on the road. It's a straight path for the next mile or so."

He removed his hands from the wheel and rolled down both front windows. The wind rushed into the vehicle and wrapped around me in a soft caress. I inhaled deeply and almost closed my eyes but remembered at the last second that I was supposed to be watching the road. The earth beneath the SUV rumbled, and the vehicle jerked forward. I yelped as the tires landed hard and threatened to turn to the side.

Alisandra, let me help. The whisper caught me off guard, and I looked around.

"Stay focused, AJ," Kellen hissed from behind me.

The vehicle lurched to one side, and I realized I veered off the narrow path. I jerked the wheel to the right and over-corrected. The back of the SUV swerved violently and panic gripped me. I spun the steering wheel in the other direction, but the vehicle didn't respond as I hoped.

Kellen's arm wrapped around my stomach as we tilted to one side.

Let me help! The whisper sounded urgent and demanding.

"Yes, please help!" I called out.

A warm gale blew through the open window and righted the vehicle. Kellen's right leg rose between my own, and I lurched forward as he slammed on the brakes. Dust billowed around us as the SUV skidded to a stop.

Kellen's arm loosened around my middle, and I leaned back against him, peeling my fingers from the steering wheel and resting them on his arms. He pushed the shifter in park and sighed.

"Holy shit," I whispered, as a panicked grin spread across my face. "That was crazy."

Kellen chuckled beneath me. "You could call it that."

"Did we lose them?"

"They won't be going anywhere for a while," he replied, his breath ruffling my hair.

A tingling sensation prickled my hand, and I lifted it in front of me. Kellen moved his arm with mine, and I watched as a tiny spark leapt from him to me. It raced along my skin, up my arm, then back down again.

"What is that?" I asked. "And why can I see it now but not before?"

Kellen shifted slightly beneath me, and my face flushed. I shouldn't have been so comfortable with his hard, muscular body beneath me.

"That's the link between us," Kellen replied. "I've heard people describe it in many ways, but most of the time it's a small spark."

"Is it yours or mine? It seems to start with you, then jump to me."

"I never noticed it until I attempted to remove your binding," he replied. "I'm not sure who it belongs to."

I watched it make circles around my hand, then disappear into Kellen's. "You don't control it?"

"Not at all," he replied. I heard the humor in his voice again as he dropped his hand back to my stomach. My pulse quickened, and I felt a flutter in places I shouldn't.

"We should probably get moving," I said.

I opened the door and tumbled out of the SUV. Kellen kept me from falling into the sand, as he climbed out behind me. My heart still raced, and I tried to tamp down the mixed emotions raging through me. I wasn't used to having someone in my personal space. They always tried to avoid me, like my physical deformities were contagious. Kellen didn't have that problem, but he also saw the new me, not the old me. Maybe things would be different this time.

"Oh my God," I exclaimed as I took in the destruction behind us. "That's terrifying... and amazing!"

The ground rose in shattered pieces ranging from ten to fifteen feet high. The setting sun cast shadows around the large boulders scattered between the upheaved earth. Dust lingered in the air, leaving an eerie sight behind.

"Should we see if they're okay?" I asked, concern replacing my amazement.

"I imagine they stopped before hitting the barricade, but we shouldn't stick around to find out."

I nodded and circled around to the passenger side of the SUV, glancing back at the destruction in our wake. A soft gasp escaped my lips at the sight of a softball-sized rock embedded in the passenger door. I contemplated whether I should tell Kellen or let him find it on his own. Not wanting to be the bearer of bad news, I climbed into my seat, and he took off while I fastened my seatbelt. "I hadn't realized the extent of your strength," I said softly, wondering if our pursuers were hurt. "Or the possible uses for our magic."

"That was not just my power," Kellen said. "The wind tore those boulders free, not me."

I looked over at him but had a hard time seeing his features as twilight closed in. I thought about the whisper in my mind, asking me to let it help. "I heard something whispering to me during our wild ride," I said.

"I heard you reply to it."

"That was the second time it asked," I explained. "The first time wasn't as urgent, and I thought I imagined it." I bit my lower lip. "I hope we didn't hurt those people."

Kellen remained silent as he followed the dirt trail across the desert. After thirty minutes, we arrived at another set of gates. Kellen leaned out and pushed a button on the console. It remained silent. He pushed it again, then again.

"Damn, Kellen," Logan's voice crackled over the mic. "Give me two seconds to get in here. I don't camp out in the security room."

The gate slowly rolled open. I assumed they had cameras mounted on the walls, but I couldn't see them. Kellen drove through and crested a small hill. The estate below lit up the darkening sky.

"Did he have to turn on all the lights?" Kellen mumbled. "He's a damn vampire. He can see in the dark."

He pulled the vehicle directly into the opening garage door. I stared at the two wide doors, wondering how I missed that detail on my first trip here. The garage hadn't materialized overnight. The door rolled closed behind us as Kellen got out of the SUV. I pushed open my door and remembered the rock lodged in the side.

"Kellen, you might want to see this," I said.

He walked around to the passenger side and a string of curses exploded from his mouth.

"And you might want to come with me, princess." Logan's voice startled me, and I glared at him. "I know, some warning next time," he said, grinning, but I doubted he would comply.

I followed him out of the garage and into the kitchen. "How did I not see this door here earlier?" I asked.

"Because you weren't looking?" he offered.

"Smart ass," I replied. "Are there any leftovers in the fridge?"

He looked at me with raised eyebrows and dropped into one of the stools at the bar.

"Oh, right," I said, realizing my faux pas. Vampire's wouldn't have leftovers, at least nothing I would want.

The fridge offered several plastic containers that looked like they might have been there too long. I opened the freezer and found a variety of frozen dinners. I picked two and dropped them on the counter.

"Aren't you the little homemaker," Logan said.

I looked at him and grinned. "These are gourmet dinners," I said, pointing to the label. "If I put it on a plate when they're done, it's almost like I cooked them myself."

He laughed, and I smiled with him. I seriously doubted his claim to vampirism. He acted like a normal man, with the exception of his really fast movement. But I was no longer in a position to deny that magic existed, so I had to assume he was more than just human. A loud, wrenching noise from the garage interrupted our silliness.

"He's really pissed," Logan said. "How'd that rock get embedded in the side of his car?"

"It's a long story," I replied, "one I should probably let him tell. I'm pretty sure there are parts of it that went over my head. Not to mention I was in a state of shock half the time."

I put the dinners in the microwave and sat down next to my 'vampire' friend. If nothing else came from today's events, the threat to my life was confirmed. The Magister wanted me dead. Victor's group wanted a weapon. I had no idea what the strange Mr. Smith wanted, but he was willing to pay a great deal of money for it. Maybe my current company wasn't that bad after all, and maybe they were trying to protect me.

"So, anything wild and crazy happen while we were gone?" I asked.

"That reminds me," he responded. "I expected you to come back in some new clothes. Yet, here you are in the same baggy blue jeans and t-shirt."

"Don't evade the question," I countered. "You and Kellen both do that. It's extremely irritating."

He swiveled on the stool and faced me, pushing a long lock of hair from his face. "Alright, fair enough. The portal room is completely destroyed, as planned. The patio garden is a disaster and three windows are broken, not as planned."

"What happened to the garden? And the windows?"

"I'm fine, princess, but thanks for caring. Unfortunately, Kellen will not be when he finds out how much damage is done."

"Did they really attack the house?" I asked, remembering Kellen's comment about people looking for us.

He nodded.

"Who was it?"

"No one you know," Logan replied, swiveling back to the counter.

"I don't know. I met a lot of people today."

He tilted his head my way. "Really? Do tell."

"Well, first was a bear, who was terrifying. Then, a pack of mutts, as Kellen called them. Their leader was even scarier. Then, some government group who wanted to buy me for a huge amount of money." I frowned, realizing he dodged my questions.

"Damn. I'm guessing the mutts were Victor's," he stated. "The bear, was it a man or woman?"

"A woman who looked like a man. She was huge."

"There are several possibilities there." Logan scratched his chin. "The government boys must have been the ones camped at the gate all afternoon."

"That was kind of fun," I said with a grin.

The slamming door drew my attention to Kellen. I covered my smile with my hand. Streaks of dirt covered his face, and large, dark stains dotted his shirt.

"What happened?" I asked, trying to smooth my features.

"We're not talking about it."

The microwave dinged, and I jumped down from my stool. I removed the two dinners and set them on the counter, then went in search of plates. Kellen eyed me suspiciously as he scrubbed his hands in the sink. I gave him my sweetest smile and started transferring the mashed potatoes and cubed steak to the plates I found.

"What are you doing?" Kellen asked, drying his hands on a towel.

"You should wash your face too," I replied, ignoring his question.

He raised his eyebrows at me and went back to the sink. I heard Logan cough and turned to see him smiling. Kellen sat down opposite of Logan, and I slid his plate in front of him.

"Thanks, I think."

"Sure thing," I replied, resuming my seat next to the vampire, chuckling at the thought.

"Looks like someone left out a few details," Logan said.

"I told you I'd let Kellen explain what happened. I'm still struggling to sort out everyone I met today." I waved my fork at him. "You two talk. I'm eating."

"She's got quite the little spark, doesn't she?" Logan asked.

I choked on the bite I'd just taken, hoping he wasn't referring to my partnership with Kellen. But Logan was a mage with a partner before he became a vampire. He would know. I decided to ignore his comment and finish my *gourmet* meal.

"Don't go there, Logan. Just tell me what happened today," Kellen said.

Logan swiveled towards Kellen. "Two teams of vampires showed up," he began. "I let the outer defenses take care of the first team. When the second witnessed the demise of their fellow blood-suckers, they hesitated. I managed to kill three of the seven before they reached the house."

He paused, and I leaned forward so I could see Kellen's expression. He stared at Logan with his fork halfway to his mouth.

"Your guardians finished off the rest of them, but the garden's a mess."

Kellen dropped his fork on his plate and rushed towards the glass doors leading into the garden. I slid off the stool and Logan grabbed my arm.

"You should give him a few minutes," Logan explained. "The garden was his mother's."

~~~~~~~~~~~~~~~~~~

I stood at the glass door, looking out into the ruined garden. The tall palm trees that once lined the right side lay on their broken branches, crushing the flowering bushes I didn't have names for. Kellen knelt beside one of the largest trees with his hand on the rough, layered bark.

As soon as my feet left the house, a sense of overwhelming sadness washed over me. I approached the nearest fallen tree and noticed multiple claw marks cut deep into the bark. The tree's sap oozed from each one and tears pooled in my eyes. Why was I getting so worked up over a tree?
~~~~~~~~~~~~~~~~~~

I dropped to my knees, placing my hand on the jagged cuts. Waves of pain assaulted me, and I snatched my hand away.

"It's one of the guardians," Kellen said, kneeling beside me. "I can't fix it. None of them." He motioned towards the line of fallen trees, and I looked over at him.

"What's a guardian?" I asked, watching his pained expression.

"They're part of the estate's defense," he replied, "and my mother's creations. They're more than just trees. They're sentient beings that protect my home and the portal to the palace." He placed his hand on the open cuts and streams of mud rose from the ground. The thick mixture coated the tree's wounds, but didn't stop the flow of sap pouring from it.

"How do you withstand its pain?" I asked.

He looked up me, a spark of hope in his brown eyes. "You can feel it?"

I nodded. "All too well."

"Would you endure it to save the guardian's life?"

I looked at him, eyes widening. Didn't he remember my pitiful display over the broken rib? I'd only touched the tree for a split second and couldn't stand it. "I'll try," I whispered, unable to deny his pleading eyes.

"I'll give you my strength if you give it your healing touch."

I nodded, not understanding a word he said. He laced his fingers through mine, and I reached towards the tree with a shaking hand. Kellen's spark raced up my arm, tickling my senses. I felt it dive towards my middle as I touched the wounded tree.

Pain surged through my body. I tried to focus on the water around me, but I could only feel the tree's agony. I jerked my hand away. "Kellen, I don't think I can do it," I said between gasps. "Its pain is unbearable."

He reached up and wiped a tear from my cheek.

"Have you tried to mix your magic yet?" Logan asked from behind us.

"No," Kellen replied, not hiding the bitterness in his voice. He rose to his feet, pulling me with him. "We haven't exactly had time."

"Your mother had earth and water, didn't she?" Logan asked.

Kellen nodded and looked back at the guardian.

"You two can do it together, it'll just be harder. More so because you haven't practiced reaching for each other." Logan looked at me with a sad smile. "Don't fight it, princess. Every instinct you have will try to fight against him. Don't."

I had no idea what he was talking about, so I just stared at him.

"Let's go to the practice room, where there are fewer distractions," Logan suggested.

"We can't leave them," Kellen argued.

"You can do nothing for them until you two can work together," Logan countered. "The emotions lingering here will keep AJ from being able to reach you."

"I feel the trees?" I asked. "This is their sadness?"

"Not just the guardians," the vampire replied. "Come on. Let's not waste time arguing about it."

He left us standing in the broken garden. For the first time, I saw true uncertainty in Kellen's eyes. A rustling of leaves drew my attention to the opposite side of the garden. All six of the uninjured trees seemed to bow, their long fronds touching the sand before resuming their full height.

"AJ, I..." Kellen's voice stuttered several times, and I turned back to him, waiting silently, realizing whatever he needed to say was going to be difficult. "There cannot be two people on this planet more different than you and I," he said. "Everything about us is on opposite ends of the spectrum. In a normal world, we wouldn't even be friends."

His words hurt. I looked away, knowing what was coming next. I'd accepted rejection so many times in my life.

He gently lifted my chin, forcing me to look at him. I tried not to scowl, but my eyes narrowed and my lips turned down on their own. A puzzled look crossed his face. "What's wrong?"

"Nothing, please just say what you need to say."

"You think I'm going to reject you? I can see it on your face."

"What am I supposed to think?" I asked, not hiding the contempt I felt. "People never accept me, Kellen. Why would you be any different?"

"Because they could not see who you are," he replied. "That's not what I'm struggling to say. Dual mages do not have partners, AJ. They don't need them. The occurrence is so rare, they're able to write them all on a single sheet of paper. In every instance, the pairs are exactly like you and I." He paused again. "Logan wants us to do something we aren't ready for. I wouldn't even attempt it before you had more training, but he's right. We can't heal them alone." He looked back at the wounded guardians. "I fear *you* will reject *me*, and I'll lose the guardians."

I didn't know what to say. Could I really have a true friend? A partner for life? My elements seemed to think so, but I resented that they made the decision for me. It felt like another entity in my life controlling me. I followed Kellen's painful gaze and shook my head. Of course, they knew better than I did.

"Let's go irritate Logan, then we can come back and fix your guardians."

Chapter 15

I sat cross-legged in front of Kellen in the middle of the dirt floor. The moonlight streamed in from the high windows behind him, casting shadows across his already dark features. It was the only thing illuminating the room. Logan sat next to me, and I envisioned a bizarre three-leaf clover. How ridiculous, the two mages and the vampire. Even if I couldn't deny this world, it still seemed a little absurd. I giggled, and both men looked at me.

"Nothing, just nervous," I said meekly, straightening my back.

"Alright, this will likely get messy, and I'll need to leave in a hurry," Logan began. "So, listen up. It's extremely important that you do not fight each other. Your opposing elements will posture and jockey for lead positions. Let them. Under no circumstance should you interfere." He took a deep breath. "Air and water created a tremendous thunderstorm during mine. I can only imagine what will happen with all four." He pushed himself to his feet and laid a hand on each of our shoulders. "Focus on the spark between you and ignore the elements. They chose each other for a reason; let them figure it out." He turned towards the door, and I grabbed his hand.

"You're not staying?" I asked.

"Nope, I just talked myself out of it," he replied. "You'll do great. See you in the morning."

"The morning?" Kellen and I said together.

"Will it really take that long?" Kellen asked. "What about the guardians?"

"I'll continue to use what little magic I have to help them," Logan replied. "They aren't as fragile as you think. Stay focused on each other."

"You already said that twice," I said to his back as he walked through the door, closing it behind him. I frowned and looked back to Kellen. "His instructions sucked. Do you know how to start this... this process?"

"No, not really," Kellen replied with a shrug. "But let's not start with fire and air, and I don't think we want all four at once."

"I got the impression we didn't have a choice."

"We might not." Kellen placed both palms on the dark soil, and I noticed it start to ripple. "Your turn," he said.

"I don't know what to do," I replied.

"Can you feel the moisture in the air?" he asked. "You called on it easily enough at Victor's."

"I was a little irritated at Victor. And you, for that matter," I replied. "The two of you acted like teenage boys, trying to see who could be more intimidating."

"Who won?" he asked.

"Seriously?" I asked. How was that even relevant? We were supposed to be connecting or something.

"Of course."

"Victor, by a long shot," I replied. "The man is enormous."

"Wow, that hurts," he said, placing a hand over his heart. "Didn't our run through the desert earlier impress you at all?"

"That was rather impressive, but I haven't seen what Victor can do." Clearly, we had arrogance issues, which surprised me coming from Kellen. I hadn't seen that side of him. Confidence, yes, but not arrogance.

"We're getting distracted. Can you feel the water in the air?" he asked.

I concentrated on my surroundings, trying to recall the heavy feeling at Victor's. "Nope. Maybe the air is just dryer here?"

"Alright, sit next to me and face the fountain. Maybe you need to start with a visual."

I scooted on my butt until I turned full circle. I looked down at my skinny thigh next to Kellen's well-defined muscles and frowned. "That is disconcerting," I said.

"What?" he asked.

I poked at his leg, making him flinch. He laughed, and I looked up at him.

"I keep telling you to eat. You're like a walking skeleton." He continued to stare at me, making my frown deepen. "Okay, as soon as you gain some weight, we'll work on building muscle."

"Don't patronize me," I mumbled.

"I'm not. You're the one who keeps pointing out how small you are. You should consider it a gift. You will always be underestimated, which gives you an advantage over your opponent."

"Maybe I don't want to fight."

"You aren't going to have a choice." His mood sobered, and he tilted his head towards the fountain. "Let's stay focused."

I followed his gaze and settled on the large stone fountain across the room. Water flowed from a spout on the wall into a half-moon shaped basin. It splashed softly into the pool, and I let the sound calm my mind. I closed my eyes and imagined the water rising from the fountain in the shape of a person. It pointed at me and drew a large circle with its arm. I had no idea what I was trying to create, but it looked cool in my head.

"Open your eyes," Kellen whispered.

I opened one eye and gasped. It was nothing like I imagined. Moonlight reflected off the narrow stream flowing over the edge of the fountain and across the dirt floor. It made a slow circle, surrounding Kellen's rippling earth. I opened both eyes when the earth sunk and swallowed the water, creating a small moat.

"That's cool," I said quietly.

"Can you feel the water's intentions?" Kellen asked.

"Sort of," I replied, concentrating on the water. "Its willingness is apparent, but it doesn't want to be, I don't know, dictated to?" I looked up at him, hoping he understood. I wasn't sure I could explain it any better.

"It's willing to help, but on its own terms," he suggested.

"Yes, exactly."

"Okay, time for the other two," he said. "The air should be easy to reach for."

I nodded, uncertain what to do with my tenuous connection to water. I closed my eyes again and listened to the breeze coming in the open windows above us. A coyote's howl followed the call of some bird I didn't know. Crickets sang to one another. How was I supposed to call to the wind? I wasn't even sure how to envision it. I suspected it spoke to me earlier without any encouragement on my part.

The smell of water-logged soil reached my nose, mixing with a tangy smoke. I sneezed and opened my eyes. Tiny tornadoes whirled around the room, picking up grains of soil as they went. A line of fire raced towards a dust-devil on my left and was consumed by it. The tornado grew and flared red. I thought I saw a set of eyes between the swirls of fire and dirt, but they vanished instantly. Another line of fire raced towards the now growing tornado. The flames stopped just short and circled the whirlwind, forming a barrier around it. The air reacted immediately, plunging into the line and sucking the fire into its raging center. Three more lines of fire burst into existence and rushed the tornado that consumed their brethren. The remaining smaller tornadoes consolidated and joined the larger one.

"Kellen?" I whispered, not taking my eyes from the stand-off between the two elements. "Should we be concerned?"

"Logan said to ignore them and find the spark between us."

I pulled my gaze from the tornado that now reached the stone ceiling and saw Kellen staring at the fire that rose to meet it. His profile intrigued me. I touched the side of his face and felt the little spark jump to my fingers. He turned towards me and took my hand in his own. The spark jumped again, and I smiled.

"They're going to be really hard to ignore," I said.

"Agreed. I'm grateful the other two seem content to occupy our little moat."

I twisted to face my partner, folding one leg beneath me and letting the other stretch out to my side.

"Can you make Sparky move, or does he have a mind of his own?" I asked.

"You named it? Really?" It was hard to see his expression with the shadows dancing across his face.

"If you can think of something better, I'm all ears." He huffed, and I smiled.

"I've never tried to make it move," he replied. "I didn't even feel it until I removed your binding."

"So, what does it feel like for you?" I asked. "I can only feel it when it's running around inside me." I strained to see his face beyond the shadows, but his expression eluded me.

"I'm not sure I can explain it," he said after several moments of silence.

A fiery tornado rushed by us, leaving behind a wave of smoke and heat.

"That was close," I gasped, leaning towards Kellen.

"Ignore them, remember," he said.

"I noticed you tensing up as well," I retorted, watching the tornado collide with the stone wall. The fire separated from it and rose into a solid barrier of flames, trapping the tornado against the stone. A thunderous roar shook the ground beneath us. The room grew unbearably hot, sweat dripping down the sides of my face.

"That can't be good," I whispered.

"Logan said they would try to dominate each other," Kellen murmured.

"Why aren't the other two joining the fight?" I asked.

"They aren't as aggressive, even though they're probably stronger," Kellen replied. "We're getting distracted again. We have yet to do anything with this spark."

"I don't even know what we're supposed to do with it," I said. "I feel like a bystander as the elements decide everything."

"Maybe they're making the decisions because we aren't," he suggested.

"You need to turn around so I can see your expression," I said, feeling my lower lip extending to a pout. "I can't tell if you're being serious or sarcastic."

"Then I'm definitely not moving," he replied. "Besides, I love watching your expressions. You hide nothing."

I pushed myself to my feet and put my hands on my hips. I knew I had control over nothing, but he didn't have to confirm it. I also knew it wasn't what he meant, but it was true. He and Logan pushed me into their possession, and now these elements dictated the rest. Regardless of the awesome display of power, I felt trapped.

"Sit down, AJ. I'm just teasing you," Kellen said, but I could still hear the humor in his voice.

"No."

I heard him sigh and saw his head shake from side to side. I reached towards his shoulder with my fingers extended.

"Here, Sparky," I said, as if I called a pet. A sardonic smile crossed my face as it tugged at me. "That's a good boy." I held out both hands and watched in amazement as a jolt of light burned through Kellen's t-shirt and jumped to my hands.

Kellen jumped to his feet and loomed over me.

"That was undignified," he said with a low growl.

"No, that was really cool," I replied. "See if you can call it back."

I held out my cupped hands and my smile grew as the spark raced beneath my skin and up my arm. I laughed as it wove circles around my stomach, fluttering against my ribs. I didn't want to be amused by this mischievous little shit, but I couldn't help it. "Oh my God, that tickles," I said between giggles. "Are you doing that?"

I looked up to see half his face illuminated by the moonlight. He was smiling when I expected him to be mad. "Nope, but I wish I was," he replied.

It raced around my ribs again, and I struggled to remain standing, wrapping myself in a hug to hold in my laughter. I couldn't remember the last time I was tickled. It hurt. "Alright, that's enough." I gasped for breath, but the little spark was relentless. "Kellen, you need do something! My ribs ache."

I raised my shirt to expose the pale skin on my stomach. A line of light raced around beneath my belly, and I assumed it was the mischievous spark. It stopped at my belly button, and I swore it was watching me.

Kellen placed his hand near my stomach, almost touching me. "Get over here, stupid." Sparky made a slow circle around my middle, then jumped to Kellen's hand.

"What does that even mean?" I asked, truly confused by the little spark.

The ground shook violently beneath my feet, and I fell against Kellen. He wrapped an arm around me to steady me, but his focus was to his left. I followed his gaze and gasped.

A wall of solid earth collapsed over top of the flames and tornado. Steam rolled out from beneath the pile of dirt until the floor leveled out once more, removing any evidence of the once warring elements. An eerie silence filled the room.

I looked up at Kellen to finding him staring back at me.

"Are they done?" I asked.

He shrugged. "I guess so."

"I don't feel like we accomplished anything," I said, looking back at the spot where a raging tornado faced off the wall of fire. "Weren't we supposed to merge our magic or something?"

"Or something," he repeated. His voice sounded odd, and I turned back to him.

"What is it?"

He grabbed both my shoulders and knelt in front of me. "Can you feel that spark inside of me?" he asked. I saw uncertainty in his eyes again, the moonlight finally shining on his face and not mine.

I thought of Sparky. A flicker of light blinked against the dark skin on Kellen's arm. "When I think of him, he appears, but I don't feel him," I replied, confused by his question. "Am I supposed to?"

He dropped his hands and looked at the dirt floor. I crouched in front of him with concern.

"What am I missing, Kellen?" I asked. "Please tell me."

He took a long breath. "I can feel it inside you," he replied. "I can feel your laughter and amazement as it races through your body."

"Why don't I feel yours?" I whispered, guilt mixing with my confusion, somehow knowing my ignorance played a role in our failure to achieve whatever we were supposed to do.

"Because you are undecided," a low, rumbling voice said.

Kellen and I both jumped to our feet, but Kellen placed himself between me and the voice. His desire to protect me soothed my fears.

"I see what you mean, brother," a deep, yet hollow voice added.

I peered around Kellen's shoulders, and my eyes widened. In front of the door stood a dark, stone statue. Flickers of fire lit its hollow eyes and wound circles around its massive torso. Next to it, a humanoid form made completely of water, lounged on the edge of the fountain. Small, wispy clouds floated in front of it, spitting droplets into the pool.

I stepped out from behind my protector. "You're our elements," I said. My voice shook, but I wasn't sure if it was fear or shock.

"We are," the water elemental replied, flowing into a standing position. Its form shifted with each movement.

"Why can't I feel the spark the same way Kellen does?" I asked. "What do you mean I'm undecided?"

"Kellen knows what he wants," the rock replied, taking a rumbling step towards us. "He knows his purpose, his strengths, and even his weakness."

"But you do not know," water continued, also moving towards us.

I laced my fingers through Kellen's, and he squeezed my hand. It was definitely fear running through my veins.

The flowing form of water stopped in front of me. "Your heart knows, but your mind refuses to see it."

A string of fire separated itself from the rock and formed into another humanoid. "Her uncertainty will prove our demise," it hissed. "We should choose another."

A blast of wind dispelled the fire and formed into yet another humanoid, shifting with its transparency. "How can she be anything other than uncertain?" the wind asked, its voice low and somehow heavy despite its irritation. "She knew nothing of us until two days ago."

The fire reformed and circled the wind. "She should trust our selection," the fire's voice crackled.

"Caution is expected," the rock rumbled, stepping between the hostile elements. "But we don't have time for unnecessary delays." It turned and faced me. "You will not feel your partner the way you need to until you accept him and your destiny."

I stared at the talking statue with disbelief. How was any of this possible? Was I really having a conversation with the elements? I shook my head and focused on the beings in front of me. "I don't know what to think, much less believe," I said. "I feel no different, even though all of you are standing in front of me. I see the living proof that magic is real and that I have some crazy role to play. I'm just..." I looked up at Kellen. "I'm no one. I've been no one my entire life. I've done everything I can to hide from a world that hates me."

"Child, you are exactly what you need to be," Water said, placing its hand on my shoulder and drawing my gaze. "Hardship has made you strong, and your partner will make you even stronger." Waves of warmth emanated from the Water's hand and filtered through my body. A smile formed on my element's ever-moving face.

"The coming fight will require complete dedication," Earth continued. "You cannot waver in your choice."

"How long do I have to make a decision?" I asked, glancing from one element to the next. "I didn't realize I had a choice."

"You must choose tonight," Water replied.

"You can choose to decline," the rumbling rock added. "But you will not be given another partner."

I frowned. According to Kellen, dual mages didn't need partners. The elements almost never chose to pair them. "What happens to Kellen if I decline?" I asked, not looking at him.

"He is a dual mage like you and doesn't require a partner," Earth replied. "But his role is already set. It will be much harder without you, but I think he'll succeed if we cannot find another."

"Do I have to tell you now?"

"No, child," Water replied. "We'll know your decision once it's made."

I nodded, still unable to look at Kellen, his sadness smothering me like a blanket. I wiggled my fingers in his hand, but he wouldn't let go.

"Can you help us heal the guardians?" I asked.

"Of course, they are needed in the fight that's coming," Earth replied.

"Thank you."

I took a tentative step forward. The elements did not move, but Kellen finally released me. A lump formed in my throat, and I struggled to hold back my tears. Why were these decisions being forced on me? Why was I so important to whatever battle they had coming? Two days ago, I was excited about cleaning up after a bunch of tourists. Now? I shook my head, unable to sort through the demands threatening to drown me.

I stepped between Water and Earth and left the room. I barely noticed the cool, air-conditioned space as I made my way down the hall and into the large living area. I crossed it as well and pushed opened the door to the garden.

A soft wind caressed my face, carrying the scent of flowers and earth. I strolled towards the first fallen guardian and looked down. Eight claw marks dug deep beneath its bark, which continued to bleed sap onto the ground.

"Give me strength to endure its pain," I whispered, unsure who I talked to, only hoping someone heard my plea. I took a deep breath and placed both hands on the oozing bark. Pain surged through my body. I cried out, but I refused to let go. "If you can endure this for hours, I can take it for the next few minutes," I said between gasps.

I squeezed my eyes shut and searched for any moisture in the air. It condensed around me as another pulse of pain rushed through my body. When it subsided, I drew the water into my hands and pushed it towards the tree. I forced my eyes open to find a tiny puddle wavering above the horrid wounds but going no further to heal it.

I pulled my hands away and sobbed. Was it my indecision that kept me from helping this creature? If I accepted my role, would I be able to heal it? I didn't even know what that role was. I didn't think to ask. "I'm so stupid," I whispered. "Why can't I make a choice?"

"Because you don't understand what's at stake," Logan replied quietly.

I sniffled and looked up at him, too upset to be startled by his sudden appearance. "Should that even matter?" I asked. "I know the mages' lives are at stake. I know the shifters are afraid of the vampire council that intends to reveal them all. I know that if we are revealed, the outcome won't be good."

He sat next to me, the long hair on the top of his head falling into his eyes. He pushed it back and looked at me. "We need your partnership with Kellen to present a strong enough front against those who want to reveal us. Without it, those who are sitting on the fence will side with the vampire council," he explained. "The elements recognize the need, otherwise they would not make this choice. It's dangerous for them to give so much power to a mage. They didn't do this without a great deal of deliberation."

"How can they possibly think I'm the right person for this, Logan?" I pleaded, trying to understand. "Look at me."

"I see a strong woman who will dedicate herself to the people she loves because she knows how precious love is," he replied, wiping a tear from my face. "I see a woman who is not afraid of pain or adversity because she has lived with both. And I see a mage who will embrace the power she is given without abusing it."

"You're so full of shit," I mumbled.

"Then prove me wrong," he argued. "Get up and walk out, right now."

I stood, and he rose with me. "I don't have a car," I said, wiping my tears with the back of my hand.

"Kellen leaves the keys in the ignition," he replied.

"I don't have a license," I countered.

He raised an eyebrow. "Seriously?"

Why was that such a surprise to everyone? I looked back at the house. The lights inside the living area illuminated the beautiful space. Kellen pushed open the door on the opposite side of the room. He ran his hands through his dark hair and looked at the floor as he crossed the space.

"Last chance," Logan said.

I turned to the line of wounded guardians, their lifeblood spilling into the sand. The glass door slid open on its runner, and I knew I wouldn't leave, couldn't leave. How did I become so attached to these people in just two days? Was it my lack of friends? My lack of social skills? My need to fit in somewhere? Anywhere?

Kellen's footsteps in the sand drew my gaze to him. He refused to look at me, turning his attention to Logan. I couldn't blame him. I did exactly what he feared. I rejected him.

"How are they?" he asked.

"Hanging in there," Logan replied. His eyes dropped to me, then back to Kellen. "Can you heal them?"

"Yes, the elements will help us," Kellen replied.

Logan raised his eyebrows in surprise. "You talked to them?"

Kellen nodded and kneeled in front of the guardian. I looked at Logan, the lump in my throat swelling to the point where I could barely breathe. I drew in several ragged breaths and knelt next to my partner. Wiping the tears from my eyes, I hovered both hands over the claw marks. Kellen said nothing as I pressed my palms against the wounds. The guardian's pain once again assaulted me. I clamped my mouth shut and stared at the open cuts.

I will do this. Not just for the guardian or Kellen or even the war that is coming, but because I need to prove to myself that I can do this. I'm not a victim of everyone's hatred. I'm not a product of my parent's abandonment. I will choose my future. It will not be dictated by my past.

And where does your future lie, child? Water's wispy voice echoed through my mind.

You know it's here. I answered. *You've known that from the beginning.*

Yes, but you needed to know.

A rush of power surged through my hands and into the wounded tree. My pain tripled, and a scream burst from my lips. Kellen's arm wrapped around my shoulders, easing some of the ache. I had no idea what he did but was grateful for it. I watched as the guardian's wounds stopped bleeding, thick layers of bark slowly forming over the deep cuts.

Waves of nausea rolled over me, and I leaned to the side, leaving my dinner in the sand. My head throbbed, and I couldn't tell if it was my heartbeat pounding in my ears or the beginning of a migraine.

The guardian next to me groaned, and I turned to see Kellen pushing it into a standing position. I watched with awe as its roots burrowed into the sand. When it was fully upright, it shuddered.

Kellen knelt beside me and laid his hand on my back. "Only five more," he whispered. "You did great."

"I don't think I can do it again," I replied. "My head is throbbing, and my stomach is threatening to rebel again."

"Then let me help."

"You did help," I stated, rolling on to my butt and looking at him. "I felt you take some of the pain."

"This time we'll start together. It will lessen the drain on you. One more, then we'll take a break." His uncertainty was still there but subdued by his determination. He stood and held out his hand. I looked at him for several seconds before placing my hand in his and letting him pull me to my feet.

"Five more," I whispered.

The thought scared me, but the sight of the healing guardian gave me courage. One of its long leaves grazed my cheek, then wrapped me in a quick hug. It shuddered once more, then stilled. A collective sigh from the guardians on the opposite side of the garden drew my attention. They also shuddered, as if it were a choreographed dance they practiced for years.

"Five more," I said again and followed Kellen to the next fallen tree.

Chapter 16

I woke to the sun streaming through my window. My head throbbed and the inside of my mouth tasted like I ate glue. My swollen tongue stuck to the roof of my mouth, and the small amount of spit trying to loosen it failed miserably. I pried open one eyelid and closed it immediately.

"Oh God," I moaned, rolling over and pulling the blankets over my head. "Why do I feel so bad?"

No one answered, not that I expected anyone to. The air beneath my covers quickly became stale, and I flipped them back. I rubbed my eyes with my palms and tried opening them again.

"Wow, that really sucks." I rubbed my forehead, squinting at the light.

I tumbled out of bed and made it to the bathroom without stubbing my bare toes on any of the furniture. The bathroom light was already on when I opened the door. I squeezed my eyes shut and palmed the wall until I found the switch, turning off the offensive lights.

Feeling better about the relative darkness, I opened my eyes and stepped into the room.

"It isn't polite to come in without knocking," Logan said as he wrapped a towel around his waist.

I squeaked and turned around, but not before getting an amazing view outlined by the light from his room. Lean, corded muscles covered his body, unlike Kellen's defined bulk. My stomach fluttered, and he laughed.

"I'm so sorry, Logan."

My ears burned with embarrassment as I stumbled back into my room and slammed the door. I climbed into bed and pulled the covers over my face. I would never be able to un-see that. My embarrassment doubled when I realized I didn't mind, then tripled when I remembered I was only wearing a tank top and panties.

Several minutes later, Logan's muffled voice drifted towards me. "It's all yours, princess."

I finished my own shower in record time, afraid that Logan would return the favor and barge in. I noticed a small trunk at the end of my bed and remembered my conversation with Kellen. I pushed open the lid and peered inside. It was only half full. Did I really have so few belongings? I already knew the answer, but it hurt to see the reality.

The left side contained my small pile of clothes, while sketchbooks and letters I wrote to parents I would never have filled the right side. Tears threatened to spill down my cheeks, but I forced them back. The events over the last few days proved I didn't need those memories. They did nothing but bring me pain and sadness. My new connection to the elements and Kellen gave me purpose, even if it did terrify me. Kellen accepted me with all my flaws and ignorance. He offered friendship, security, and protection. Even Victor and his people respected Kellen, despite their obvious dislike for each other. I needed to set aside my insecurity and move forward. If Kellen had wanted to hurt me, he'd already had more than enough opportunity to do so. I pulled my clothes from the chest and closed the lid on my past.

"I'm not crying over people who never loved me."

I dressed quickly, combing my fingers through my short hair as I walked down the hall. I considered styling it now that it wasn't hidden all the time.

The smell of food greeted me when I opened the door to the living area. My stomach rumbled, and I quickened my pace towards the kitchen. Kellen smiled at me from his seat at the bar and tilted his head towards the stove. I followed his gaze and felt heat rush up my neck. Logan leaned over a saucepan with a large, wooden spoon in his hand. All I could see was his naked body, not the man standing before me wearing blue jeans and a t-shirt.

"Glad to see you finally decided to get up," Kellen said.

I pulled my eyes from Logan's back and climbed up on the stool next to Kellen. "How long was I asleep?" I asked, swiveling the stool so it faced my partner.

"All day," he replied, raising an eyebrow at me. "Is something wrong?"

"Nope. Well maybe," I replied. "I feel like I've been hit by a truck. My head is pounding, and food smells really good, even if it's being prepared by a vampire."

"How many trucks have you been hit by?" Logan asked, not turning around.

"It's a figure of speech," I retorted, knowing he was trying to bait me. I could imagine the irritating grin on his face. "I've never been hit."

"Do you like chili?" he asked, apparently choosing to ignore my mood.

"Yes, so long as it isn't really spicy. Is that what I smell cooking?" I drew in a deep breath and recognized the chili powder and onions.

"Yep." Logan ladled the chili into two bowls and set them in front of me and Kellen. He winked at me, and my eyes dropped to the chunks of tomatoes and kidney beans. I was so stupid.

"We have a lot to discuss and even more to do," Kellen said, digging into his own bowl. If he noticed my discomfort, he chose to ignore it as well.

Logan leaned on the counter in front of us. "The guardians are doing remarkably well, by the way."

"What other defenses are there?" I asked. "Are there more like the trees?"

"No, the trees are the last line before breaching the house," Kellen replied. "The others are more mechanical and less magical."

"But just as effective," Logan added. "They took care of the first group easily."

"We need to talk about Mr. Smith," Kellen said, changing the subject as he scraped the bowl with his spoon. "He probably won't wait three days for an answer."

I chased a kidney bean around in my bowl. I wasn't sure what he expected me to say. It's not like I knew enough about this supernatural world to strategize for intrigue and war.

"Do you know anything about him?" Logan asked, breaking the silence.

"Not a thing," Kellen answered. "I'm reluctant to reach out to any of my normal contacts for information. Their loyalties have always been suspect, probably more so now the Magister has a price on my head."

"I'll see what I can find out tonight," Logan offered.

"Be careful, Logan. The target on your back is not any smaller than mine."

They both glanced at me, making me squirm. I didn't think they would give me up, not after last night, but when someone's life was at stake, people tended to change their minds.

"I'll leave the dishes for you two," Logan said, pushing away from the counter. "I'll be back before sunrise. And you might want to put a lock on our bathroom door." He winked at me again and left the room.

Kellen turned to me, eyebrows raised.

"I don't want to talk about it," I said, scooting off the stool and taking my empty bowl to the sink. "What do you think we should do about Mr. Smith?"

"I believe he's on our side," Kellen said, walking up beside me. "I don't see any human wanting the vampires to reveal themselves since humans are the vampires' most efficient means of food." He placed his bowl in the sink and leaned against the counter next to me.

"I don't understand why the vampires want to be revealed," I said, pouring dish detergent into the running water. "Won't they be hunted down and killed?"

"Not likely, not if they have their way. They'll reveal all of us, not just themselves." He pulled a hand towel from the drawer next to him, and I handed him a clean bowl to dry. "It's hard to tell how the major governments will react. Some will decide to ally with whomever they believe will come out on top." He put the dry bowl in the cabinet over his head and took the next one. "Others will band together and try to eliminate all the supernatural races."

"So, our best chance is to stop them from spilling the beans." I pulled the plug from the sink and watched the soapy water swirl down the drain. I supposed it made sense, but how did it benefit the vampires? "Do the vampires intend to eliminate all the other supernatural races?" I asked.

"I don't think they want to eliminate them, but they would see everyone bowing to the vampire council," he replied. "If they could take control of both the humans and supernaturals, they wouldn't have to worry about food supplies or anything else for that matter."

"And they aren't like Logan, are they?"

Kellen shook his head. "No, he is very much the exception."

The thought of vampires ruling the world soured my mood. I had visions of humans being farmed like cattle and shuddered. Kellen placed his hand on my shoulder, and I looked up at him.

"Unless Logan comes back with really bad news, I think we should meet with Mr. Smith," Kellen said, handing me the towel.

"At a place of our choosing?" I asked, drying my hands.

"You got it," he replied.

I twisted the towel between my fingers. There were more questions I wanted to ask but couldn't form the words.

"Let's go practice harnessing your magic," he suggested. "There's a lot you need to learn."

~~~~~~~~~~~~~~~~~~~~~~

Sweat covered my aching body, and a thin layer of dirt covered every inch of my exposed skin. I didn't care as I stretched out in the middle of the room, exhausted. I practiced recognizing my elements within my environment and calling to them. After three hours, I could call one or the other, but not both together. The smallest distraction undid all my hard work. How did I manage the enormous task of healing the guardians and now be completely unable to focus?

I gazed at the ceiling and frowned. Moonlight from the high windows revealed scorch marks covering the stone above. I suspected they were a tribute to Kellen's practice sessions.

The buzzing of his phone on the bench near the door drew my attention.

"Yeah."

I rolled over on my stomach and propped my chin in my palms.

"How much time?" Kellen asked, his voice rising with concern. "And what about you? Do you have someplace to go?"
~~~~~~~~~~~~~~~~~~~~~~

I rose to my feet and dusted my hands on my blue jeans.

"Alright, I'm locking it down. Text me as soon as you can." His hand dropped to his side, and the screen on his phone went dark. I didn't move as he stared at me.

"We're leaving," he finally said. "We have less than thirty minutes to lock down the estate and get out."

He picked up his shoes and left the room.

"Wait," I called after him, stopping to pick up my own sneakers. "What happened? I assume that was Logan."

"I'll explain everything once we're on the road," he shouted over his shoulder as he jogged down the hall in front of me. "Pack a bag and be ready in fifteen minutes."

He disappeared around the corner, and I stopped in front of my door. My hands shook as I turned the knob and hurried into the room.

I pushed open the trunk at the end of my bed and noticed my filthy hands.

"Five minutes." I ran to the shower, shedding my dirty clothes on the way.

Seven minutes later, I stood clean and fully dressed by my pile of clothes and toiletries, realizing I didn't have a bag to put them in. Should I take the time to search Logan's room or throw them all in a pillowcase? The thought of carrying around a flowered pillowcase made up my mind for me.

I rushed through the bathroom and into Logan's space, feeling guilty for a moment, but not enough to have second thoughts. I jerked open the closet door and found two backpacks. I snatched the closest one and ran back to my room.

I stuffed all my clothes, hair brush, tooth brush, and shampoo into the bag, then looked around the room one last time, hoping I could come back to it. Surely Kellen's concern was temporary.

I jogged down the hall to the large living area. It was dark and quiet, lit by a single lamp next to one of the small seating arrangements. I strolled towards the glass doors and realized they were blocked by large sheets of metal. My gaze darted to the windows to find the same. Was the entire house covered in metal sheeting?

The door leading to the garage opened, drawing my attention. Kellen's look of determination and control reminded me of the first time we met.

"Are you ready?" he asked.

I nodded, adjusted my borrowed backpack on my shoulder and followed him out. Dirt still covered his clothing, and I felt a little guilty for taking the time to shower and change. Apparently, he didn't have the same luxury.

I tossed the bag in the back seat. Kellen barely waited for me to close the door before he backed out of the garage. My eyes widened as the garage door slid down, and four sheets of metal unrolled across it. Maybe the whole place was covered.

Kellen sped across the desert until we reached the back gate. He pushed a remote on his visor, and the gate rolled open. When his vehicle cleared it, he put the car in park and jumped out. I twisted in my seat and watched the gate roll back into place. Kellen placed his hands on the stone wall, standing perfectly still. After several moments, a low rumble shook the SUV. A slab of rock sheared off the wall and slid over the metal gate, covering it completely.

Kellen's shoulders shook violently, and he slumped to his knees. I pushed open my door and stumbled from the SUV, reaching his side within seconds.

"What's wrong?" I asked, placing my hand on his shaking shoulder.

He didn't answer as he pushed himself to his feet. I stepped in front of him and took in a sharp breath. Tears rolled down his face, but he didn't try to brush them away.

"We need to go," he said, his voice strained.

I nodded and got back in the car.

We rode in silence for nearly an hour, giving me too much time to think about all that had happened in the last three days. How had I gone from a penniless, unemployed nobody to this? I still struggled to know what *this* even was.

I glanced over at Kellen's permanent scowl. I knew I should say something, but I couldn't think of anything that didn't sound petty or ungrateful. He had done so much for me, and now he was running from his family home because of me.

"I'm sorry," I whispered.

He glanced at me, and his features softened. "You shouldn't be. This isn't your fault."

I almost started to argue with him but held my tongue. It would be petty and selfish. He didn't need to hear me whine about events that he experienced with me. "Where are we going?" I asked instead.

"We really only have two options," he replied, looking at the darkness in front of him. "We could go to the nearest portal and hide in the Magister's Palace, or we can go to Victor's."

"You really think Victor's is an option?" I asked. The man was totally intimidating and tried to keep me there against my will.

"You really think seeing the Magister is an option?" Kellen asked, glancing my way again.

"Oh, yeah, five hundred thousand dollars and death threats." I leaned my head against the window, watching the dark desert roll by.

"Yeah, him too," Kellen said, tapping his long finger on the steering wheel. "Why now? Are they trying to flush us out of the estate where we're relatively safe? Or are they forcing the other players to take sides by accelerating the timeline?"

"Why didn't we stay?" I asked. "Logan and your defenses kept them away last night."

"I'm not Logan," Kellen stated. "He can match their speed and strength. The guardians only had to fight against a handful of vampires. The council is sending fifty tonight."

My eyes widened. Would the guardians I just healed be there when we got back? "What about the guardians?"

"I told them to stand down," he replied. "The vampires will breach the walls, but hopefully they'll assume we ran when they find the house sealed."

"This isn't just about me, is it?" I asked. "This isn't about some bounty on my head. This is about starting their war."

Kellen nodded. The lights from passing cars illuminated his features. His deep scowl resurfaced, and I wished there was something I could do to help. I thought of my decision to commit to Kellen's cause. Not just Kellen's, but the elements as well, which also meant the mages. Although, according to Kellen, only some of them.

My thoughts wandered to Kate, who didn't have a partner yet, and the Magister, who destroyed hers. Was being a vampire really a better option than going insane? Logan seemed normal, but maybe he was the exception.

What was I doing to my own partner by not totally committing to him? Earth had said Kellen didn't need a partner, but his role in this fight would become harder without me. Could I abandon him like that? Could I deliberately make his job harder and possibly risk his life because of my indecision?

I looked out the window again, not really seeing the endless desert that passed. How could I commit to someone I'd only met three days ago? I assumed it was a lifetime commitment, and it wasn't like I could just get a divorce if things didn't work out.

I sighed and leaned my head on the window, staring out into the darkness.

Chapter 17

The slowing vehicle woke me from a fitful sleep. I peeled my face from the window and looked over at Kellen. He rubbed his eyes with his palm, blinking several times.

"I'm sorry, Kellen. I should've stayed awake and talked to you," I said, sitting up in my seat.

"Don't worry about it," he replied gruffly. "We need gas."

He nodded to my right, and I followed his gaze as he pulled into a small gas station. The lights above the pumps were the only ones on.

"No hope for a bathroom," I grumbled.

"At least it's dark enough to go behind the building without being seen," Kellen suggested. "Go while I pump the gas. I'll wait for you to get back before I do the same. There should be something in the glove box for you to use."

I flipped the latch on the glove box and found a pile of napkins and a couple of packaged wet wipes. Was he always this prepared? Reluctantly, I slid out of the SUV and walked towards the small brick building. I passed by a door with the unisex bathroom symbol on it. I jiggled the handle, but it wouldn't open.

"Damn."

I circled the back of the building to find the silhouettes of two large garbage cans overflowing with trash and what looked like an old metal chair. My nose wrinkled at the smell.

"At least they won't notice anything I'm leaving behind."

I took care of business and headed back the way I came. An arm wrapped around my middle, pinning my arms to my side, and a rough hand stifled my scream. I stomped on the foot behind mine and threw my elbows backwards into a solid stomach.

"Well, well," a harsh voice whispered in my ear. "Quite the little fighter."

I bit at the fingers that covered my mouth, and they moved a fraction of an inch, far enough that I couldn't reach them, but still too close to let out my muffled cries.

"Keep fighting, and I might have a snack before the boys get here," he whispered again.

His tongue ran across my neck, and I quit moving. Was he a vampire? Is that why I didn't see him?

"AJ! Are you done?" Kellen yelled from around the corner. "You're not the only one who needed a break."

My captor's hand clamped so tight across my nose and mouth, I could barely breathe. I kicked his shins and stomped on his feet. When that didn't work, I kicked outward, knocking over one of the garbage cans.

"AJ?"

I could hear the worry in my partner's voice and knew he'd come around the corner any minute.

"Don't move, lover boy," my abductor called out as Kellen rounded the corner. "I haven't eaten in two days, and she would make a lovely treat."

The darkness prevented me from seeing Kellen's expression, but I was sure he was scowling.

"Let her go, and I won't kill you," Kellen replied in a low voice.

"You won't kill me before I drain her dry," the vampire countered. "So be a good boy, get in your truck, and leave."

"Not going to happen," Kellen said. "AJ, ninety percent of your body is made of what?"

"This isn't trivia night!" the vampire shouted, his hot breath blowing across my ear. "Don't push me into killing her."

I knew the answer to Kellen's question, and I also realized what he implied. I needed to use my connection to water to make the vampire let go.

"You won't kill her," Kellen stated. "If you do, you won't last until morning. You and I both know you need her alive."

The vampire's huff blew through my hair, and I thought I heard a whisper as it passed.

"You'll be dead in five minutes when my back up arrives, so keep talking, little human."

Five minutes and Kellen would be dead. I didn't even want to find out if he could fight against a vampire, let alone several. I focused on the hand pressing against my lips. How was I supposed to move it? I closed my eyes and called to the moisture beneath his skin. It was sluggish and slimy, but I pulled it anyway. I could deal with slimy for a few minutes if it gave us time to leave before reinforcements showed up.

"What the hell?" the vampire exclaimed in my ear. Was that panic in his voice?

I ignored him and continued to pull against the sluggish slime. As soon as his grip loosened, I pushed his arms away and ran straight towards Kellen. I opened my eyes just in time to trip over the metal chair, falling to my knees. I crawled farther away and turned to look at the vampire.

A trail of fire soared over my head, illuminating what looked like a mummified corpse. I gasped in horror, watching as Kellen's fire consumed it within seconds. That thing had just had its dead arms wrapped around me.

My partner pulled me to my feet and grasped my shoulders. "I still need to piss," he said. "Stand right here and don't move."

I nodded, still in shock over what I'd seen. I thought it was a vampire, not a mummy. No—he'd been a vampire, and I sucked every drop of moisture from him. I clapped my hand over my mouth, trying to swallow the bile in my throat. Kellen turned his back to me. When I heard his zipper, I turned and ran towards the SUV.

"Damnit, AJ!" he yelled from behind me, but fear and revulsion over what I'd done drove me to the car.

I jumped in and locked my door. A few moments later, Kellen joined me and sped back onto the highway. I clasped my shaking hands in my lap and looked out the window, trying to slow my ragged breaths.

"You okay?" Kellen asked.

"I don't know," I replied. "I wasn't trying to... I was just trying to get him to let go."

"He would've killed you," Kellen said. "And if he didn't, his buddies would have. You did what you had to."

"I thought they wanted me alive?" I asked. "Isn't that what you said, and he all but agreed?" I turned and looked at him. "They would've killed you and taken me."

He glanced at me, but his expression was unreadable.

"I couldn't let them kill you," I whispered. "But I thought I could just make him let go, and we'd run for the car before the others showed up."

"Do you really think he would've let us leave?" Kellen asked.

I knew the answer, but it didn't make me feel better. Why did I feel guilty about killing a vampire, anyway? I knew that answer, too. Logan. But he wasn't a normal vampire. He was Kellen's friend and trusted ally, at least that was the way I saw it. Logan was committed to their cause just as much as Kellen.

So, why was I still avoiding a commitment to my partner? It was obvious, even to me, that I didn't want to see him hurt or killed. I couldn't walk out on him the night before when Logan told me to. The thought of not having him there scared me. Was it because I hated feeling so incapable of taking care of myself?

"We won't stop again until we reach Victor's," he said, interrupting my thoughts.

"Okay, I just hope we have a better welcome this time," I replied.

"Don't count on it. He's going to be pissed when he finds out we're running."

"And bringing all our new friends straight to him," I added.

"You got it."

"Lovely."

Chapter 18

Just as the sun started to rise, we wound our way towards Victor's lodge.

"We need to be united when we reach them, AJ," Kellen said, breaking the silence that still hung between us.

"I know," I replied. "That's exactly what they'll see."

He opened his mouth to reply, then snapped it closed. I could see the frustration on his face, but I couldn't force myself to do something I wasn't ready for.

"Only our combined strength will prove our worth. Unfortunately, we *will* have to prove it."

"What are you saying?" I asked.

"We'll be challenged," he replied. "And losing isn't an option."

"But I can't fight!" I protested. "Surely they know I just discovered all of this three days ago. How can they expect me to fight?"

"Because they'll assume we've accepted our partnership, which gives us an advantage."

"And I haven't." I looked out the window and sighed. My guilt strangled me.

"The last thing I want is to force you into this decision," he said, his voice calm. When I glanced at him, his expression had changed from frustrated to sympathetic, making my guilt surge forward. "But we can't decline the challenge, and losing—well, I'd rather not find out."

"Is there no other place for us to go?" I asked. "Somewhere you can have time to train me, and I can have time to adjust to all the demands."

He glanced at me, then pulled his SUV off the road and put it in park.

"I would love to tell you there is," he replied. "But if they can find us at the only gas station within fifty miles, one that I didn't even know I would stop at, there is no place we can go on our own." He turned toward me, and I saw the frustration in his brown eyes. "If we can satisfy Victor's challenge, he'll make sure we have time and space to train."

I pulled my gaze from his, knowing what he was asking of me. When I didn't reply, he let out a long breath, put the car in drive, and started down the road once again.

Victor's lodge came into view twenty minutes later. I marveled at its size and beauty, like a private retreat for the wealthy tucked away in the mountains. Several men lounged on the porch in nothing but sweatpants. I stared at their muscular chests with awe. Were they all built like Mr. Universe?

Kellen parked next to an old pickup truck. "Don't stare," he said, glancing over at me. "They're already arrogant enough."

My ears grew hot with embarrassment. I pushed open my door and fell into Matt.

"Well, hello," he said, grabbing my shoulders and setting me on my feet. "Back again so soon?"

"Yep, we couldn't stay away from your amazing hospitality," I replied, pasting a smile on my face.

He chuckled and opened the back door, grabbing my bag. "You know the requirements for staying, right?" he asked, looking down at me.

"Sort of. Kellen tried to explain, but you know…three-day-old mage couldn't figure it out."

His smile grew as he turned to Kellen. "Is she ready?"

"As she'll ever be," Kellen replied, pulling two large bags from the back of the SUV.

"You should leave those there in case you lose," Matt replied, his grin growing even wider. "Come on, let's see what the boss has in store for you."

I didn't miss the fact that he carried my bag and told Kellen to leave his in the car. I glanced between Kellen, Matt, and my bag. Maybe we should've tried our luck with the Magister.

I followed Matt up the steps and onto the porch, and I couldn't help but notice the bare-chested men staring at me as I walked by. I tried to ignore them but knew I didn't pull off the nonchalant stroll I was going for. Kellen's hand on my lower back gave me a little reassurance as we entered the great room once again.

I was surprised to find it empty. My stomach rumbled at the sight of the long dining table, empty and clean.

"Has Kellen not fed you?" Matt asked. "We'll have to fix that when we're done."

I could feel Kellen's irritation without looking at him and knew Matt was goading him on purpose. We walked down the wide corridor to Victor's study. Matt knocked and waited to be acknowledged.

"After you, princess," he said.

I looked at him, my eyebrows raised. Why did he call me that? That was Logan's nickname for me. A surge of anger rushed through me, and I stopped in front of him.

"You will call me AJ," I stated.

His eyes widened. "You got it."

I continued to stare at him, uncertain where my anger originated from. It was just a name, but I was relieved he agreed so easily.

"Ms. Johnson, please come in."

Victor's deep voice pulled me from my staring match with Matt. I stuck my tongue out at him and waltzed into the room.

"Kellen will wait outside," Victor said when my partner followed me. "I can see you are not full partners. We'll discuss her options alone."

Kellen started to protest, and I placed my hand on his chest. "I got this," I whispered, looking up at him, but not feeling as confident as I sounded. "Maybe I'll bring Sparky with me."

He wrapped his hand around mine and a small trail of light rushed from his hand. I smiled as it raced towards my ribs.

"Be careful," Kellen said, "and commit to nothing." I saw the concern in his eyes as they focused on nothing but me.

"I think that's the only thing I've managed to master," I replied, smiling to soften the hurt that surfaced with my comment.

"We don't have all day," Victor stated.

Kellen released me and walked out. Sparky fluttered in my abdomen, and I placed my hand against it, thinking it would make a difference.

We got this.

Victor sat in the same place he had when we met a couple of days ago.

"Sit down," Victor commanded. "You and Kellen have put me in a very difficult situation."

I sat in the chair across from him but remained silent. How did he already know our circumstance? He stared at me for several moments, and I stared back. His eyes reminded me of chocolate milk, a smooth, light brown without the typical striations of darker shades. My stomach rumbled again, and I clasped my hand over it.

Victor raised his eyebrow. "I assume you are being pursued and seek refuge here?"

I nodded.

"Did he explain the challenge requirement?"

I presumed he meant Kellen. "Yes, sort of," I replied. "He said you would make us fight in order to be granted a safe place to stay."

"Eloquence is not his strong suit," Victor said. "But yes. Normally, both of you would participate in the challenge, but your life is too valuable to risk. If you had even the smallest amount of training and a solid partner, I might consider it."

"You're foregoing the challenge?" I asked in surprise.

"No. Kellen will complete it without you." He stood and offered his hand to me, as if he hadn't just presented me with an awful situation. A flood of emotion rushed through my core. Here I was again, allowing someone to dictate my future. How much more did they think I could take?

"You will take into consideration that I am not with him," I stated, taking his hand and letting him pull me from the chair.

"You will not command me, Ms. Johnson, regardless of your station." He released my hand and started towards the door. What was he talking about, 'my station?' When I didn't follow, he turned to look at me. "Do you not wish to be present for his challenge?"

"You're doing it now? We've been up all night, with no food or rest. I imagine your people have at least had breakfast." My voice continued to rise with each statement. "It's hardly a challenge if your challenger is fighting against a severely weakened opponent."

His stare hardened, and with three steps, he was towering over me. "Did I not say that you will not command me?"

I straightened my back, trying to appear taller and glared back at him. "I didn't hear a command anywhere in my statement. I was merely pointing out the obvious."

He drew in a deep breath and let it out several seconds later. His hot breath ruffled the top of my head. "Fine."

He stormed from the room, leaving me alone in his extravagant office. Sparky raced around my middle, and I smiled. Did I really just stand my ground against the most intimidating man I'd ever met?

Yes, you did, princess. The wind's voice drifted by my ear, and I jumped.

Victor's bellowing startled me more, and I ran from the room and down the hall.

"Marissa! Food. Now."

I met Kellen at the entrance to the great room. Victor continued yelling for more people, and Kellen dragged me to one of the small seating areas.

"What happened?" he asked in a harsh whisper, still grasping my forearm.

I looked at his hand, and he let go. "He is making you do the challenge on your own," I replied, rubbing my arm even though it didn't hurt. "Something about not wanting to risk my life." I frowned as I realized the implication. Kellen was expendable.

Kellen took a step back and turned his gaze towards Victor, who was now surrounded by three others.

"Kellen, I can't sit back and watch you do this by yourself," I said.

"You have to, or they will force us to leave," he replied, still watching Victor.

"No, he won't," I argued. "He'll watch you die, then keep me prisoner. He wanted me here from the beginning." I huffed and put both hands on his face, forcing him to look at me. "We should leave. We're no safer here than we are with the Magister."

He looked down at me, and the lines of worry between his eyes softened. "There's something going on here that we're missing. I'm not disposable. My value to him may not be as great as yours, but he can't afford to throw me away, either. We'll play his game, for now."

He wrapped his hands around mine and pulled them away from his face.

"You should give Sparky back," he said with a grin.

"How can you be smiling right now?" I asked. "And you know you can take him back anytime you wish."

He chuckled and leaned towards me, pressing our folded hands against his chest. "Come on, stupid. We have stuff to do."

"Are you talking to me?" I asked, feeling my ears start to burn. Sparky's flutter in my stomach answered my question as he raced through my core, up my arm, and back to Kellen.

Matt appeared next to Kellen, who straightened his posture and his expression at the intrusion. "Sorry to interrupt a tender moment, but the boss says you have fifteen minutes to eat."

"Thanks," Kellen replied, dropping one of my hands but keeping hold of the other as we walked towards the long dining table.

Two plates graced the table at one end, looking completely out of place. I didn't spend any energy thinking about it as my stomach growled once again at the sight of real food. Two slices of thick ham, three eggs, hash browns, and toast covered the ceramic platter. I dropped into the seat and devoured my meal.

~~~~~~~~~~~~~~~~~~~~~~

Twenty minutes later, I sat on a wooden bench, sandwiched between Victor and Matt. Mike took the place on the other side of his brother and a tall woman, with long
~~~~~~~~~~~~~~~~~~~~~~

blond hair sat on the other side of Victor. She glared at me every chance she could. It got really annoying, really quick.

Twenty or so of the same wooden benches surrounded a clear patch of dirt about fifty feet across. Men and woman of all shapes, sizes, and colors filled the benches, and dozens more stood behind them. No one wanted to miss out on the mage's challenge.

Long gouges covered the hard-packed earth. I suspected they were claw marks, since everyone here was supposedly a shifter. I hadn't seen any of them in animal form and wasn't sure how I'd react to it. How big were they? What color fur did they have? Did their fur match their hair or skin color? I hoped it was their skin color as some of the women dyed their hair in wild, florescent shades.

Cheers and shouts interrupted my musing. A man and woman entered the little arena. He wore only black sweatpants, exposing his dark, muscled chest and arms. His black, curly hair hugged his scalp, and his blue eyes scanned the crowd. They landed on me, and he bowed.

The woman next to him slapped his arm and scowled at me. Her curly black hair was also shaved close to her head, framing her perfectly shaped skull. A well-fitted tank top and yoga pants covered her muscular body.

The pair turned to my right and stepped closer together. I followed their gaze, my stomach twisting in knots when I realized they were looking at Kellen. He emerged from the crowd and approached his challengers. He wore a black t-shirt tucked into loose cargo pants, and black leather boots covered his feet. A leather vest wrapped around his torso, and I cringed. Would a simple leather vest protect him from their claws? I had no idea. I didn't even know what animal they were, but I doubted they'd shift into docile, spoiled house cats.

He stopped ten yards from his opponents, and the arena fell silent. Victor stood, but my focus remained on Kellen. I couldn't imagine being as calm and relaxed as he appeared. My own pulse raced, and fear poked at my determination to stay calm.

"Everyone knows the rules!" Victor bellowed. "Begin!"

The man and woman nodded at Victor, then focused on Kellen. The air warmed, and the ground beneath my feet rumbled. I gripped the edge of my wooden seat.

The man shifted mid-stride from human to an enormous black wolf, his shoulders easily reaching Kellen's waist. My eyes widened when the woman did the same, changing into a slightly smaller version of the same wolf. My heart pounded against my ribs, and I had to force myself to breathe. I'd never seen Kellen fight. Could he really win against these two? I realized I didn't want to see him hurt, and I knew he would be, even if he won.

The bench beneath me shuddered, and I cried out as four slabs of earth rose from the ground surrounding my partner. The wolves paused and tilted their heads, then leapt backwards as the walls raced towards them. Kellen's hands rose into the air and circles of fire chased the stone slabs. The wolves dodged them, racing around the arena until they reached the edge. The walls of rock disappeared, but the fire surged back towards Kellen, surrounding him.

A soft whisper shifted my focus back to Kellen, who now kneeled in the dirt.

Be ready, the wind whispered to me.

The wolves paced around the fire's protective shield.

"He cannot hold it forever," Victor said. "I can feel him pulling a large amount of magic into himself. I wonder what he has planned."

I looked up at the man next to me and found his strange chocolate eyes staring back.

"You will not interfere," he said.

I scowled at him. "You will not command me."

"The rules of the challenge cannot be disobeyed," he retorted.

"Since no one told me the rules, then they don't apply to me," I replied.

His eyes narrowed and the milk chocolate shifted between lighter and darker shades, reminding me of creamer making its last stand against the coffee it mixed with.

The rumbling ground interrupted his response. Several benches overturned as the shaking became more violent. The flames surrounding Kellen rose, and the ground split open around him, creating a trench in the earth over two feet wide. His fire dove into the crevice and disappeared.

The male wolf leapt over the fissure easily, raking his claws against Kellen's chest. They ripped through the leather vest, but I couldn't see any blood. I bit my knuckles, trying not to cry out. I couldn't sit back and do nothing as they tore him apart.

Kellen grabbed the fur around the wolf's neck and tried to toss it on its side. The wolf rolled with the momentum, pulling Kellen with him. My partner released him and jumped to his feet the same time the shifter gained his own balance. They circled one another, the wolf baring his teeth and growling.

I gasped when the female wolf rushed towards the fissure, but Kellen's fire surged from the trench as she was about to leap. She stumbled trying to stop her forward momentum, then disappeared into the crater with a howl. The fire fell into the crevice with her, and the crowd roared.

Two men leapt from their seats and raced towards the crevice. My focus darted back to the fight between my partner and the male wolf. Kellen brought his elbow down on the wolf's snout as it turned to look for its companion. It snarled and snapped at Kellen's arm. He backed up several steps, leading the wolf away from the two men hanging over the edge of the fissure.

They slowly pulled the woman out and helped her walk toward the benches. Scorch marks covered her naked, human body, but her pain didn't stop her look of hatred directed at Kellen.

I snapped back to Kellen as the male wolf locked his jaws on my partner's forearm. He smashed his fist into the wolf's head several times, but it wouldn't let go. I jumped from my seat, ready to intervene, but Victor grabbed my arm.

"You will not interfere," he stated. I glared at him until he finally released my arm.

I watched in horror as blood dripped from the wolf's mouth, still attached to Kellen's arm. My partner dropped to his knees and placed his free hand on the bare earth. The ground opened beneath the wolf, and it fell into the gaping hole, dragging Kellen with it.

Dozens of shifters surged to their feet and converged onto the arena floor. I shot forward, sprinting across the space as fast as I could, knowing that Victor would be right behind me. I barely cleared the crevice and reached the hole at the same time as the other shifters.

Kellen's head and shoulders hung over the gaping pit. He didn't move when I touched his shoulder. One by one, the men and women around me shifted into their wolves. I didn't have time to be amazed by the myriad of colors and sizes as they formed a loose circle around me and Kellen.

I'm with you, Alisandra. Do not fear them. The wind's whisper brought only a small amount of comfort.

The sound of claws scraping against rock caught my attention. I glanced around to see Kellen's opponent clambering his way out of the hole. He bared his bloody teeth at me when his snout reached the ledge, then he lunged.

Without thinking, I swept my hands to the side. A gust of wind buffered against me and threw the wolf to the ground. I looked at my hands, then at the circle of wolves. Kellen's opponent shifted into his human form, standing before me completely naked. I forced my eyes to stay above his chest with effort.

"Your partner broke the rules of the challenge," he growled. "He tried to kill my sister."

"If he wanted her dead, she would be," I snapped. I stepped back until my heel touched Kellen's side.

"Someone will pay the price for her injuries." He snarled, and his human form shimmered with magic. I knew he would shift again soon. What was I going to do against a dozen wolves?

"Kellen followed your stupid rules when he fought," I replied, raising my hands. "I will not."

"So be it."

Within seconds, he shifted to his wolf and lunged again. I pushed him to the side once more, this time with greater force. He rolled twice before regaining his feet and immediately surging towards me.

Say the word, and I will end him, the wind whispered to me.

I ignored its tempting offer and whipped another gust of air in the wolf's direction. He dodged it and plowed into me. I fell on my ass, the wolf on top of me.

He lowered his jaw within inches of my face and drew in a deep breath. I dug my fingers into the fur around his neck and pulled him closer.

"Do you know what I did to the last monster that threatened my partner?" I whispered. "I pulled all the fluid from his body, leaving a dried-out husk behind."

I watched his blue eyes widen at the implied threat. My blood rushed through my veins, pulsing in time with my anger. How dare they issue a challenge that threatened Kellen's life? Did they really think I would stand by and do nothing? I suffered at the hands of bullies my entire life, but that part of my past was gone. I finally had the strength to fight back, and I would.

"I have water *and* air, you bastard. Step back, or I'll kill you." I shoved him once again, using the wind to knock him away.

I pushed myself to my feet and looked at the wolves surrounding me. They ranged from gray and black to light brown. Most were the same size as my opponent, but a few were larger. The blue-eyed wolf glared at me, growling softly.

The shifters directly in front of me parted to allow Victor to walk through, still in his human form.

"I told you not to interfere," he said.

"I believe my partner has endured a more severe injury than your wolf," I replied. "I don't see how it matters."

"It matters because you disobeyed," he responded.

"What is it you like to say to me?" I asked, tapping my chin. "Oh, yeah. You don't command me."

Several growls erupted around me, and I struggled to tamp down my fear. Victor took a deep breath, but I didn't miss the way his eyes shifted color.

"You've put me in another quandary, Ms. Johnson. There are penalties for what you've done, but the consequences are more than I'm willing to sacrifice." He took several steps towards me until he was just out of reach. "What is a leader supposed to do?"

"If you were the leader I thought you were, we wouldn't be having this discussion," I snapped. "You claim to be our allies, but here we are playing your stupid games. An ally would be providing us sanctuary against the evil that hunts us." I waved my hand at the arena and several wolves cringed. "But here we are, fighting against our so-called friends."

The sky clouded over, muted lightning flickering between the clouds. The wind whipped around me, pulling at my clothes and whispering in my ear. I ignored its pleas for destruction.

"If I didn't completely trust Kellen's judgement, I would say you're working *for* the damn vampires, not against them." I took a step closer to him as thunder followed the lightning across the sky. "So, what are you going to do, *Victor*?"

His eyes narrowed, and a low growl passed his lips. "Are you challenging me?"

"Do I look like I want to be in charge of something this archaic?" I asked in return.

"You look like a lost child playing in a world you know nothing about!" he yelled.

"Because you won't give me the opportunity to learn!" I bellowed back. "We've wasted precious time with this stupid, whatever this is, when Kellen and I could've been training." Lightning struck a nearby tree, shattering the limbs at the top. Swirls of wind gusted through the arena, creating small dust devils that disappeared in seconds. "Call off your mutts or kill me now. I'm done with your games."

"How dare you command me!" Victor roared.

"You stubborn bastard!" The wind once again buffeted me, and Victor leaned into the gale.

"Give them to me, Alisandra," the wind said as its translucent form appeared next to me. "I will teach them to respect their betters." It disappeared as quickly as it appeared, and I wondered if I really saw it. I balled my hands into fists to hide their trembling. I suspected the wind was reacting to my rage, and while I welcomed it now, I would need to learn how to control those emotions later.

"So, what will it be?" I asked, turning back to Victor.

He stared at me with an unreadable expression for several moments. "Bring your mage to our medical wing, and we'll see to his injuries," Victor replied.

"I'll take care of my mage," I retorted. "Are you allies or enemies? Tell me now, so there is no confusion later when the vampires show up at your door."

His lips pressed into a thin line, and he lowered his eyes. "We are allies."

"Then let me heal Kellen in peace."

I turned my back to him, a move I'd seen in dozens of movies over the years. I knew it was overly dramatic but not nearly as impressive as the storm threatening to break loose. I hoped Victor was sincere about our new relationship, but for now, I had more important things to worry about, like healing my partner.

I knelt next to Kellen and brushed my hand across his sweaty brow. My eyes drifted to his chest, and I shook my head. The leather did nothing to protect him from the wolf. Three long slashes ran from his collar to his stomach. His bloody arm rested across his abdomen, and I swallowed the bile that rose in my throat. Dirt and blood covered the puncture marks that still oozed.

"You better hope that damn dog doesn't have rabies, or I'm going to be really pissed," I called over my shoulder. There was no response as I wrapped my fingers over the wounds on his forearm. "A little rain to wash this away would be really nice."

I focused on the abundance of moisture in the air without closing my eyes this time. It formed into small drops that merged together as they floated towards me. With my free hand, I guided them towards Kellen's open wounds, watching in awe as they settled over him. I pushed what I now knew to be my healing power into Kellen's arm. I embraced his pain as warmth and fatigue washed over me, but I gritted my teeth and kept going.

A small light beneath his dark skin jumped from him to me.

"Sparky, I need to know if there's any internal bleeding. Will you tell me?"

It moved up my arm to my elbow, then turned back and slowly returned to Kellen.

"Procrastination is not attractive, little one," I scolded.

More rain fell from the sky, and I looked up at the still darkening clouds. The drops turned to a steady rainfall, coating my face and seeping into my clothes within seconds. I ignored it and focused on the punctures beneath my fingers. I felt them slowly shrink until they were nothing more than angry welts.

"Wow, I feel like shit," Kellen said, raising his head. "Damn, that hurts."

"Which part?" I asked, smoothing the water from his forehead. "Does your arm still hurt?"

He gasped as he tried to sit up and fell back. "Sort of, but my chest is killing me."

"Be still, Kellen," I ordered as I unbuttoned the leather vest and peeled it off his chest.

The rain had already soaked his clothes, mixing the blood and dirt. I pressed my hand against the three open wounds and frowned. Blood and grit stuck to my hands. What if the cuts started closing with pieces of dirt and linen in them?

"Damn." I looked at his face and found him staring at me. "What?"

"Nothing," he replied. "Please continue."

"I might need help getting your shirt off or at least pulling it above the cuts on your chest."

Kellen lifted his arms and grimaced as he gripped the collar of his shirt, then ripped it down the middle. He flinched as it peeled away from his shredded skin. Water cascaded off his shirt and across his chest.

"Or... that works," I said.

He let out a long sigh and closed his eyes, his head lulling to the side. A large, purple bruise covered his left jaw. Rainwater dripped from my chin and hair as I leaned over him, once again placing my hands over his chest and pushing a pulse of healing into his wounds. A flood of warmth surged toward me along with his pain. But something else was there as well. A sense of contentment?

"Sparky, what are you seeing?" I whispered, hoping Kellen wasn't conscious.

My pain increased as the little spark floated beneath my hands. Is this what Kellen was talking about when he said he could feel my laughter when the little spark raced around my ribs? I squeezed my eyes shut, trying to focus on my connection to Kellen. Each time Sparky passed an injury, I felt his level of concern or anguish depending on the severity. We made a quick run through the rest of Kellen's major organs. There was lots of bruising, but nothing broken.

I leaned back and sighed. "Thank goodness."

"For what?" Kellen whispered, placing one of his hands over mine. He pushed himself into a seated position next to me, and waves of emotion washed over me. Gratitude, dedication, longing. My face flushed, and I looked away from him. I knew I cared for him, or I wouldn't have risked myself, but were these emotions his or mine? I had no idea.

"I don't think anything is broken," I replied. "Sparky helped me check everything."

He raised his eyebrows, and hope and uncertainty assaulted my overrun emotions.

"Sparky, I'm done now," I said, attempting to stand. Kellen grabbed my hand and forced me to stay by his side.

"You can feel it?" he asked.

I nodded and pressed my lips together as more emotions flooded me. They had to be his; mine were never this strong.

"We need to find Sparky's shut off switch," I said. "Those feelings are more than I'm capable of dealing with."

I pulled my hand from his and stood. His fear of rejection surged forward, igniting a wave of guilt from me. I'd dealt with that fear my whole life, and now I'd subjected him to the same feeling twice. He rose beside me and swayed.

"Wait. Logan's comments make sense now," he said. "We were supposed to experience this the first time. I've always been able to feel yours, but they were not usually directed at me." His face flushed, but he continued. "I imagine you're overwhelmed right now. Take Sparky so you'll have a break from me. It will give me time to..." He paused and looked at me. I felt his emotions subside, and he held his hand out to me.

"I don't want you to know what I'm feeling right now," I replied. "I'm pretty sure I can't subdue any of it the way you just did."

"And I can't keep it under control forever. I need time to sort it out," he responded.

I bit my bottom lip, uncertainty weighing on me. Should I even worry about what he thought? Maybe if he could feel it, then I wouldn't have to say it out loud. Maybe he could help me decide what I really wanted. And maybe I was dreaming.

"Come on, Sparky," I relented. "Let's humiliate the new mage for a while."

Sparky soared across the space between us and Kellen laughed. "I might be a little jealous," he said, still chuckling. "Am I that unpleasant to be around?"

"No, he just endured a lot of pain and agony for you. I imagine he needs a break."

I turned towards the muddy arena, the steady rain still falling around us. The large, gaping holes Kellen created were still there, but the wooden seats were abandoned. The shattered limbs from the lightning strike smoldered on the ground just outside the ring of benches.

The earth rumbled beneath my feet as the craters closed. Kellen sighed, and I looked over at him.

"Too much magic," he said. "I'll be worthless for at least a day."

"I feel like this was all a waste, Kellen," I said, looking around the arena. "Why would he make us do this?"

"It is tradition for new wolves who wish to join the pack," he replied.

"I'm not a wolf, and I have no desire to join the pack," I argued.

"True, but we're asking for his protection."

"Which he should've given willingly as your ally. Why all this?" I waved my hand around the space.

Kellen narrowed his eyes at something behind me, making me turn. Matt wound his way through the benches and stopped a few yards away.

"Your room is ready at the lodge," he said, looking at the ground.

I stomped towards him, my anger rising with each splash of muddy water. "Why?" I demanded, stopping inches from his chest and craning my neck to look up at him.

"Please, pr...AJ," he stuttered out my name and continued. "Victor didn't believe your true heritage until today."

"What does that mean, Matt?"

He looked past me to Kellen, then back to me.

"Didn't he tell you about your family?" he asked, motioning towards my partner.

"Yes, I know. I'm the Magister's daughter. My looks alone prove that," I replied, not hiding my bitterness. "It has nothing to do with what happened here."

Matt looked over my head again, confusion clouding his features. "Your family has ruled the mages for centuries, AJ, but that isn't all. Your great-grandfather united the supernatural races, creating alliances that were not broken until the Magister took over."

I turned and looked at Kellen, then back to Matt. "Still not clearing it up for me."

Matt sighed and sat on the nearest bench, ignoring the puddles of water on its surface.

"Victor thought you might have been a bastard child, one that didn't carry the blessings of the elements," he began. "Your mother is the first in your line that only has one element which is probably why she made the choices that have led us here. I imagine she resents the elements for rejecting her. Today's test was to prove you had both elements. He knew you had water, he watched you use it the other day."

I dropped onto the bench next to him, my wet clothes squelching beneath me. "He could've just asked," I said. "I would've gladly shown him without anyone getting hurt."

"He also needed you to make a commitment," Matt said reluctantly. "We all did. We can't fight the army the Council has created."

Thunder rumbled across the sky again, and I took a deep breath. "I don't like being forced into anything," I hissed.

Matt looked over at Kellen again and shrugged.

"Say it, Matt," I stated.

"My God. Can't you do something about that, Kellen?" he asked, then turned back to me. "You were probably the only one who, well... Everyone else could already see your attachment to him. It's obvious. You just wouldn't admit it to yourself."

I deflated. Was I really that transparent? If everyone else already knew how I felt, why was I so undecided? Because I didn't want someone dictating my future. Without the prison of my deformity, I should've been able to make my own decisions. But here I was, trapped in my ignorance and fighting a battle I couldn't win.

"There's a lot I'm still missing," I said. "Will I have time to learn? Will Victor stop being an ass and leave me alone?"

Matt chuckled. "Victor will be Victor. He's been the one to keep our pack safe from the Magister and the vampires for a very long time. He isn't used to someone challenging his authority."

"I didn't challenge him," I insisted. "He was being an idiot."

"She doesn't know," Kellen said. "I'll tell her when we're someplace where we can't be overheard."

Matt nodded, and I felt my eyes narrow with my patience. "You'll tell me now," I said, my anger flaring again. "I'm tired of the secrets, Kellen. You sprinkle information on me as you see fit, but all it does is leave me ignorant and pissed off."

"Fair enough, but it's a conversation we should have in private." He looked down at me with the familiar impassive gaze. "Not here."

Matt chuckled and rose from the wet bench. "I'm glad it's you and not me, man. Come on, I'll take you to your room."

Chapter 19

"Are you kidding me?" I asked, standing in the middle of a lavishly decorated suite, looking at the door to the only bedroom. Did they really expect us to share a bed? We were partners, but that didn't mean I was sleeping with him. My face flushed at the thought, and I turned my back to them.

"Is something wrong?" Matt asked.

"Nope, it's perfect," Kellen answered, walking him to the door. "Thank you for bringing up our bags. I really need a change of clothes."

"No problem," Matt replied. "Victor gave us instructions to leave you alone until tomorrow. Dinner is at seven if you're interested." He closed the door behind him, and Kellen leaned against it looking at me.

"Don't say it," he said. "I need a really hot shower and dry clothes. We'll discuss the sleeping arrangements afterwards, as well as answering all your questions."

He walked past me, picking up one of his bags. I glared at his back until he closed the bathroom door. I couldn't argue with him. He'd just fought a battle for me, one that left him injured and exhausted. I could at least let him shower in peace.

I looked around the extravagant suite. A small kitchenette took up the corner by the door, equipped with a mini-fridge, microwave, and narrow pantry. A Keurig rested on the black granite countertop, and wine glasses hung from the overhead cabinets. A round hardwood table and four chairs occupied the space next to the kitchen and a tan, leather sectional sofa faced patio doors that led to the balcony. A thick oriental rug covered the hardwood floors, and two doors flanked each side of the room, one for the bathroom and one for the bedroom.

I dropped into the short end of the sectional and stretched out, ignoring my wet clothes and shoes. I needed time to think about everything that happened. I was making too many rushed decisions I knew I'd regret later. Again, I went back to the same question I asked myself the day before. How did I go from being nobody to the most important person in a fight between supernatural beings? I had no idea they even existed until now, yet my family seemed to be the key to it all. Why wasn't I allowed to know them? Did my mother abandon me, or did she really believe I was dead? She didn't act like she cared, and she was willing to pay to have me killed. I shook my head. No, she abandoned me. I was an idiot to think otherwise.

I closed my eyes, trying to remember my life three days ago. Was Sharon looking for me? Did she know I abandoned my apartment and skipped town? Did the vampires have my best friend? Would they hold Sharon hostage to get to me? My eyes popped open. What a terrible thought. Surely I would've heard something if that were the case. It wouldn't do any good to have a hostage if no one knew about it.

My thoughts drifted to my partner. He'd been more of a friend to me than anyone before, even Sharon. He could have abandoned me or handed me over to any number of bad guys several times, but he didn't. He always stuck by, defended me, and made sure I ate. I smiled, and my eyes drooped again. But he also kept so many secrets from me. Did he really think I couldn't handle all the information at once? He kept using the excuse that he wanted me to be more familiar with my magic, but that shouldn't keep him from telling me about my family. It wasn't up to the shifters to tell me about my family uniting the supernatural races. Kellen should've told me that.

A jaw-breaking yawn interrupted my thoughts. When was the last time I slept? Maybe on the drive up here, and I'd used so much magic...

Kellen's hand brushing my forehead startled me awake. I rubbed my eyes as he sat down on the edge of the sofa beside me.

"Have a nice nap?" he asked.

"How long was I sleeping?"

"About an hour," he replied. "I thought you might want a shower and clean clothes. You cannot be comfortable."

I shifted on the couch and moaned when my wet jeans stuck to the leather sofa. Kellen stood, and I slid my feet to the floor.

"You're right," I said. "Thanks."

"Your bag's in the bathroom, but there are more clothes for you in the bedroom if you want them."

I raised an eyebrow at him as I walked towards the bathroom. I wasn't opposed to hand-me-downs. Most of my wardrobe came from second-hand stores, but I didn't see anyone my size in the group of shifters.

"A couple of the teenage girls made donations," he explained. "Some of them have pretty good taste in fashion."

I huffed and closed the door, looking in the mirror that covered the wall above the double sink. I was a mess. My mostly dry shirt was covered in blood and clumps of dirt. My short hair stuck out at odd angles, and streaks of mud ran across my face.

I struggled to peel the jeans from my legs and wound up sitting on the cold tile floor to get them off. I tossed my t-shirt in the waste basket, knowing it was ruined, then removed everything else and got in the shower.

~~~~~~~~~~~~~~~~~~

Kellen lounged on the sofa, watching a large screen TV that hung from the wall. I dropped next to him, taking the remote from his hand. I hit the power button and tossed it to the other end of the couch.

He eyed me suspiciously, then smiled.

"What's so funny?" I asked, crossing my arms over my stomach.

"Your expression," he replied.

I scowled at him and held my hand out. He looked down at my upturned palm then back to my face.

"I'm not ready to take him back yet, but I am ready to talk." He folded my hand back over my stomach and smiled.

My scowl deepened. What was he so happy about? "Tell me about my grandparents."

"Can we talk about that command first?" he asked.

"It wasn't a command," I argued, then bit my lip. "Okay, maybe it was, but I need to know."

"Yes, you do." He rubbed his chin, and I noticed the five o'clock shadow emerging on his jawline despite the raw bruising on one side.

"I won't repeat what you already know about how long your family's been in charge," he continued. "What's important is that your line has a unique ability to convince people to do what you want them to do. I'm not certain where it comes from, but your family is the only one who possesses it."

"What do you mean?" I asked. "I can manipulate people's minds to convince them to obey me?"

"No, not really," he replied. "A few moments ago, when you told me to explain your grandparents, I could feel the command in your voice, compelling me to tell you. The only reason Matt revealed as much as he did earlier is
~~~~~~~~~~~~~~~~~~

because of that same command. You can compel people to do things, though I would advise you not to. They can feel it and will resent a command they don't agree with."

"That's why Victor was so upset with me," I said, dumfounded. I pulled my knees to my chest and hugged them. "He kept telling me I could not command him, but I think he was trying to convince himself, not me." I rested my chin on my knees and thought about my fight with the blue-eyed wolf. "That's also why your opponent didn't kill me. I told him to back off, or I would kill him." I looked over at Kellen to find him staring at me. Concern and curiosity poked at the edge of my mind.

"I don't think I was awake for that part," Kellen said.

"No, you weren't," I replied cautiously. The concern converted to curiosity and amusement. "Do you have Sparky?" I asked.

"Nope," Kellen replied.

"Then what do I feel?"

"I'm not sure Sparky has anything to do with it," he answered.

"Then take him back, and let's find out," I suggested, turning towards him and folding my legs beneath me. I extended my hand to him and waited.

His amusement faded to apprehension. He didn't want me knowing his emotions either. Did we have a choice? It didn't look like it.

"AJ, I know how you feel about being forced into any decision," he said, keeping his hands to himself. "Knowing my emotions will only make it harder for you."

"Do you really think I don't already know?" I asked, dropping my hand in my lap.

"It's not the same as hearing it or feeling it," he replied. "I can't turn it off, but that doesn't mean it should be forced on you either."

"I think I can feel it regardless," I said and took a deep breath. "Apparently, my own feelings are obvious to everyone but me."

"But you're the one that matters. We've connected. That's all we need. Anything more than that can wait until this is done."

I took in his brown eyes and long lashes, his perfectly straight nose that met his full lips in exactly the right place. How did I end up with someone who was not only easy to look at, but actually cared about how I felt? Didn't Logan tell me not to fight against my partner? I couldn't trust a vampire, but he used to be a partnered mage. He had more experience with that than either of us.

"Thank you for understanding," I whispered.

"Thank you for accepting me," he said.

I tried to swallow the lump forming in my throat. I had accepted him and without realizing it, finally admitted that I was in this fight, but I wasn't alone. He wasn't the only one grateful for acceptance.

"Let's get some rest," he suggested, pushing himself from the couch. "Neither of us has had quality sleep since the night before last."

He held his hand out to me, and I remembered the single bedroom.

"Where are we sleeping?" I asked, my stomach fluttering as I took his hand.

"I'll do my best to stay on my side of the bed," he replied, smiling.

"Okay, I'll try to do the same."

Chapter 20

The tantalizing smell of fresh coffee roused me from sleep. Nothing compared to the aroma of fresh-brewed coffee. I stretched, rubbing the sleep from my eyes. I'd managed to stay on my side of the bed, and so had Kellen. A tiny drop of disappointment joined my drowsiness, but I didn't dwell on it. He could have taken advantage of me, and he didn't. I couldn't be mad because he behaved like a gentleman.

I rolled out of bed and got dressed, then wandered towards the coffee bliss calling my name.

"Good afternoon. Coffee?" Kellen asked, dropping a K-cup into the Keurig, a smile lighting his face.

"Yes, please," I replied. "What's on the agenda for this afternoon?"

"More practice. You need to be able to call both elements at the same time."

I frowned, thinking about how insistent the wind was. Kellen pushed a steaming cup of black coffee towards me, and I wrapped my fingers around the warm cup.

"What is it?" he asked.

"I don't really need to call the wind," I explained. "It's more like trying to restrain it. It constantly whispers to me, offering its destruction."

"And Water doesn't do the same?" he asked, raising an eyebrow at me.

"No, not at all. I have to ask Water to help me," I replied. "It always does, but I have to ask." I tentatively sipped my hot coffee and sighed. How did people survive without it?

"Let's go down to the arena and see how we can make that work. After coffee." He smiled, again, pouring cream and sugar into his own cup.

"Have you heard from Kate?" I asked.

"Yes, she texts me every day," he replied.

I should have known that. She *was* his sister. "Is she at the palace?"

"She was until yesterday. She and several others are going to pick up more mages," he explained.

"You mean ones captured by the vampires?"

"Yep. They're in a small town in Vermont." He looked at the watch on his wrist. "She should be texting again in a couple hours to let me know their status."

"What about Logan?" I asked, taking another sip of coffee.

"Nothing," he replied, frowning.

"Is that normal?"

"We've gone months without speaking."

"But he said he would let you know when he reached his safe house," I said, feeling his worry.

"Yeah."

Kellen seemed sure Logan could take care of himself earlier, but his concern for the vampire floated through our connection. I finished my last drop of coffee with reluctance and pushed away from the counter.

"I'm guessing Victor doesn't have a room like yours to practice in."

"No, not likely." Kellen finished his as well and put both cups in the sink. "The arena may be best anyway. It will force you to maintain control in a confined area rather than letting everything get out of hand."

"Are you saying I have no control?" I asked, walking towards the door. I woke up feeling more in control of my life today than I had all week.

"Not at all," he replied, opening it for me.

I narrowed my eyes at him. Did he mean I had no control, or did he imply that wasn't what he said? He smiled at me and nudged me out the door.

Raised voices greeted us halfway down the stairs. A young girl sprinted by the bottom of the steps, and I turned to see her making a path to Victor's door.

"You should have killed it on sight," a man's voice growled.

A woman's panicked voice rose above his. "Don't bring it into the lodge!"

"Wait for Victor," another shaking voice echoed above the others.

Kellen and I reached the bottom of stairs and ran into a large group surrounding three men. Two shifters held an unconscious form between them. Kellen's sharp intake of breath preceded his rush through the crowd. I followed on his heels, along with shouts and protests. My partner knelt in front of the center man covered in dirt and blood.

"Logan," I whispered and dropped to my knees next to him. I looked between the two men carrying him. "What happened?"

Their eyes narrowed at me. "We found him on the road. He said he was a friend of yours and brought grave news."

I looked back at Logan's face. Bruises covered his left side, and blood dripped from the corner of his lip.

"Did he tell you the grave news?" I questioned, placing my hand on his bruised face. Did the shifters inflict these injuries or someone else? I wasn't in a position to ask, my own presence teetered on the verge of hostile.

"No. He fell unconscious after he insisted we bring him to you."

"Take him to my room," I ordered, then thought about my conversation with Kellen and commanding people. Too late.

"Please, take him upstairs," Kellen intervened. "There's no reason for you to continue carrying him around."

Victor's deep voice drifted across the crowd. "I will not have a vampire in my house."

Kellen placed his hand on my shoulder and shook his head, then rose and turned to Victor. I knew what he meant. Don't command Victor to do anything.

"He's my friend and the only insight I have to the vampire council," Kellen began. "If he risked himself to come here in the middle of the day, then his news is dire."

"He likely led the Council's army to us," Victor stated. "I'll not have him in my house."

"The council already knows where you are," Kellen argued, his fists clenching at his sides. "They didn't need Logan to show them the way."

I rose from Logan's side and stepped beside Kellen, forcing his fingers apart and lacing mine in his. Neither of us needed to irritate our host. "Please, Victor. We need to hear what he has to say. I'll assume full responsibility for his actions." I avoided meeting Victor's intense stare, trying to appear inoffensive. "You can lock him in our room if you wish, though I imagine he'll leave as soon as he's strong enough."

Silence filled the space for several moments, and I glanced at Victor. His chocolate eyes bore into me, and I dropped my gaze.

"He will leave at nightfall," Victor demanded.

I nodded, trying to keep the scowl from my face. I wasn't good at playing his stupid games. The two shifters dragged Logan's body up the stairs, his feet banging against each step. Kellen opened the door, and they tossed him on the floor.

"We better not see him again," the same man said. "Next time we won't give him the benefit of knowing you." He slammed the door, and I cursed at him.

"Remind me why we're here," I said, looking down at Logan's battered form.

"Because it was better than the palace," Kellen replied.

He bent down and wrapped his hands beneath Logan's arms, pulling him away from the door. I shut the blinds on the glass doors leading to the balcony, then sat on the floor next the vampire. I picked up his arm and pressed my fingers on his wrist, surprised by the faint pulse beating against my finger.

"I didn't know vampires had a pulse." I turned his arm over and gasped at the puncture marks lining the inside of his elbow. I pulled the collar down from his shirt to reveal more bites around his neck. "Kellen?" I looked around but didn't see my partner. "Isn't that lovely. Leave me with the wounded vampire."

I gently laid his arm on the floor and lifted his black t-shirt. Red, swollen welts covered his stomach and chest. I placed my hand over the cuts and called to the water to heal them.

I cannot heal him, child, Water's voice whispered to me. *He is no longer mine.*

I scowled and removed my hand.

"Because you abandoned him. I'll just do it the old-fashioned way, with band aids and peroxide," I mumbled, and rose to my knees, but Logan's hand snatched my arm. His grip hurt. I turned towards him to complain, but my words caught in my throat. Red swirling irises replaced his hazel eyes. He stared at me with a deep hunger, sending shivers down my spine.

"Logan," I whispered. "You're hurt. Let me help you."

His grip tightened, and he jerked me towards him. I fell against his chest and tried to push away with my free hand. He grabbed the back of my neck and pulled me towards him. The tips of his fangs peeked out from behind his cracked and swollen lips. My heart raced, and I pushed harder against him.

"Logan, you do not want to do this," I stuttered, putting as much emphasis behind my words as I could. I didn't feel the least bit guilty trying to command him not to bite me. It wasn't working.

My face brushed against his, and he inhaled deeply. My heart thumped against my ribs, and I wriggled uselessly under his grasp. I wasn't getting away from him.

"Stop," I commanded. "I will help you, but not like this."

To my surprise, he loosened his grip on my arm and neck, but didn't let go. "I'm so sorry, princess," he breathed against the side of my face.

I dropped my forehead on his shoulder and let out a long breath. A shiver ran through my body when he released me. I pushed myself off him and backed away, watching the color of his eyes as they darted around the room. Blue and brown rolled through the red swimming in his eyes.

"Where's Kellen?" he asked, his voice harsh and cracking.

"I'm not sure," I replied. "He was here a few minutes ago."

Logan's gaze returned to me, and I saw his pain and guilt.

"Who did this to you?" I asked, ignoring his need to apologize again.

"I really need to talk to Kellen." He pushed himself onto his elbows and groaned. "And I need to get out of here before I do something I'll regret."

"What do you need, Logan? How can I help you?" I asked, fearing the answer.

"You cannot give me what I need to heal from this," he replied. "Where is your damn partner? He never should've left you alone with me. What the hell is he thinking?" The ring of red circled his hazel eyes, and he squeezed them shut.

"Tell me what you've learned. I'll pass it on to Kellen when he gets back," I suggested, knowing he needed blood. I didn't want to be the donor, willing or otherwise.

"Two hundred vampires will be here tonight," he said, opening his eyes but avoiding looking at me. "Seventy-five of them are like me. I know you don't understand the implications, but Kellen will. Victor needs to be ready for them. As soon as I take care of my needs, I'll be back to help you."

He rose to his feet, and I rose with him, keeping my distance. Not that it would matter. He moved way faster than I did.

"Logan, you can't come back," I said. "The wolves won't think twice about killing you. They only spared your life because of our friendship. They will gladly mistake you for just another vampire the next time they see you."

The ring around his eyes grew, and he looked towards the door. I followed his gaze. It opened quietly, and Kellen entered. He carried two large, glass bottles with deep, red liquid swirling inside. A low snarl erupted from Logan.

"Stop, Logan," I commanded, unable to keep my voice from quivering with fear. Not just for me, but for Kellen too.

Logan's whole body shook. Kellen closed the space between them quickly, handing one of the bottles to Logan. He snatched it from Kellen's hand, then grabbed the other jar. The bathroom door slammed shut before I realized he moved.

My knees buckled, and I fell to the floor. Kellen scooped me up, and I wrapped my hands around his neck.

Tears poured from my eyes, as I buried my face in his collar. He let me exhaust my tears and rub my nose on his shirt. There's no way I deserved this man.

"Did he hurt you?" Kellen asked, resting his cheek on the top of my head.

"No, he just scared me," I replied.

"I didn't expect him to wake up so soon, or I wouldn't have left you."

Kellen's guilt and anger mixed with my fear. He couldn't have known how quickly Logan would have recovered. I shouldn't have approached a wounded vampire. I shivered again, and Kellen rubbed my back. I'd spent the last several days trying to convince myself that Logan wasn't a vampire, but all those arguments just went out the window. He terrified me.

I looked up into Kellen's eyes. He wasn't afraid of Logan; he was worried about me and berating himself for leaving me alone.

"This is not your fault," I said. "He's okay now, right? I assume those bottles had blood in them?"

"Yes, but it's not human. He'll still need to leave, but that will calm his thirst long enough to talk."

I took a deep breath, trying to calm my still pounding heart. I didn't even want to know where Kellen got that much blood in a shifter camp. "He has bite marks all over him, Kellen. Why would they do that?"

"I don't know," he replied. "I'm not sure why they let him live."

"I guess... he just acts so normal. I forget that he's a vampire." Kellen pulled me closer, wrapping an arm around me.

The bathroom door opened, and Logan emerged. I could see the pain and guilt in his red eyes. I tried to see the man I'd grown to trust, but I couldn't get past the vampire.

"What's happened, Logan?" Kellen asked.

"She didn't tell you?"

"No. I assume they're coming. When and how many?"

Logan continued to stare at me with a haunted look. The dirt and blood covering his clothes only added to the stranger who took my new friend. "I'm sorry, princess. I thought I could protect you, ensure you took your rightful place, and bring the mages back to where they need to be." He dropped his gaze to the floor. "This monster I've become controls everything. When you need me most, I cannot be here for you."

I took a step towards him, but he raised his hand to stop me and turned to Kellen. "Don't leave her with me, Kellen. I'll continue to fight for you, but I cannot risk her life."

The two men stared at one another for several seconds, then Kellen nodded. "How many are coming, Logan?"

"Two hundred," he replied. "Seventy-five like me. They'll be here before midnight. They assume they'll win by sheer numbers. Victor doesn't have two hundred fighters here, and there isn't time to summon more."

Kellen pulled me closer. "We'll tell Victor and let him make the choice to leave or stay."

"Don't sacrifice her life for these mutts, Kellen."

"I think you know better, my friend."

Logan's expression softened, and one corner of his mouth turned towards a smile. I held my breath—the Logan I knew must still be in there somewhere if he could manage his infuriating grin.

"I see she's discovered her ability to boss everyone around," he said.

"Did it work on you?" Kellen asked.

"Just barely," he replied. "If I weren't like this." His eyes narrowed again, the smile vanishing. "If I were in control, it might have been different."

"Be careful, Logan. I still need you in this fight," Kellen stated.

Logan nodded. The shades covering the patio doors fluttered, and he was gone.

I turned to my partner and rested my forehead against his chest. I tried focusing on his warmth and strength, but all I could see was Logan and his warning about the army of vampires descending on us.

"I can't do this, Kellen," I whispered, tears falling again.

His arms snaked around me, pulling me tight against him. "You can do this," he said. "You've survived a childhood of anguish, and your short attempt at adulthood hasn't been any better. But you've never given up." His voice softened. "I know you've been thrown into this with most of the choices taken away from you, but we can do this together."

As he started to pull away, I blinked away the last of my tears and squared my shoulders. Kellen was right. I had survived for a long time, through situations and people nearly as nasty as vampires. "Okay," I said finally.

"We need to go to Victor," he said.

"I know."

Chapter 21

"I will not abandon my home!" Victor thundered.

"Did you not hear what I said?" Kellen asked, raising his own voice. "How will you defend against them? They aren't just vampires."

"This is my pack!" he yelled. "I know our strengths and our weaknesses. You can leave if you wish, but we will fight."

We were once again in Victor's office, the two men standing within inches of each other in the center of the room. Kellen glared at Victor, then turned his back and walked towards the door. I joined him as he stomped down the hall and through the great room. I understood Victor's unwillingness to abandon his home. As much as I didn't like him, he was a proud leader with a lot of responsibility. I wasn't sure what I would do in his place. Would I risk my people to defend my home? Maybe if I thought they could win, but Kellen seemed to think otherwise.

Several people watched with open curiosity as we left the lodge and crossed the yard to the arena. Kellen stopped in the center of the circle, removed his boots, and sat crossed-legged in the dirt.

I stared at him for several seconds before doing the same.

"We're staying, aren't we?" I asked.

"I'm not sure," he replied. "That arrogant bastard irritates the shit outta me, but I understand why he won't leave. I'm..."

"If you were alone, you would stay," I offered. "But I'm a liability. You feel compelled to protect me from everything that's coming."

"You are not a liability," he replied. "You are the key to our success. You're the hope that will keep everyone fighting. You are the last of your family. If you die..."

"Someone else will take over the mages, Kellen. I'm not destined to do it." I placed my hand on his knee. "It won't be the end of the world if someone else takes control. Governments change leaders all the time."

"It will be the end of life as we know it if the Magister keeps control," he replied. "She will give the mages to the vampires. I can't let that happen."

I pulled my hand away and looked at the scarred earth between us. I didn't know the answer, but I knew I couldn't fight against a bunch of vampires. I could barely fight against one wolf.

"I want to teach you a few offensive and defensive techniques," Kellen said, breaking the silence between us. "You can help protect the kids, and your ability to heal will surely be needed."

"Where will you be in all of this?" I asked, raising an eyebrow at him.

"I'm going to assume your elements respond similar to mine, even though wind seems to be a little more aggressive than I suspected," he said, ignoring my question. "As you've seen several times, the earth provides very nice protective barriers. Let's see if water can do the same."

"You didn't answer my question," I stated, crossing my arms. That little trait was getting really irritating.

"Where do you think I'll be, AJ? I won't sit in the back when I can fight."

I pressed my lips into a tight line and stood, glaring at Kellen. "My friend, the one who seeks to destroy, what do you choose?" I asked, knowing the wind would answer my overly dramatic question. Its translucent form flitted into view next to me.

"You already know that answer," the wind replied. "It appears your partner is the one who requires reassurances." It circled me twice. "And please, call me Niyol, if you must call me."

Niyol disappeared, leaving a shocked expression on Kellen's face. A satisfied smirk spread across my lips as I beckoned Water to answer the same question. It did not reply, and I frowned.

"Will you not protect these people from the very thing you chose me to fight against?" I asked. "Will you remain silent when I call for your aid?"

A pool of water formed at my feet and rose into the fluid, humanoid form I witnessed at Kellen's home.

"You call me with anger in your heart. Remember who you are to these people," it replied with its slow whisper.

"I don't know who I am," I said. "And I'm angry because I've been forced into a role I don't want and a fight I know little about."

It rolled to my other side, losing its form for a moment as it moved. "You are exactly what your partner told you," it continued. "Call me with love and compassion, and I will come." The water fell to the ground with a splash and disappeared into the earth. I followed it, falling to my knees and placing my hands on the damp earth.

"I can't believe they talk to you," Kellen said, drawing my attention. He still sat crossed-legged in front of me, but he leaned back, bracing himself with his hands. His wide-eyed expression startled me. "They've never spoken to me, AJ. Not until the other night when we summoned them together. I just watched the wind tell you his name." He leaned towards me, brushing his hands on his pants. "I didn't even know they had names."

"What does it mean, Kellen?" I asked. I didn't know my relationship with the wind was so unique. It felt completely natural to me. Was I so different from everyone else?

"It means so much more than I realized." He unfolded his legs and stood. "There are rumors that your family could do what you just did, but like everyone else, I never believed it. We've only ever known the Magister, who doesn't have that gift."

I frowned. Besides hours of practice, I really needed a history lesson about my family. I dropped my gaze to the damp earth beneath my fingers. Maybe Kellen couldn't teach me what I needed to know. Maybe my lessons needed to come from my elements.

"AJ." Kellen's voice drew my attention again. I looked up at his outstretched hand and took it, allowing him to pull me to my feet. He turned me around, and my eyes widened in surprise.

Dozens of people lined the arena, staring at me in wonder. Had they just witnessed the exchange with my elements? Victor's imposing form stood in front of the group. He nodded to me and lowered himself to one knee.

"I can no longer deny what my eyes have just seen," he said, his voice echoing across the space between us. "You have our strength, loyalty, and protection."

The other shifters dropped to one knee, and my mouth dropped open. "What the hell?" I whispered.

"You are the chosen ruler of the mages, AJ, whether you like it or not," Kellen said.

"What does that have to do with Victor?"

"The shifters have been the mages' allies for centuries...until the Magister," Kellen responded quietly. He nudged me forward, and I realized they expected me to say something. I barely spoke to one person effectively. How was I supposed to speak to a group? *Focus on Victor, ignore the others.*

"Thank you, Victor," I said. "I'll try to be worthy of your strength, honor your loyalty, and be grateful for your protection."

He looked up at me, and his chocolate eyes swirled. "I will treasure the day that you replace her."

I didn't know what to say. I didn't want to replace my mother, but it's what everyone expected. They somehow thought I was the answer to this mess the Magister created. How could I be when I knew so little about this world?

Kellen placed a hand on my shoulder. "Let's prepare for battle."

Victor rose and started barking orders at his people. I watched in amazement at his ability to direct them so efficiently. I couldn't do that. I had no idea how to lead anyone, much less a community of magically gifted people. I wasn't doing any of this without my partner.

The arena emptied, leaving Kellen and I alone. My mind whirled with questions, but the looming battle dominated my thoughts.

"Let's get something to eat," Kellen suggested.

"Shouldn't I be practicing more?" I asked. "I feel helpless. All these people are going to fight, and I barely understand why."

He gently squeezed my hand. "You need to save your strength, and I think your unique connection to your elementals is your greatest asset. I'm not sure the small amount of training I can provide in an hour or two can compare."

"I disagree. Niyol, that's a cool name..." I said, then shook my head. I didn't need to get distracted. "Anyway, Niyol is really demanding. I don't know if he would bother distinguishing between the good guys and bad guys."

"I think you underestimate your elemental." Kellen started towards the lodge, pulling me after him. "Let's see what's for dinner. I assume they'll feed their fighters early."

Commotion filled the great room when we walked in. People rushed through with large crates, leather bags, and several spools of wiring. Children stacked plates and utensils on the long counter lining the wall beyond the dining table. The smell of roasting meat floated through a swinging door every time it opened, and my stomach rumbled. How did I ever survive on one meal a day?

"What are all the crates and wiring for?" I asked as two more rolls of wire passed by, carried by well-muscled shifters.

"I imagine they're setting traps." He followed their progress out the door, then turned back to me. "I'm going to help," he said. "I'm sure you can find something to do."

Uncertainty flooded me. These people had just tried to kill me a few hours before. How was Kellen letting that go like it meant nothing?

"I think I'll come with you," I said, gripping his hand.

He moved around in front of me, placing his free hand on my shoulder. "They will not hurt you," he said. "Victor's pledge to you will ensure that."

"But."

He put his finger on my lips. "Marissa will show you around. I need to help them set up their defenses. I think your talents will be better utilized in here."

A woman walked up beside him, and I recognized her from the specialty shop in Reno. Kellen leaned down and brushed his lips against mine. It was gentle and personal, but not demanding or passionate. "See you at dinner."

I turned and watched him walk away, stuffing my trembling hands into my pockets. What was wrong with me? I never had separation anxiety, not even when my foster parents dropped me in the office of my apartment complex and left. I'd spent my entire life with them and felt no loss when they were gone. But Kellen walking out into the nearby forest left me feeling empty.

"I'm so stupid," I mumbled. I spent my whole life taking care of myself. A few days with a man who seemed to care, and all of a sudden, I couldn't do it anymore. I shook my head in disgust.

"Sorry for the way we met last time." The woman's voice next to me interrupted my moment of self-pity. "I'm Marissa." She held her hand out, and I accepted the friendly gesture.

"Thanks."

"We've got a ton of work to do and could certainly use another pair of hands." Marissa looked at my hand in hers and smiled. "Even ones as small as yours."

We spent the next two hours prepping food for the evening meal. Marissa kept me busy, but my restless brain constantly mulled over my situation and the coming battle.

"Does your mind ever stop?" Marissa asked, placing a platter of sliced venison on the serving counter.

"What do you mean?" I asked, setting my own platter next to hers.

"I've been trying to talk to you for the last half-hour, but you've completely ignored me." She placed her hands on her hips and looked down at me. "What do you want to know? I hear everything, so there isn't much I couldn't tell you."

"I'm sorry. I don't even know where to begin," I replied, feeling a little guilty for ignoring her. "Last week I was a complete outcast to society. I couldn't keep a job, and I think my landlord was only charging me half the rent of everyone else in the building because he felt bad for me. He knew I couldn't afford to go anywhere else." I looked around the extravagant room. "Now I'm here."

"Come on. We can chat and work, as long as you stay focused." She led me back into the kitchen to get another round of serving plates. "There has always been an alliance between us and the mages," Marissa began, "at least as long as anyone here remembers. All of that changed with the current Magister. I don't completely blame her, though." She handed me a large bowl of pasta and picked up a basket of dinner rolls. "Your grandfather fell in love with a normal human, one without magic. He went against every tradition the mages had and married your grandmother. The mage community was furious. Generations of Rosewynns had always arranged their marriages carefully to ensure the dual-mage trait would continue."

"Rosewynn?" I asked, following her through the swinging door. "Is that their name?"

"That's your name, too," she replied, arranging her basket and heading back to the kitchen. "Anyway, your grandparents threw it all out the window. Many of the Magister's advisors and council abandoned him, stating that he threatened the stability of the entire magical community. Of course, the Magister wouldn't hear it. His love for your grandmother was all that mattered to him. He insisted that the elements decided who was worthy of power, not the mages."

We collected another round of plates. I tried not to drool over the enormous apple pie she gave me. The soft heat from the bottom of the pie plate warmed my hands, and the tempting aroma wafted into my face as I walked. My stomach growled in response.

"When your mother was born with only one element, those who remained loyal to your grandfather started having doubts as well. Your mother grew up as an outcast, an oddity that should not have happened and an unwanted heir to the throne."

Marissa put her plate of food on the counter and looked at me.

"She blamed her parents for her lonely childhood and the rejection of her people. When they died, she put all her efforts into proving the people wrong. She took the helm of Magister and did amazing things." She brushed back a strand of hot pink hair drifting across her face. "Some say her success came from her partner. He was also a single-element mage, but he was strong and devoted to her. I hear he loved her deeply, but she didn't return his affection. I don't think she could. They say she isn't capable of love." She paused, and her frown pulled at her strong features. "When she killed her partner, it all but sealed her fate as a heartless leader who cared nothing for her people."

I bit my bottom lip and looked at the floor. I knew bits and pieces of the story, but Marissa filled in many of the gaps. Did the shifters know that Logan, the vampire who was just here, was also the Magister's former partner?

"She told me she thought I was dead," I said softly. The revelation still hurt. I needed my mother to want me. "Someone told her I died shortly after she gave birth."

"That's what we all thought," Marissa confirmed. "No one knew you were alive until a few days ago. Even then, many of us doubted your heritage until today."

Someone knew I was alive. They kept me bound and veiled my entire life. If it wasn't my mother, then who?

"What made her change from proving everyone wrong to betraying her people?" I asked.

"I don't know," Marissa replied, pushing away from the counter full of food. "It happened before she lost her partner, or I would say madness consumed her. Some say it was because her father abandoned tradition, and the elements punished her for it."

"But that doesn't make sense," I argued. "According to Kellen, most mages only have one element, and they don't go crazy as long as they have a partner. I've spoken to my elements. I can't see them punishing a child for her parents' wrongs. I honestly don't even see it as wrong. How is following your heart ever wrong?"

"Kellen is right, and I agree with you, but it doesn't change the fact that we're fighting a battle tonight without our allies." Marissa looked across the room. "There was a time when the mages would've been here within hours."

"Momma! The guys are on their way, and they're hungry." A young girl of thirteen or fourteen years with bright green hair burst through the door. "Oh! Sorry, princess, I didn't know you'd be here."

"Just AJ, please."

"Sure thing. I'm Tara." Another girl with purple hair, obviously her sister, followed right behind her. "This is Tia."

"I'm glad to meet you," I said.

"Get washed up, girls. You're going to help serve," Marissa ordered, corralling the girls towards the kitchen.

"Momma, did you ask her?" Tia questioned as she walked by.

"No, now get moving."

"But Mom."

Marissa gave her the 'mom look,' and the young girl relented.

"What does she want to know?" I asked, following the exchange with a smile and a significant amount of jealousy. I wanted that closeness.

"They love the color of your hair. They want to cut and style it for you," Marissa explained.

"Really? I'd love that!" I exclaimed. The thought of being the sole object of their attention warmed my heart. No one had ever told me they loved my hair, and nobody had ever wanted to style it.

Marissa chuckled. "Be careful what you ask for. You'll end up with hot pink." She pointed at her own hair. "Did you think I did this on purpose?"

"But it looks great on you." I allowed a smile to cross my face. Marissa had a life I wanted, and I would help her protect it tonight.

"Me and every other woman here," Marissa mumbled, smiling to soften her words.

The door opened again, and a line of people flowed through it, heading straight for the serving counter. Dirt and sweat covered their clothing, but they didn't look even slightly winded.

"Get a plate before there isn't any left," Marissa said, pushing me in that direction.

"It's okay. They need it more than I do," I replied. "They'll be out there fighting to protect us."

"And you won't?" Marissa asked, handing me an empty plate. "What was that demonstration for earlier if you don't intend to fight?"

"I..." I looked down at the plate in my hand, unsure of my answer.

"You'll know when the time comes," Marissa said.

I helped myself to a little of everything, then sat down at the far end of the table. A few minutes later, Matt and Mike joined me.

"They didn't make you cook, did they?" Matt asked before shoveling a spoonful of potatoes in his mouth.

"No," I replied, pushing my food around my plate. It smelled and looked great, but I wasn't sure I could eat without throwing it all back up. "I just helped set up the buffet."

A plate piled with food appeared on the table beside me. I looked up as Kellen sat down. He smelled like dirt and sweat. I tried not to wrinkle my nose, knowing they worked hard for the last few hours.

"I don't want to see a single crumb left on your plate," he said, picking up his fork and pointing at my food.

"Then you might have to eat it," I said.

He raised an eyebrow and brought a forkful of steak towards his mouth. "Have you forgotten our deal about building muscle?"

"Nope." I took a bite of venison and frowned. I'd never tried it before and decided I really didn't like it.

"It's an acquired taste," Matt said, between bites, apparently noticing my soured expression. "I'll eat yours if you don't want it."

"Please, by all means." I pushed my plate towards him, and he stabbed the small piece of venison with his fork, adding it to his already full dish.

"Is everything okay?" I asked.

"If you're asking are we ready, the answer is no," Kellen replied. "You and I have a few things to do before sundown."

"Damn, I was hoping to have the chance to show her my talents," Matt said, grinning and raising his eyebrows at me.

Kellen rolled his eyes. "Hurry up. It'll be dark in an hour."

"And you say I'm bossy," I mumbled, wondering what we needed to do before sundown.

Chapter 22

I closed the door to our room and leaned against it as Kellen pulled his shirt over his head. He looked at it with disgust, opened the door to the kitchen pantry, and tossed it in the garbage.

"Are you okay?" I asked.

"I'm exhausted, and I smell," he replied. "I'd forgotten how much stamina they have. They never seem to tire."

"Can I help? You can't go into this fight worn-out."

"I don't know. I'm taking a shower first, then we'll figure something out. But you're right. I can't fight like this."

He ambled into the bathroom, leaving the door wide open. I collapsed on the sofa, trying not to watch his reflection in the bathroom mirror. Was there anything I could do to help him? Would my water elemental revive his energy, or did it just heal his wounds? He'd already exhausted himself during their stupid challenge. Whatever they did out in the woods only made it worse. But I was pretty sure he wouldn't stay at the lodge while the others risked their lives.

You can offer him your energy and strength during the battle, Water's voice whispered.

How do I do that? Through you?

No, child. Through your connection to him.

I thought about what it said. Sparky traveled between us all the time. I didn't even know if he was with me or Kellen at the moment. Could he carry my energy?

So, I can revive his strength before the battle? I asked.

No, you must go with him and feed him your strength. Through you, he can be strong.

Logan did that for my mother, didn't he?

You are not your mother, child. Don't ever compare yourself to her, and don't insult your partner by doing the same to him.

The element's voice was harsh and left me feeling reprimanded. Its presence faded, leaving me with more questions than answers.

I got up and went into the bedroom. A stack of clothes sat on the tall chest of drawers near the window. I stood on my tip-toes and moved the pile to the bed. A multi-colored tie-dyed shirt graced the top of the pile. I set it to the side, revealing a pair of camouflage cargo pants. I picked them up and shook them out. They might actually fit and would certainly be better than my blue jeans.

I kicked off my sneakers and wiggled out of my jeans, then pulled on the cargo pants. They were baggy but comfortable. I rummaged through the rest of the pile and found a black, long-sleeve t-shirt with a fluorescent print of some music band I'd never heard of. I swapped out my own shirt to advertise for my new band.

"That's a new look."

Kellen's voice startled me, and I turned towards the door. He stood there with a towel wrapped around his waist. The scars on his chest from earlier drew my attention, and I knew my face flushed with embarrassment. He'd been a perfect gentleman up to this point. Was he waiting for me to initiate something?

"You need some rest before they get here," I said, walking towards him.

"I know. Don't let me sleep for more than an hour," he said, his bare shoulder brushing against me as he passed.

"I thought we needed to talk or something before sundown?" I asked, trying not to watch him crawl into bed.

He pulled the blankets over his chest and I heard the towel hit the floor on the other side of the bed. I snapped my gaping mouth closed at the thought of him being naked in the same room with me.

"I don't think I can I stay awake," he mumbled. "Matt made too many suggestive comments to leave you down there."

My embarrassment and longing turned to anger. He didn't own me. What made him think he was the only one I could spend time with?

"I'll be in the other room, making sure no one disturbs you," I said between my now-grinding teeth. He needed sleep, and I didn't need a dictator.

"Okay, thanks." He closed his eyes and yawned.

I stomped out of the room, refusing to be baited. Lives were at stake. I didn't need to waste energy on jealousy or irrational attractions. I needed to figure out how to transfer my strength to Kellen. Would it be similar to what he did when we healed his guardians? He helped me endure their pain, but I wasn't sure which one of us was giving. I assumed it was him. All my focus was on healing the trees. I didn't know enough about my abilities to come up with a solution, and Water refused to talk to me.

An hour later, I flipped through the channels on the TV, finding nothing to maintain my interest. My mind constantly returned to my partner. How was I supposed to transfer strength to him? Logan would know, but he wasn't here, and I wasn't sure I wanted to see him. Should I risk waking Kellen up by trying now? Could I afford to wait until the heat of battle to find out?

The bedroom door opened on silent hinges, and I peeked inside. Kellen laid in the middle of the bed, flat on his back. The sheet wrapped around his waist, leaving his chest exposed in the dim light. I once again wondered how I ended up with him after being unwanted by everyone my whole life.

Crawling into bed, I got as close as I could without touching him. He stirred but didn't wake. My fingers hovered over his chest, and I thought of Sparky. His faint light dropped from my fingers and landed on Kellen's skin.

He flitted around over Kellen's chest but didn't enter his body. I looked at him with narrowed eyes. Did Kellen have to invite him in? I didn't think so. He'd jumped back and forth several times without either of us asking.

"I need to make him stronger, Sparky," I whispered. "How do I make that happen?"

I thought about where my own strength originated from and realized I didn't know. The tiny amount of magic I used so far came directly from my elements, but I must have been channeling it somehow. I traced one of the long scars on my partner's chest, Sparky chasing my finger.

"What are you doing?" Kellen's voice startled me, and I drew my finger back, along with Sparky.

"I'm sorry. I wasn't trying to wake you," I said, trying to gauge his expression.

"You were trying to do something. I could feel it."

I sighed. "Water says I should join you in battle and feed you my strength."

His eyes widened as he sat up, frowning at me. I scooted away from him, waiting for his response.

"No."

"I thought it was a good idea," I mumbled, a little hurt by his immediate rejection.

"How is you being weakened in the middle of a battlefield a good idea?"

"My point exactly," I said. "You are the fighter, not me. But you're in no condition to fight. It only makes sense that I would help by giving you the strength I cannot use."

"And who will protect you while I'm fighting against a horde of vampires?"

"Niyol."

He frowned, but I could feel him recognize the wisdom in it. Would he risk me in battle to receive my strength?

"I need to know how to transfer my strength to you," I said.

"This is a bad idea," he muttered, shaking his head. "Your ability to feel the magic in our world starts here." He leaned forward and placed his fingers above my heart, then trailed down my stomach, stirring up emotions I tried to ignore. "In the very core of your being. It's why Sparky always races for your ribs. He is drawn to the magic that resides in you. You draw strength from your elements and channel it through your body. It's released when you focus your will."

"Like when I threw that wolf around the arena with the wind?"

"I wasn't awake for that, but I would've enjoyed seeing it." A smile crept across his face. "But yes, just like that."

"And how do I give it to you? We won't have physical contact."

"It's tied to your will," he replied. "You have to force it from your reserves to me. Like when we healed the guardians. I gave you the strength to endure the guardian's pain."

"Can I try it now?"

"It might be a good idea."

I placed my hand on his chest, and a warm sensation filled me.

"I don't think that's the one you were going for," Kellen said with a smile.

"I'm sure it was, but it's not the one I need right now." I smiled, and my ears grew hot. "I probably shouldn't touch you anyway. I won't have that luxury in a fight."

I pulled my hand away reluctantly and focused on my center, where he said my magic originated. My middle grew warmer, and I imagined the magic following through my hand and to my partner. Nothing happened. I squeezed my eyes shut and tried again, focusing on the small well of magic in my center until it burned, then once again tried to move it to Kellen. Nothing happened.

"Well, that sucks," I said. Why can't I do this?

"You didn't expect to do it on the first try, did you?" Kellen asked. "There's a reason mages spend years practicing."

"But I don't have years," I protested. "I might have thirty minutes, maybe an hour."

"Or you can stay here."

I glared at him, poking my finger into his chest. "No, I will not. I can see the weariness in your eyes and feel it in our connection. I won't let you go out there alone."

"I won't be alone. Over a hundred wolves will be joining me, along with another twenty or more shifters that Victor was able to contact in the local area."

"I've seen how fast Logan moves," I said, feeling my resolve crumble. I wasn't a fighter and we both knew it. "Are they all that quick?"

"No, only the mages turned vampire."

"What else can they do that makes them more dangerous?"

Kellen laid back down with a sigh. "Their magic enhances the vampire's magic, making them stronger and faster. Their venom works faster as well."

"So, don't get bitten," I said, thinking of my all-too-close encounter with Logan. "What happens if a shifter gets bitten? Is there such a thing as a vampire wolf?"

"No, the shifters' bodies reject the venom, and the vampires cannot drink shifter's blood without being weakened." Kellen raised his arms above his head and yawned, then clasped his hands behind his neck. His muscle stretched and rippled with the action, and I blushed. "They are nature's way of balancing the two species."

"I'm going to keep trying to feed you my strength," I said. "Go back to sleep while you can."

"I won't be able to sleep with your magic poking at me," he said, his lips twitching.

"Then I'll leave you alone. "

He glanced at me with a strange expression. Was he inviting me to stay, and I was too dense to know it? No one ever flirted with me and certainly never suggested an intimate relationship. Unless he came right out and said so, I wasn't sure I'd get the hint. My face reddened again, or maybe the embarrassment just intensified. He smiled, and my heart stuttered. Did I have the courage to approach him and endure the rejection if I read this wrong?

A knock on the door kept me from finding out. Waves of disappointment rolled across me, and I couldn't tell if it was mine or Kellen's.

"I'll get it," I muttered, rolling out of bed.

I opened the door to Marissa's worried but determined face.

"They're here," she said.

"We'll be right down." So much for trying to help my partner. Anxiety and fear replaced my disappointment. I needed to make a decision about joining Kellen or staying here. I was certain Niyol would help me and could almost hear his huff of annoyance that I would think otherwise. But would it be enough? Would I have time to figure out how to transfer my strength to Kellen? Or would I be totally distracted by a battle raging around me?

"It's time to go, isn't it?" Kellen's voice interrupted my internal argument.

It didn't take him long to dress in a pair of cargo pants much like my own, a long sleeve t-shirt, and black boots. A wide leather belt wrapped around his waist, with a long sword hanging from one side and pistol holster on the other. He was ready to face this. How could I do any less? Because he'd obviously done this before, and I hadn't.

"Together?" he asked, holding out his large hand to me.

I grabbed his hand. "Together."

Chapter 23

We waited in the darkened tree line with twenty of Victor's pack already in their wolf form, except for Matt, who stood next to my partner in a pair of black sweatpants. I was beginning to think that was the standard wardrobe for them. Maybe because they were easy to get in and out of or because they were cheap to replace. Maybe both.

"How many scouts have been spotted?" Kellen asked in a low whisper.

"Six," Matt replied.

"Do you know how far away the main group is?"

"About half a mile."

"So, they should hit the wall any minute now," Kellen stated. "Are they surrounding us or just flanking our sides?"

"Flanking both sides," Matt said. "Our feathered friends haven't spotted anyone coming from the mountains."

"They answered Victor's call?" Kellen asked, not hiding the surprise in his voice.

"They were the first ones to arrive this evening," Matt replied with pride.

"People can shift into birds?" I asked, then covered my mouth when I realized I hadn't whispered.

Neither of the men answered. I huffed. It wasn't my fault I was so naïve about the supernatural world. A snapping twig to my left drew my attention, and my pulse raced. Kellen and Matt didn't react to the noise, but it didn't settle my nerves. I could barely see the outline of the thick pines surrounding us, blocking out the moon's light. I wanted to bring a flashlight, but Kellen convinced me it would be futile to try to carry it while fighting. It made sense, but the darkness wore on me.

The unusually quiet forest accentuated even the tiniest of sounds. The long, low hoot of an owl startled me again, followed by three short chirps. I opened my mouth to ask what it meant, but a booming explosion threw me to the ground. A blinding light and screams of pain quickly followed. A dozen or more howls filled the night, and a chorus of thundering roars joined them, making the hair on my arms stand on end. My increased pulse turned to full, heart-thumping adrenaline.

The blinding light faded, leaving behind flickering flames that raced through the trees, illuminating the forest in front of us. My breath caught in my throat as swift, agile bodies leapt over a stone wall I hadn't seen before. The wolves around me growled, and within seconds I heard snapping teeth and ripping flesh.

Two vampires appeared in front of me, and I froze, staring into their red eyes. I watched in horror as one of them raised a clawed hand, bared his fangs, and cackled. His grating laughter pierced my soul, and I knew I'd made a mistake. I couldn't defend myself against them.

I raised my arms to cover my face and screamed, waiting for a fatal blow that never came. I peeked out from beneath my arm to see Kellen standing next to me with a bloody sword in his hand and a scowl on his face. The second vampire fell to the ground, with a wolf's jaws locked around his leg. Kellen's sword swept towards the vampire's neck, removing it in one clean sweep.

We should not be idle, Niyol whispered.

What should we do? I have no idea how to fight.

Will you trust me to fight for you?

I thought about his question. There was no reason I could think of why I shouldn't trust him. Weren't the elements responsible for keeping the earth safe?

Yes, Niyol. I trust you to keep us safe... without destroying the forest.

His laughter echoed over the howls and screams, drawing the attention of the nearest wolves and vampires.

"What did you do?" Kellen asked, grabbing my arm.

"I told Niyol to have at it," I replied, allowing him to drag me further from the stone wall.

"Are you sure that's a good idea?"

"You're the experienced mage. You tell me."

I heard him mumble incoherently as the wind picked up around us, tossing leaves and branches into the air. Four more vampires cleared the wall, and I swept my hands towards them, stopping their forward momentum. Three wolves raced to intercept them, but the fourth recovered quickly and lunged towards me. I pushed another gust of air at him, but he leapt, soaring over my head and disappearing.

I spun around, barely catching his movement to my right. I spun again, but he was gone. The hairs on my neck tingled as I slowly turned. Kellen fought with a light brown wolf against two more vampires. He wasn't using magic, instead wielding his sword like a gladiator. I was impressed and jealous. I needed to learn to do that.

An arm snaking around my waist brought me back from my distractions, and I yelped.

"I've heard mage blood is better than a normal human," the vampire whispered in my ear. "The magic in it is like a drug we can't get enough of."

"You won't be having any of mine," I hissed, squirming.

"I think I'll be having plenty."

I felt his fangs on the back of my neck and panicked. No matter how much I kicked and fought, I couldn't get free of his grasp. I remembered the vampire at the gas station and focused on my attacker's blood. The same slimy sensation greeted me, but I pushed past it, drawing on it as quickly as I could. The vampire's fangs loosened on my neck, and I doubled my efforts, feeling my legs weaken and my mind cloud over.

A raging torrent of wind surrounded me as the vampire released his grip. Kellen appeared below me in a raging fire, surrounded by wolves. I felt myself being pulled into the air away from him, but I couldn't do anything to stop it. He screamed at me, but I couldn't hear him above the wind howling in my ears. Darkness surrounded my partner as I lost consciousness.

~~~~~~~~~~~~~~~~~~

My head bounced against something hard, waking me from my nightmare. The smell of leather and dirt greeted me first, then wet dog and Kellen. I never noticed how nice he smelled before. Kind of like brown sugar and cinnamon, which went great with coffee.

I opened my eyes and saw his filthy shirt. My gaze lifted to his face, set in a hard scowl. I turned my head and cried out as pain shot into my neck. Panic flooded through me as I realized it wasn't a dream. That damn vampire bit me.

"Don't move, AJ," Kellen said.

I reached up and felt the thick bandage on the back of my neck. I couldn't stop the tears from streaming down my face.

"Kellen," I whispered. "He just bit me, right?"

"I don't know," he replied. "We're going to find out in just a few minutes."

He ran up the steps to the lodge, and then took the stairs to our room two at a time.

"What about the others?" I asked. "Are they still fighting?"
~~~~~~~~~~~~~~~~~~

"No, the vampires retreated." He kicked open the door and turned sideways so he didn't smack my head on the frame.

"Really? It didn't feel like we were winning. More were coming over the wall when—" I stopped and shuddered, remembering the vampire's fangs sinking into my neck. A burning sensation flared down my shoulder, and I whimpered.

"Niyol got a little pissed off when he saw that vampire hanging on you."

I closed my eyes and grimaced as another surge of fire ran down my shoulder. The door slammed shut, and a different smell greeted me. It was cool, like spearmint, and a little familiar.

"Kellen." Logan's voice forced my eyes open.

"Is his venom in her?" Kellen asked, his voice thick with emotion.

"Most definitely," Logan replied. "I could smell her when you entered the house downstairs."

Kellen sat me on the sofa and removed the bloody rag from my neck. Logan's eyes widened along with the red ring around his iris.

"Is there anything you can do to remove the venom?"

I watched Logan's gaze move from me to Kellen. I knew I should've had some reaction to Logan's red eyes and hungry look, but all I could do was stare at him. He was so different from Kellen. His tall, lean body fit nicely in his tight jeans and t-shirt.

"I can try to remove it, but she cannot afford any more blood loss," he replied. "I can't just remove the venom."

"You have to do something! I can't..." Kellen stuttered, and I turned my face towards him. His eyes pooled with tears as they drifted across my face and landed on my neck. "If we wait, she will change."

"What are you two saying?" I asked, hoping my suspicions were wrong.

Kellen sat down beside me. His pained expression made my heart ache. "He didn't just bite you. Logan can try to remove the venom from your body, but he'll also need to remove more blood, which you can't afford to lose."

I looked back at Logan who now stood across the room. The red ring around his hazel eyes seemed to grow by the second. I felt drawn to him, almost as if nothing else in the room mattered.

"Don't, AJ," Logan said. "I'm barely in control of myself right now."

Kellen's hands on the side of my face turned my head to face him. Tears ran down his cheeks, but I struggled to stay focused on him regardless of his raw emotion.

"It can't happen this quickly," he said. "Logan please, I cannot lose her. She is the key to everything."

Logan was at my side a moment later, looking down at me and Kellen. "If I kill her, you will take my life," he said. "I can barely live with myself now. I won't live knowing I killed her."

Kellen nodded and leaned into me, pressing his lips against mine. I responded with an urgency that surprised me, wrapping my arms around his neck and pulling myself into his lap. He ended our kiss abruptly, and I felt my lower lip puff out in a pout. I never pouted. What was wrong with me?

"We'll finish that later," Kellen whispered, gently pushing me away. He stood and turned to Logan. "I'm not leaving."

"You can't be here for this," Logan insisted. "Someone needs to keep the wolves away from us. They will only smell her blood and not understand." Logan's gaze drifted to me, and my stomach fluttered. "This will be hard enough for her.

It's best if you don't know what she's about to endure. If she decides to tell you afterwards, it will be on her terms."

Kellen turned back to me but with a different expression. Sadness and guilt filtered through our connection. Why did he feel guilty? It was my stupid decision to join him.

"I'm sorry," I whispered. "I should have stayed here, like you said."

He reached down and cupped my face with one hand. Sparky immediately jumped from me to him. "There's a lot I should've done and didn't. This is not your fault."

I watched him walk across the room and out the door, closing it softly behind him. Logan followed, turning the lock and pulling the chain in place.

"Can you walk?" he asked, strolling back across the room.

I placed my feet on the floor and stood. The room swayed, and I sat back down. "Yes, but only with some help."

Logan scooped me up before I could protest and carried me into the bathroom.

"Why the bathroom?" I asked as he set me on my feet.

I leaned against the counter, and he locked the door. My eyes narrowed as he pulled his shirt over his head and unthreaded his belt from his pants. The burn in my shoulder flared with the same intensity as my desire.

"What are you doing?" I asked, my hands fidgeting at my sides. I wanted to reach out and touch him but knew I shouldn't. My heart thundered and my head swam, and I blinked a few times, trying to regain control.

"This is going to be messy, and the shower is the easiest place to clean."

His blue jeans slid to the floor, leaving him in a pair of striped boxers. My face flushed, remembering the last time I saw him in the bathroom. Heat rushed through my middle, and I knew it wasn't Sparky.

"You're welcome to remain dressed, but you'll probably have to toss your clothes when we're done," he said, turning on the water in the shower, appearing to avoid my roaming eyes. "I don't have anything to change into, and it's a bad idea to walk around in blood-stained clothing."

"What exactly are we doing?" I asked, trying to calm my raging hormones. Where did this desire for Logan come from? Was it the vampire's bite?

He stood in front of me in a flash, his hazel eyes nearly consumed by the red ring. Did he just abandon his control? "I'm going to try not to kill you," he said, under his breath. "I need to bite you in the same place the other vampire did."

"Okay. That doesn't seem so bad." Even as I said it, the flare in my shoulder pulsed again, rushing into my chest and down my arm. It had to be the venom infiltrating my system.

"You will need to do the same to me in order to keep from dying."

"Excuse me?" Did he just say I would need to drink his blood?

"My blood will replace what you've lost while I attempt to remove the venom from you." He glanced at my neck, and his fangs lowered below his top lip.

"I'm pretty sure I won't be able to bite you, Logan," I said, watching his eyes turn completely red. Rather than being repulsed, a shiver of desire rose from my middle.

"Your fangs are no different than mine, princess." A smile spread across his lips, exposing more of his long fangs.

I ran my tongue over my teeth and yelped. I turned to the mirror and pulled my lips back. Short, curved fangs replaced my canines. "Is it too late?" A moment of panic replaced my desire and fascination.

"I hope not." He grabbed my shoulders, forcing me to face him. "I'm willing to try to save you from what I've become, but you have to be willing as well."

"Is that why everyone smells different? Why is it happening so quickly?"

"Yes, your senses are heightening rapidly because the vampire who bit you was a mage. His magic increases the toxicity of his venom, accelerating everything."

"Okay." If the venom was moving this quickly through my system, I knew we needed to get it out of me and quick. I took a deep breath and looked up at him. "You bite me, I bite you, and all this goes away."

A frown spread across his face. "Don't fight against me. You'll experience sensory overload before this is over. You need to accept it." He paused. "Don't fight against me."

"Yeah." I ran my tongue across the pointed teeth once again. A shiver ran through me as Logan leaned towards my neck. Apprehension mixed with my raging desire. I leaned towards him, and his lips brushed my skin. His hands trailed down my arms and wrapped around my fingers.

"Breathe," he said, "And don't wait to take my blood."

I exhaled as his fangs sank into me. It didn't hurt, not like the first time. I leaned my head to the side and looked at his bare shoulder. His smooth skin moved with his muscle as his hands released mine and wandered past my waist, cupping my butt. He hoisted me onto the counter, and I pressed against him.

My hormones spiked as he pulled me closer. I felt light-headed and woozy, but my desire to be with him kept my eyes open. His lips pulled away from my neck. I stared at his tongue slipping from his lips and catching a drop of my blood. I should have been repulsed by it, but found myself becoming even more aroused. A moment of guilt assaulted me as I thought of Kellen.

"You are not helping," Logan said, his voice husky.

"What was I supposed to be doing?" I asked, still watching his lips, completely mesmerized by him.

He tipped my chin with one of his fingers, forcing me to look up. The red in his eyes swirled, drawing me even closer. "Follow my finger," he said, tracing it down his neck along his jugular, then making a sharp left at his collar bone. "Right here." He tapped the small vein that pulsed beneath his skin.

My mouth watered with the overwhelming urge to bite him. Isn't that what he just told me to do? I couldn't remember, my mind too foggy and overrun with emotion.

"Now," he demanded, pulling my head to his neck.

I sunk my new teeth through his skin and tasted the coppery fluid flow over my tongue. A new urge flooded through me, eliminating any reservations I may have had before. All thoughts of Kellen, wolves, and mages vanished as I became lost in Logan's need for acceptance, love, and devotion. I laced my fingers into his hair and pulled him closer. I had no idea how long I stayed attached to him, only focusing on eliminating the space between us. My fingers explored every inch of his neck and back, before he gently pulled away.

"I think that's enough," he whispered in my ear.

Reluctantly, I released his neck and kissed away the lingering blood. His hand ran up and down my spine, sending shivers through my body. His boxers did nothing to contain his own desire. I wrapped my legs around his waist and looked up at his red-swirling eyes. He started to speak, and I kissed him. He returned it immediately with unbridled passion.

nds lifted my shirt over my head, interrupting him unsnap my bra as I slid off the counter. He go pants off my narrow hips, and I let them and my panties fall to the floor. Two seconds later, we were in the still running shower.

He made love to me with a passion that brought tears to my eyes. Logan held nothing back, allowing me to experience his loneliness, sense of betrayal and abandonment, as well as his need to be with me. My own sense of abandonment and loneliness mingled with his, along with my need to be accepted. I didn't just want to belong, I needed someone to *want* me. My body, mind, and soul ached for something I thought I would never have. Love. He made me feel complete.

I stood in silence as he leaned over me with his hands against the tiled shower on either side of my head. I rested my forehead against his chest and sighed. The water running across his back was no longer hot, but he didn't complain. I reached behind me and turned it off. My hormones calmed down, but my feelings for him had not.

"Did you know this would happen?" I asked, using my fingers to catch the streams of water running through the ridges on his stomach.

"Yes, I suspected it would."

"Why?" Had he just entranced me? The intensity of being with him still pulsed around me. Was it real or something forced on me? My fear of his answer kept my head buried against his chest.

"Vampires are complicated, princess," he replied, cupping my chin and forcing me to look at him. "Exchanging blood is personal."

What did that mean? His hazel eyes looked down at me, but I couldn't decide if they held remorse, regret, or sadness. Maybe all three. "And that's the only answer I get?"

He nodded, and water dripped from his hair across my face. I tried not to frown and knew I failed. Why would he keep this from me? It couldn't be any more traumatic than the rest of my night.

"Is the vampire venom gone?"

His eyes never left mine, still drawing me in. "Yes, it's gone."

"And what about us?"

"You were not mine to take," he replied, pulling one hand away from the wall and brushing the wet hair from my face.

"I'm not so sure," I said cautiously. "I feel more connected to you than Kellen."

"But you shouldn't. I cannot be what you need. He isn't just your partner, he's your soulmate. I've tainted that for you, and I'm sorry."

I pushed against his chest and glared at him. He didn't move. "Are you sorry for making me feel complete? Sorry for giving me a part of yourself? Or sorry for not letting me become a vampire like you? *Or* are you deliberately trying to piss me off right before you walk out on me?"

Logan smiled and left me standing in the shower. He was *not* walking away. I would have answers from him. He wasn't going to leave me with bread crumbs the same way Kellen did. What was this bullshit about a soulmate? Kellen even said we could be partners, not lovers.

"You don't get to leave without answering my questions," I hissed.

He slid his boxers over his hips and covered them with his blue jeans, then pulled his t-shirt over his head. He leaned into the shower and kissed my wet forehead. "Get dressed."

He unlocked the bathroom door and left me standing there gaping at him. I didn't know what to think. He'd just saved my life, but also made it extremely complicated. My feelings for Kellen were real and sincere, but not like the emotions that raged through me about Logan. Did he entrance me, forcing me to feel that way about him?

I got dressed and stormed into the living area to find it empty.

"Of course, he would leave," I said, feeling tears swell in my eyes. *Stupid bastard. Saves my life, throws my emotions into chaos, and leaves.* My shoulders slumped and exhaustion washed over me. Why was all this happening to me?

"I'm not gone yet," he whispered in my ear, startling me. He scooped me up and carried me into the bedroom. I looked up at him with anticipation but noticed his sadness. He was really abandoning me. I could see it in his eyes. How could he do this to me?

He laid me in the bed and sat on the edge next to me.

"I cannot leave you like this," he said. "Kellen has been my best friend for years. He gave me purpose when I was broken. I promised myself, and you, that I would be your protector. Nothing more and nothing less. I've broken that promise to you, and I've betrayed my friend's trust."

He brushed my hair away from my face, and his remorse washed over me.

"Sleep, princess, and forget."

I felt my eyelids get heavy as his lips brushed against mine. "Don't you leave me, Logan," I mumbled, fighting against the unnatural sleep that took me.

"I will never leave you," he whispered.

Chapter 24

"Good morning, sleepyhead," Kellen whispered in my ear, the smell of sugar and cinnamon tempting my taste buds.

I smiled and tugged the blankets over my head. He pulled them back and sat on the bed next to me. I opened one eye to find his intense stare.

"Is it morning?" I asked, rubbing both eyes with my palms.

"It is. How do you feel?"

"I'm not sure, I was just rudely wakened by a handsome man who is completely dressed."

A smile replaced his intense look. I blushed, uncertain where my sudden forwardness came from.

"So are you, little girl."

I lifted the blanket and looked at myself. I never slept in pants. "Why am I fully dressed?" I dropped the blanket and rubbed my eyes again, trying to remember when I got in bed.

"Do you remember anything about last night?" he asked.

"No." I glanced up at him, nervous energy flooding me when I saw the concerned look on his face. "Why don't I remember? What happened?"

Kellen shifted, giving me space as the same intense look returned. "Do you remember fighting against the vampires?"

I pushed myself into a sitting position and hugged my knees, shaking my head to clear my foggy brain. "Oh, that's right. Everything is so hazy." I paused. "They were jumping over that wall in the woods. The wolves pinned three of them, but the fourth one got to me." I clamped my hand over my mouth, remembering the vampire that bit me.

"Do you remember anything after that?"

I shook my head again. "Sort of. I felt weird and tired. Logan was here, and you left me with him." Fear crept at the edge of my consciousness. I pointed my finger at him. "You weren't supposed to leave me with him."

"The vampire who bit you was a mage," Kellen said, his gaze falling to his hands folded in his lap. "I had hoped... it doesn't matter. His venom was already turning you in the short time it took me to collect you from Niyol and carry you here. Logan removed the venom, preventing you from becoming a vampire."

I stared at him. How did I not remember any of that? What did he have to do to remove the venom? I thought I knew, and it terrified me. My whole body shivered beneath the blankets.

"Logan said he tried to make you forget what happened, as it was very painful and unpleasant." He looked at me, searching my face for something. "He wasn't sure it would work, but apparently it did."

"Were you there?" I asked. "Do you know what he did to me?"

"He saved you from his fate," he replied, his frown deepening. "I was downstairs keeping Victor from barging up here to stop him."

I slid back down beneath the covers, pulling them over my head. Kellen left me alone with Logan even after the vampire said not to because he couldn't control himself. I was nearly a vampire, saved by another who tried to bite me earlier that day. Another shudder ran through me, and I pulled the blankets tighter. Why couldn't I remember any of it?

"What can I do to help?" Kellen's muffled voice asked.

I pulled the blankets off my face and looked at him. "I don't know."

"Coffee?"

"Yes, thank you."

He stood and looked at me for several moments before leaving the room. Something felt off, like a barrier between us. Was it because of whatever happened last night? Did Kellen know and not want to tell me?

I tossed the blankets aside and followed him out, making my way to the bathroom. My bladder screamed at me the closer I got. I took care of my immediate needs, then went to the sink, stepping in a puddle of water. I pulled a towel from the rack and dropped it on the floor, silently cussing Kellen for not cleaning up after a shower.

I washed my hands and looked in the mirror. A startled laugh escaped my lips. The entire left side of my hair was flattened on the side of my head. "Did I go to sleep with my hair wet?"

I dunked my head in the sink, soaking my hair, then felt around the counter for another towel. My fingers found my bra, and I paused. What was my bra doing on the bathroom counter? Maybe I did shower before I went to bed, but why was I fully dressed except my bra? What did that venom do to me?

I grabbed the last towel from the rack, dripping water across the floor. I scrubbed my short hair and looked in the mirror again, tilting my head to the side. Two small puncture marks graced the side of my neck. I tentatively poked them with my fingers. They were a little tender but didn't hurt. I huffed and tossed my towel on the floor, scooting it around with my bare feet. I slipped my bra beneath my shirt and threaded my arms through it, then picked up the towels and tossed them in the hamper.

Dozens of questions ran through my mind as I made my way to the kitchenette. I didn't like the thought of missing an entire night, especially one with a vampire. I'd have to ask Logan about it eventually.

Kellen pushed a cup of black coffee towards me and smiled, but it lacked his usual sincerity. Something unpleasant definitely happened.

"Maybe it's better that we don't know," he said, seeming to read my mind. "I trust Logan more than anyone else. If he says we don't want to know, then I have to accept that."

I frowned and looked at the coffee swirling in my cup. I knew he was right, but I still hated the blank spot in my memory.

"How many of Victor's people were hurt?" I asked, avoiding the subject still eating at me.

"He lost eight. A dozen or so are injured, but not critically."

The Keurig bubbled and hissed. He poured cream and sugar into his cup and stirred it.

"I'm sorry. I should have listened to you and stayed here. I was completely useless." I'd forced both of us into a difficult situation. Had it been tough for Logan too?

The corners of Kellen's mouth twitched before turning into a full smile. What could possibly be good about this?

"Actually, Victor is demanding to talk to Niyol," he said.

"Really? What did he do?" I remembered giving him free reign to fight for me, but everything after that was lost.

"He is the reason the vampires retreated," Kellen explained. "His rage over seeing you hurt was unstoppable. I think he took it as a personal failure that the fiend got to you." Kellen reached over and closed my gaping mouth with his finger. "Victor really wants to talk to your element. They wouldn't have won without him."

"I don't know what to say." And I didn't. The thought of Niyol so angry left me speechless.

"Let's go see Victor, then we'll get breakfast."

~~~~~~~~~~~~~~~~~

"Ms. Johnson, it's good to see you up and well," Victor said, greeting us at the bottom of the stairs.

"Thank you."

He wrinkled his nose as we approached, and his chocolate eyes narrowed at me. "You still smell like him," he said.

"She will for another day or so," Kellen stated. "It's the price for saving her."

"I suppose it's worth it," Victor said with a heavy sigh. "Did Kellen tell you I wish to speak to your elemental?"

I nodded. "He did, but I can't promise he'll agree."

"I understand." Victor turned and walked across the great room, pushing one of the large wooden doors open. "Let's ask."

I shrugged and followed him out.

Niyol, you do not have to speak to the pompous windbag, unless you really want to, I thought, hoping he would hear me. He didn't respond.

We stopped in the arena, and Victor looked at me expectantly.

"I've been asking him to come the entire way here," I said. "I have to assume he declines."

He stared at me. "Ask out loud, for my benefit."

"I will not put him on display for you," I replied. "It's his choice to show himself or not. I am not his keeper nor do I command him."

A low growl floated across the space between us, and I rolled my eyes. Still the arrogant bastard.
~~~~~~~~~~~~~~~~~

"Please, Victor," I said as diplomatically as I could manage. "According to Kellen, the fight was won. Your pack fought bravely, and you should be proud of what they accomplished. There are those who need time to grieve for their loved ones and others who need time to heal. I won't waste mine posturing when there are more important things to deal with." I turned my back on Victor and faced Kellen. "Can I go home now? Is the vampire threat quelled for now?"

Kellen looked over my head at Victor, then back to me. "There are a few people here who would like to see you first. Two little girls swear you promised to let them do your hair." He laced his fingers through mine and led me away from the arena.

I should've said something to Victor rather than leaving him standing alone, but I'd had a really bad couple of days. I wasn't in the mood to argue with him.

Instead of turning towards the lodge, we made our way around a small group of trees that opened into a clearing. Several log homes filled the space. Kellen led me to the largest one and pushed open the door. The smell of antiseptics greeted me, along with the feel of a hospital.

"AJ." Matt strolled towards us with one arm in a sling. "Glad to see you're up and moving." He wrinkled his nose as he got closer and stopped several yards away.

"Yes, I know. I stink," I said, anticipating his remark.

He waved his free hand in front of his face and smiled. "Kellen, you know you can take care of that with a little lovin', right?"

I blushed and avoided looking at my partner. "How is everyone?" I asked. "I can help heal them."

"Nah, we heal pretty quick," Matt replied. "I'll be outta this sling by tomorrow."

"Must be nice," I mumbled.

"You've got that cool water thing going, so don't act like you're disadvantaged." He grinned and pushed past us through the door. "I'm getting breakfast. You should join me."

I looked around the room at the injured shifters. They appeared well attended to, but what did I know? Would they ask for my help? Would my magic work on them? It refused to heal Logan, after all.

"Come on," Kellen said. "If they needed your help, Matt would have said so."

We walked back across the clearing, through the trees and into the lodge. Marissa greeted me with a smile and a plate of food.

"Sit down here, and I'll have Kellen get you a cup of coffee." She winked, and I did as she asked.

I still envied her life and was glad the vampires didn't take it. I didn't feel like I contributed much, but apparently Niyol had. The food on my plate disappeared quickly, and I washed it down with the hot cup of coffee Kellen brought me.

"Do you really want to go back to my place?" Kellen asked.

"Most definitely," I replied. "I know Victor made promises to be allies and all that, but he and I are not fit to live in the same house."

Kellen chuckled and took the last bite of bacon from his plate. The barrier between us was still there, but it was good to see him smile. I hoped it would go away sooner rather than later.

"AJ!" Tara's small voice called from the kitchen door. "Are you really leaving?"

I swiveled on my chair to face the young girl. "Not before we do something with my wild hair."

Tara beamed at me. "Tia! Get the salon ready."

Chapter 25

"Why are you staring at me, Kellen?" I asked, knowing the answer.

"I like it, really," he replied, turning his focus back to the road. We were less than thirty minutes from his estate. I glowered at him, but he didn't see me.

"I'm glad they went with blue and not pink," he continued "and just the tips, not a full color. It adds a little... I don't know." He grinned at me.

I pulled down the visor and looked in the small mirror. The sides and back of my hair were cut short, and thick gel coated the top, making it stand straight up. The baby-blue tips stood out against my white hair, but it was kind of cute. It made the girls extremely happy; they even made me sit through pictures.

"Do you really think the vampires are done for now?" I asked, my reflection forcing me to think of the Magister and the mage-vampires.

"I'm not sure," Kellen replied. "And without Logan, I don't know if I can find out."

"Is he gone?" I asked. I had questions for him, but I wasn't sure I could face him. Not yet, anyway.

"No, he can no longer go back to them, which means I've lost that line of information."

"Oh." I bit my bottom lip and stared out the window. The desert raced by in endless monotony. "He scares me, Kellen. Every time I think of him, I see his red eyes looking at me like I'm dinner. I know he saved me from becoming one of them, but all I remember are the bite marks all over his body and the way he snatched those bottles of blood from you."

"The reason you fear him is the same reason he was able to save you."

I looked over at my partner's profile, once again reminded of the Egyptian Pharaohs.

"You were dying, no matter what I did," he continued. "It was a huge risk, but also the only option."

"I guess I understand," I mumbled, but I didn't understand.

My body ached everywhere in ways I couldn't explain. Sure, I'd just been viciously attacked by a monster who wanted my blood, but I'd also been saved by a monster. I rubbed my tender neck and warmth flooded my body. What the hell? Was that a residual effect of the vampire's venom? I hoped not. There was no pleasure in the way he attacked me and ripped into my neck. I shivered at the memory, chasing away the warm pleasure. I wasn't quick enough or strong enough to get away. I failed to draw that creature's blood from his body in time to save myself.

Was that the reason for my fear of Logan? Did this other vampire replace my image of the man who had become a complicated friend? No. Seeing my complicated friend's red eyes and primal urge to bite me solidified my fears. I shook my head, trying to dislodge the image of Logan's battered body from my brain.

"What's next for us?" I asked, moving away from Logan and vampires.

"We still have to meet with Mr. Smith," he replied. "I'm surprised he isn't blowing up my phone with calls and messages."

"He probably knew about the attack on Victor," I said. "I imagine he was also watching your house, so he knew we ran."

"Most likely."

"What are the chances he's waiting for us at the gate?" I asked.

He glanced at me and raised an eyebrow. "I hadn't thought of that, but you're probably right."

Twenty minutes later, the front gate came into view. Kellen cursed like a sailor. The iron hinges had been torn from the stone wall, and the gate itself lay to the side, leaving the road to his home wide open. He stopped the SUV and jumped out, walking back and forth across the road several times looking at the ground, then getting back in the car.

"The vampires don't normally use vehicles, but there are several new tire tracks leading to the house." He put the car in drive, then looked over at me. "We'll have company."

I wasn't sure how I felt about that. Mr. Smith was a huge anomaly and potentially a huge risk. He hadn't helped us defend Victor's home, and if he were really a player in this, he would've known about it.

As we crested the low rise just before Kellen's estate, the sun reflected off the metal sheeting covering his house. The blinding glare forced my eyes closed.

"How can you see where you're going?" I asked, feeling the SUV continue down the road.

"I'm not looking at the house," he replied.

"Smart ass."

We drove around the side of the house to the garage, where one black sedan waited.

"Well, shit," my partner mumbled.

I followed Kellen's pointing finger to the garage doors. A gaping hole in both the metal and the garage door greeted us. Not large enough for a vehicle, but just the right size for a person.

"Let's see if Mr. Smith is still in the car, or if he let himself into my house."

Kellen left me in the SUV and quickly approached the sedan. The driver's window slid down revealing a woman's face with large, dark sunglasses. I exited the car and jogged the few yards between the two vehicles. The back window rolled down and an older man's deep, blue eyes stared at me.

"More than one vehicle has been here," Kellen said, drawing my attention. "Don't tell me you only just arrived."

"We've had people patrolling for the last twenty-four hours," the man in the back seat said.

Kellen turned to him, and his eyes narrowed. "Has anyone else been here since the vampires?"

"No, and I don't believe they breached your house. We should all have defenses as effective as yours."

"Let's go inside." Kellen didn't wait for them to agree, and I hurried after him. He crawled through the hole in the garage door and jogged across the large open space.

"I didn't realize the metal sheeting covered the door to the kitchen as well," I said, gaping at the protective barrier still covering the door to the kitchen.

When I reached him, he'd just finished punching numbers into a panel on the wall. The metal panels retreated like a pocket-door, and I tried to contain my amazement. Kellen sighed, relief rolling off him in waves.

"I would love to have the name of your engineer," the older man said from behind us.

"Not happening," Kellen replied as he disappeared into the dark kitchen. I followed on his heels and flipped the light switch next to the door. The lights above my head flickered on, and I sat next to Kellen at the bar.

"Jonathan Smith," the man said, holding out his hand to me.

I looked at it, not sure why I hesitated. Something about him felt weird. Magic buzzed around him, drifting towards me, almost as if it wanted to touch me. That wasn't going to happen. He nodded and dropped his hand. "This is my assistant, Ms. White."

She nodded but remained silent, removing her sunglasses and putting them in the breast pocket of her jacket.

Kellen and Mr. Smith stared at one another for several moments.

"What do you want, Mr. Smith?" Kellen finally asked.

The man glanced at me, then back to Kellen. "This young lady has the means to stop your Magister from creating an army for the vampire council. I want to make sure that happens."

"And you think kidnapping her and forcing her to fight against her will is the best path?"

Like Kellen hadn't just done the same thing? Sure, he also saved my life a couple of times, but in the end, he wanted me to be a weapon against my mother.

Smith scowled at Kellen, and that strange buzz drifted towards me again. "No. My sources tell me that you are allied with the shifters north of here, along with a small group of mages at your Magister's palace." He shifted his weight where he stood, but Kellen didn't offer him a seat. "My own allies include a small group of vampires and the European mages."

Kellen's eyebrows rose, and he tapped the granite counter with his forefinger. "I thought the Europeans wanted nothing to do with us."

"That has been true for some time, but the Magister's latest antics have changed their minds. None of them want to be revealed."

I glanced at him. It made sense there were other mages across the globe, but I assumed there was only one ruling party. How was Mr. Smith connected to the European group? He appeared to be American, with no noticeable foreign accent.

"What are you proposing?" Kellen asked.

"Can we move to a more comfortable setting?" Smith asked in return. "I'm not young and have no desire to stand here while you question me."

"Follow me," I said, sliding from my stool.

A single lamp was the only light in the large living area, besides what spilled over from the kitchen. The metal sheeting still covered the windows and glass doors, preventing the sunlight from illuminating the space. I sat down on the nearest chair, while our guests sat on the sofa across from me.

"Thank you, Alisandra," Smith said.

I didn't correct him. "You're a mage, aren't you?" I asked.

"Sort of," he replied. "I'm a cross-breed of mage and shifter."

"Really?" I didn't try to hide my surprise. I didn't realize it was possible, but all kinds of people fell in love. I found it interesting that none of the mages or shifters I'd met gave off the buzzing magic coming from Mr. Smith.

"Only the royal families are bound by arranged marriages or pairings." He smiled, softening his wrinkled features. "But I'm not accepted by either of my parents' families. As far as most are concerned, I'm an outcast doing a job no one else wants."

"And what job is that?" Kellen asked from behind me. He hadn't sat with our group but remained standing behind my chair.

"I gather intelligence for the supernatural families and provide a place of belonging for those like myself."

That was an interesting revelation. How many people did Mr. Smith have in his employ? It must be quite a few if the families were scattered across the globe.

"You work for our Magister?" Kellen continued.

"No, not anymore." His gaze drifted back to me, making me uncomfortable. "When she killed her partner, I left."

I once again wondered how many people knew Logan wasn't technically dead. That would also make Mr. Smith really old. Logan had been a vampire for forty years.

"And you will share information with me and my allies if we help you overthrow the Magister," Kellen stated.

"Yes, but the European mages will also recognize the princess as the rightful heir to her mother's throne and you..."

"Why would they do that?" Kellen interrupted. "They've been looking to implant one of their princes for years."

"They would have called for a marriage between their prince and Alisandra had it not been for you." Smith tilted his head and flicked his eyes between me and Kellen. "They assume you are uniting the Middle Eastern and North American mages."

I suspected Kellen wanted me to take over, but I hadn't put two and two together when it came to his role.

"I haven't spoken to my uncle in fifteen years," Kellen said, his voice barely above a whisper. "He knows nothing of my partnership with AJ."

I twisted in my chair and looked up at him. He avoided looking back at me. Yet another secret he didn't share.

"I imagine he does know, just like everyone else. Word travels quickly nowadays," Mr. Smith stated.

"You're royalty and didn't bother to tell me?" I asked.

"I'm not royalty," he replied, looking down at me. "My father was the fifth son, and my uncle has three of his own. I have no claim to his throne."

"But you carry your family's blood line," Smith interjected, "which satisfies the royal's requirements for your princess."

"You and I will talk about this later," I stated, feeling the command in my voice. I turned back to our guest. "I'm not very good at having my decisions made for me, and the last several days have stretched that to its limit. If you're telling me to raise an army and overthrow my mother, you've lost your mind."

"Your army is already raised," Smith replied. "You merely need to present a strong front and tell her to leave. It's possible to do it without bloodshed, especially if you meet her at the palace. Her vampires cannot use the portals, so the only resistance will be those at the palace. I can't imagine there are many who will support her."

"You obviously know nothing about me," I argued. "A week ago, I was barely keeping myself from being homeless. Now, you expect me to lead a group of magical people who have no reason to trust or follow me."

"They have every reason," Smith countered. "Your Magister's destruction is first and foremost. You're gifted with both air and water. And your partner's bloodline ensures the continuation."

How did he know about my dual powers? I'd only found out about my magic in the last few days, and nobody had known about my existence before that.

"That's ridiculous!" I rose from my chair and stared down at the older man. "None of those qualify me to be a good leader. My social skills suck. I can barely think past my own needs and selfish desires. What makes me any better than my mother?"

"Your elements would not have chosen you if you had any of your mother's traits," he replied, remaining seated and much calmer than me. "Do you really think they rejected her because of your grandmother?"

I stared at him. I said the same thing two days ago. But how did he know all of this? Were his contacts embedded that far into each supernatural society?

"How would they know she was a bad person as an infant?" I asked.

"They didn't." He leaned forward in his chair and looked at his hands. "Her anger and hatred of her parents prevented the elements from accepting her fully. Water and Earth refused her before she was five. Even at that young age, she was cruel."

"Why did the wind stay with her?" I asked, sinking back into my chair.

"Because of her partner," he replied. "They found each other in their early teens. I think she was twelve or thirteen."

I thought of Logan, dedicating his life to helping his friend, only to have her betray him.

"Was she upset about his death?" I asked quietly, my anger subsiding with the thought of Logan's life with my mother.

"Not the way you would think. She was angry that his element abandoned him. She raged through the palace, cursing all the elements." He looked over at me, sadness crossing his face. "If she mourned his loss, she didn't show it."

"You know what really happened to him, don't you?" Kellen asked.

"Yes."

"What?" I asked, not hiding my surprise. "How do you know so much?"

"Thank you, Mr. Smith, for your candor and your offer," Kellen interrupted. I scowled at him. I wanted answers, but he continued. "We accept the offer from the European council and will make plans for our Magister."

"When can we expect your arrival at the palace?" Mr. Smith asked.

"I need several weeks with AJ," he replied. "She cannot take her mother's place without being prepared for a challenge. Right now, she is not the least bit ready."

"She'll be ready in a few weeks?" he asked.

"Possibly, if we can remain undisturbed," Kellen replied. "The last few days have been a whirlwind, and everything she's learned has been haphazard at best."

"I'll see what I can do." He stood and extended his hand to me once more. I took it tentatively and a surge of power rush through me with our contact.

"What did you just do?" I asked, pulling my hand away.

"Confirmed your heritage, princess."

Chapter 26

I stood outside the ruined garage door as the sedan drove away, plumes of sand following in its wake.

"I'm going to seal the front gate," Kellen said, leaning his head out the window of his SUV. "I'll be right back."

I turned my back on his retreating vehicle and made my way into the house, heading for my room. My head swam with the new information thrown at me, but two things stood out in my mind. Mr. Smith knew Logan even though our vampire claimed ignorance when Mr. Smith made his first demands. Was Logan really an ally, or was he working for both sides?

And Kellen's family ruled the mages in the Middle East. It explained his heritage, but what did it mean for me? I knew nothing about the people who ruled the mages or how the supernatural races were governed. Beyond the vampires, shifters, and mages, I didn't even know who the others were. Were there others? Kellen suggested there were, but he liked to keep secrets from me.

I stopped in front of the of large wooden doors leading to Kellen's training room. "Seriously? This was not where I wanted to be."

Maybe it was. Would my elements have answers about my family? Would Niyol explain what happened between my mother and her wind elemental?

I pushed open the door and let the warm air surround me. Sheet metal still covered the high windows, leaving the room almost completely dark. A small fire burned in the hearth, illuminating the space a few feet from it. I sat down on the bench and removed my shoes and socks, digging my toes into the cool dirt.

"What am I doing here? Am I really supposed to lead a group of magical people? Had I not seen it with my own eyes, I wouldn't even believe all of this existed."

"Your destiny has already been written, child," Water's voice replied, seeming to come from everywhere.

"Shouldn't it be my choice?" I asked. "I want to have some say in what happens. My whole life has been dictated to me. For once, I'd like to have the final say."

Water's fluid form coalesced in front of me, reflecting the flames from the small fire. "You are destined to take your place within your family's heritage. You cannot avoid that responsibility."

"But I don't want it. Can't I just give it to someone else?"

"You could, but you would be abandoning the people who need you at a time when they cannot be abandoned." Water slid to my side and sat on the bench beside me.

I didn't understand why it had to be me. Governments changed leaders all the time. If it wasn't my mother or another tyrant, why did it matter? Good rulers had qualities I didn't possess.

"Why does a dual mage have to lead them? Why can't it be a single mage?"

"Do you know why we speak to you in this form?"

I shook my head. I had no idea. And what did its question have to do with mine?

"I am one of many. The others are the same. We work together because we must, or the consequence is unthinkable." Water lifted a hand towards me and touched my shoulder, sending a soothing warmth throughout my body. "We speak to you because of your connection to Kellen. The link between two dual mages can allow us to take this form. It has been that way, always."

"But it doesn't explain why a dual mage has to rule," I insisted.

"The mages and elements are strongest when we are paired together that way," it replied. "Do you really want a weak mage governing those with the power to destroy everything around them?"

It made sense. I was trying to compare normal human politics to magic, and maybe it wasn't the same.

"Kellen didn't know about the connection between dual mages and our ability to speak with you," I said, letting go of my question about politics. "Is it because he has been away from his family?"

"He knew it as a gift to your family, but his parents did not share that it extended to all the royal families."

"But his mother was also a dual mage," I said, remembering she had earth and water. "Who was his mother?"

A rippling laughter surrounded me as Water slid to the other side. "You miss very little, child. His mother was from Australia and also carried royal blood. Her line is nearly gone, as is yours."

"Who rules the mages in Australia?"

"No one at present. Kellen or his sister could, if they would accept."

I was surprised and worried. Would Kellen go to Australia if he knew? "They're all that's left?" I asked.

"There are others in Asia who also carry the line but do not realize it."

"How don't they know? Are they not dual mages?" I looked at my element, tilting my head to the side. Shouldn't a dual mage expect to have royal blood and wonder where it came from? How could they leave an entire area without leadership?

"What has your heart told you of our selections for dual mages?"

"You didn't choose my mother because she was broken. Would you choose someone who didn't have royal blood to be a dual mage?"

"There have been many dual mages that are not recorded, because they feel the same as you. They do not wish to rule, but they have been our strongest defenders over the years."

"But do they have royal blood? Is it possible for a dual mage to not be royalty?" I asked, that little detail still not clear in my mind.

"I know of none, but that doesn't mean it hasn't happened."

"I see. The difference between them and me is that I don't get that choice," I mumbled.

"As with all choices, denying your destiny will have consequences, child."

My element fell to the ground at my feet and disappeared. I cradled my head in my hands. How was I supposed to accept this? What were the consequences for running away?

"My mother refused to tell us." Kellen's voice startled me, and I jumped to my feet.

He stood in the doorway, with his shoes hanging from his fingers. The sadness on his face kept me silent.

"She said we were the only family she ever needed." He dropped his shoes and pulled his socks from his feet, then walked to the middle of the room. I joined him, sitting across from him as I had every time we came here. He looked at me and smiled. "My father was the poster child for how not to be a fire mage. He and his element were volatile on their own, but together?" He chuckled and pointed at the ceiling. "They were always trying to create new ways to make themselves a better weapon."

"He was a single mage," I said.

"Yes, which is the reason he left Egypt. Two of his four brothers were dual mages. He would never inherit the throne, which was probably best. He planned nothing and allowed his anger and emotions to react for him, something a leader cannot do."

"And your mother balanced him perfectly."

"Yes. It's rare for a mage to have water and earth. They are the balancing elements for air and fire. I think the elements knew she would be destined to tame my father."

"They seem to know a lot about destiny." I didn't like destiny. It felt like a dictator.

"Yes."

He reached out and took my hand in his. The contrast between us was exactly as he had described the night we healed his guardians. Not just our differences in appearance, but everything.

"I will be whatever you need, AJ," he said. "Your advisor, friend, and warrior mage. Maybe one day, we'll have more, but I won't force myself on you."

I frowned, focusing on our hands. I didn't really know if he wanted more. I suspected it, but he was right—he never forced himself on me. I was the one making demands.

"That makes me sound really shallow," I said.

"I just poured my heart out to you, and you think I made you sound shallow?"

"That's not what I meant." I bit my lip. "You're willing to be whatever I need, but I'm not willing to look past myself to see what you need. Well, damn. That didn't come out right either." I pulled my hand away and stood. "I can barely comprehend the demands being placed on me. I have this undeniable attraction to you, but I don't know if it's me or our partner thing. Are they my emotions or something put there by my elements?"

I started pacing back and forth in front of Kellen. He leaned back, supporting his weight on his hands.

"And this thing with all these royal people. I grew up a step below poverty. How could I possibly ever speak to any of them without looking like a complete idiot?" I waved my hands above my head and looked down at Kellen. He was smiling, which made me angry.

"How is this funny? I have a hundred decisions to make, and I have no idea what to do."

"You're cute when you're frustrated."

"That doesn't help."

"I told you. I will be whatever you need. If you decide to take your mother's place, I'll be by your side, helping you with those decisions, which I think is your best choice, by the way." He pushed himself to his feet and closed the gap between us. "If you decide to abandon your destiny, I will also be by your side to accept the consequences. That's not the best choice, but I understand why you're thinking about it. I'll do everything in my power to convince you not to make that choice." He smiled, and I wondered if he really meant it. "As for these royal people, we'll cross that bridge when we get there. I've had some experience dealing with snobby rich people." He reached out and traced the edge of my jaw. "And your emotions are your own. Our elements have nothing to do with it."

Chapter 27

Two weeks later, light from the full moon illuminated the barren desert that stretched for miles in every direction. The occasional scrub brush cast eerie shadows across the sand. It was the perfect hiding place for the vampire I knew stalked me. I could smell his signature spearmint, cool and breezy.

I smiled as I tried not move a single muscle to give away my location. The light breeze shifted, blowing my hair into my face, along with a gust of spearmint. I jabbed my elbow straight back and was rewarded with a satisfying grunt. I rolled forward and spun on the balls of my feet, but he wasn't there.

I silently berated myself for reacting so quickly. Patience was something I still needed to work on. The wind caressed my arms and whispered to me as it drifted past. I smiled again, still crouching low to the ground. My hands slowly met each other at my knees, then drew apart, forming a short, slender spear, pointed at both ends. It was my favorite weapon, made completely of condensed air.

Niyol taught me how to make several weapons, but I liked this one best. It was long enough to give me reach without being cumbersome.

"Stay focused, princess," Logan hissed in my ear.

Rather than jab backwards with my pointed spear, I spun on the balls of my feet once again, then thrust the weapon up as I stood.

"Clever," he said, grabbing my wrist and forcing it behind my back. His other arm wrapped around my waist and pulled me into his chest. "You almost caught me by surprise."

My heart raced with adrenaline. I tamped down the surge of desire that continued to get stronger in his presence. Two weeks ago, when Kellen informed me Logan would be part of my training, I had a panic attack. Nothing Kellen said could convince me I wanted to be around the vampire, until Logan returned. All signs of the crazed man lying on the floor, covered in blood and violence, were gone. He was again the quirky man who called me princess and made me laugh.

Things changed again when we started spending our evenings training. The more time I spent with him, the closer we became. We didn't just train. He answered my questions about my family, my magic, my connections to the elements, everything that Kellen wouldn't.

"I knew you were there," I argued. "But I'm not as fast as you. There's no way I can catch you by surprise." I was grateful he couldn't see my pout.

"Then we'll try again." He released me, and I stumbled forward.

"It's pointless, Logan. Once you are in my personal space, I'm done." I put my hands on my hips and faced my so-called trainer.

His dark hair had grown in the last couple weeks. It brushed the tops of ears on the sides, and he pulled the top back into a ponytail. "A month ago, I could follow you around for hours without you noticing. You've made progress. So, we'll try again." He crossed his arms over chest and shifted his weight to one side, his lean, muscular body outlined by the moon's light.

"The only reason I know you're there is because I can smell you," I countered. A gust of wind blew sand into my face, making me cough. "Okay, Niyol helps too." I waved my hand over my face several times, trying to remove the specks of dust.

A second later, Logan was inches from me, the moonlight reflecting off the flecks of green in his brown eyes. "What do mean you can smell me?"

I took a deep breath, enjoying his scent. "You should quit chewing gum. You smell like spearmint."

"I don't chew gum, AJ," he replied.

"Really? Well, that's odd." I stuffed my hands in my pockets to keep them from reaching out to him. Did he feel this too, or was it just me?

"How long have you been able to smell people?" he asked.

"A couple weeks?" I shrugged, trying to make light of it, but I knew why he was concerned. He and I still hadn't talked about that night. Every time I brought it up, he refused to answer. But little things, like his smell and my desire to be close to him, fueled my need to know what happened.

"Ever since your fight with the vampire?"

"Yeah, maybe."

"AJ, this is serious. Why haven't you mentioned it before?"

Because you won't talk about it, I nearly said but held my tongue.

"I thought you were chewing gum," I lied. "How was I supposed to know it was actually you?"

"Who else?"

I kicked the dirt at my feet like a child in trouble. Why should I feel guilty about it? I didn't ask to be bitten, and I didn't want the side effects that came with it, except the smelling part. Logan and Kellen both smelled amazing.

"Just you and Kellen," I replied.

"Come on. We're going back to the house." He grabbed my elbow, but I jerked it away.

"Who put you in charge?" I asked, refusing to move.

"I'm in charge of your safety, and right now, I'm concerned there is part of a vampire lingering in your blood."

"Whatever. So, I can smell the two men in my life. Big deal."

His eyebrows met in the middle, and I glared at him. Would he really open up this time?

"I'm not done with my training," I said. "I haven't managed to stab you."

"You'd like that, wouldn't you?"

"Very much."

"Well, I'm done. See you back at the house."

A puff of sand was the only sign of his leaving. I kicked the rocks at my feet and started walking back towards the estate. He wouldn't really leave me. He stuck to me like glue unless Kellen was there. Then, my partner was my permanent attachment. Between the two of them, I never had any time alone.

I missed it, sort of. The feelings of rejection and loneliness were buried in my past, as recent as it was, but having time to daydream, read, sketch, or anything whimsical would have been nice. All my time was monopolized with training.

At least I was no longer ninety-five pounds of skin and bone. Kellen forced me to eat three meals a day, and every morning was consumed by some type of cardio workout, then weight training. The rigid schedule then jumped to lunch, immediately followed by history lessons and a nap. At sunset, Logan took over with weapons' training and teaching me how to communicate with Water. The wind, Niyol, reveled in my combat training, enjoying every minute of it. But Water was reclusive, unwilling to be part of any offensive training. I still failed at convincing it to help me learn.

I felt stronger physically and magically. But all my magical training came from Niyol and Logan. Kellen and I still hadn't really worked at using our elements together. He talked about it a lot, but that was it. I hoped we would take the time to do it before we went to the palace.

"Where is your mind tonight, princess?" Logan asked, materializing next to me. I knew he didn't really just appear. His movement was faster than I could see, making it look that way.

"Everywhere," I replied.

"That takes a lot of brain power."

I smiled, knowing he could probably see me despite the lack of light. "In case you hadn't noticed, I am fairly intelligent," I quipped, feeling his shoulder brush against mine. I shivered, but not because I was cold.

"I did notice," he replied, not putting distance between us.

I sighed, forcing my thoughts away from him and returning to my element. "I feel like I've failed Water somehow," I said. "Niyol is so willing to teach me anything, but Water... I don't even know his name."

"Maybe he realizes that Niyol is not as volatile as he could be, so he doesn't need to interject into your training," he suggested.

"Was that how yours was?" I asked, then regretted it. Logan wasn't always agreeable to talk about his lost magic. "I'm sorry, Logan, you don't have to answer that."

"You shouldn't be sorry," he replied. "I would love to talk about my element tonight, even if he is no longer mine."

"Are you sure? I can't imagine how painful it would be." I hung my head and kicked at the sand as I walked. "Niyol and I have become so close in the last couple weeks."

"My relationship was much like yours and Niyol, except mine didn't speak to me. We focused on calming your mother rather than encouraging her to fight."

I looked up at him when he didn't continue. He stared at me with a strange expression.

"What?" I stopped walking, and he stopped beside me.

"You are everything she should have been."

I pulled my gaze from his, feeling his sadness and longing. So, I wasn't the only one experiencing this. And where did that come from?

"I'm sorry, AJ. I'm supposed to be helping you learn, not forcing my self-pity on you."

He started walking again, but I didn't follow him. How did I feel his emotions? I expected it with Kellen, because of our connection, but not Logan. Yet every day, it became stronger. I hadn't told him because it helped me know where he was during our training, giving me an edge I didn't have before. He stopped a few yards away and slowly turned back.

"You're the little bit of vampire still in my blood, aren't you?" I asked.

His shoulders sagged in the moonlight. "Possibly. Probably."

"How did it get there?"

"You don't want to know that answer," he replied.

"Yes, I really do. Kellen is satisfied with not knowing, but I'm not."

I felt his indecision… and was that guilt?

"I had to give you some of my blood to keep you alive," he said. "I believe it's lingering for some reason. I didn't expect it to. Your body should have filtered it all out."

I shivered at the thought of having drank his blood. Maybe it *was* better I didn't remember it. "What is it doing to me?"

"I'm not sure." He closed the space between us and looked down at me. "I'm a baby vampire, as far as they're concerned. I don't know enough about my kind to give you an answer."

"Is there no one you can ask?" My thoughts went to Mr. Smith, but I wasn't sure I wanted to have that conversation. Kellen approached Logan about it and told me he was satisfied with the answer, but he wouldn't share. He said it was Logan's story to tell.

"Yes, but it would require me to leave," he replied. His finger traced my jaw and warmth bloomed in my middle.

"Am I slowly turning into a vampire?"

"No, that would've already happened, if you were going to," he replied.

"Then what? You must be feeling the same thing I am."

"I have all kinds of theories, but I'd rather have an answer, not a guess." He looked towards the estate, a shining beacon in the darkness. "Kellen's back. Let's go." His hand drifted down my arm and caressed my fingers before he stepped away from me and towards the estate.

I sighed and followed. I wouldn't get any more answers tonight.

~~~~~~~~~~~~~

"How was training?" Kellen asked as Logan and I entered the kitchen. "I don't see any blood, so I'm guessing you failed to stab him."

Humor danced in his brown eyes, and I forced a smile. "No, he won't hold still long enough. It's almost like he's afraid it'll hurt." I climbed onto one of the bar stools and rolled my eyes at the vampire.

"Imagine that." Logan took the seat beside me. "Just because I can heal from it doesn't mean its painless."
~~~~~~~~~~~~~

I waved my hand at him and smirked. "What's a little stabbing amongst friends?"

"You are not funny, princess."

"Are you kidding? That was hilarious. Don't you watch any TV?"

Kellen chuckled and leaned on the counter across from me. His eyes shined with a happiness I didn't feel; at least one of us had a good evening.

"Are you two done for the night?" he asked.

I looked at Logan, my smile waning.

"Yeah, we're done," he said. "She's as fast as she's gonna get. I think more practice summoning her weapons will help with control and finesse, but she doesn't need me for that."

I tried to block out his sense of resignation but failed. Kellen looked at me with narrowed eyes. Did he feel it too? Was he getting it from me?

"So, what do you have planned for me?" I asked, trying to stifle the uncomfortable atmosphere.

"If you feel up to it, I was thinking of a late dinner and a movie," Kellen replied.

"Someone wasn't here to wake me from my nap, so I had plenty of sleep."

"Did you miss dinner?" he asked.

"Nope. Mr. Vampire woke me up with a plate of bacon and fresh coffee."

Kellen's eyebrows rose as he turned to Logan. "Breakfast in bed?"

"Hell, no," I chimed in. "He walked by my door, waving the aroma around, then went back to the kitchen."

Kellen laughed, his smile lighting up his eyes.

"We can't have her spoiled, can we?" Logan asked, winking at me.

"Whatever," I replied, waving my hand in his direction.

"I'll be gone for a few days," Logan continued, catching my fluttering hand. "Enjoy your movie and dinner, princess." He kissed my fingers and walked away, disappearing down the hall.

I winced, something tugging at my heart as I watched him walk away.

"You okay?" Kellen asked.

"Yep, I'm good," I lied, forcing the connection to Logan to the back of my mind. "What's for dinner? I assume we're eating in."

"I brought home fried chicken and potatoes," he replied. "We'll have to warm it up, though."

"Sounds great." I looked towards the door, still feeling my vampire.

"Is everything okay between you two?" Kellen asked.

"I don't know."

"Anything I can do to help?"

I frowned trying to decide what to say. I couldn't hide my feelings from my partner; I knew I should probably just tell him. "I think something happened when he drew the vampire venom from me," I replied cautiously, not certain how he would react.

"A lot of things happened."

"No kidding, smart ass." I rolled my eyes. "Seriously, though. I think I can feel his emotions the way I feel yours. It's not as strong, but it's there. I know when he's around, almost like I can feel him. I can also smell both of you."

His eyes narrowed as he leaned towards me. "What do you mean?" he asked, his good mood vanishing in an instant.

Wonderful, now both of us would have a rough evening.

"You smell like brown sugar and cinnamon, which is very nice, by the way. Logan is like spearmint."

His frown deepened, and his uncertainty wrapped around me. "I was referring to his emotions, not the smell, but that's interesting. I didn't realize I had an odor other than my cologne."

"I asked him to find out what's happening," I said. "It's hard enough to deal with my own emotional constipation. Adding the two of you is a little stressful."

"I imagine so."

"There's no imagining. I know you can feel it. I just don't know what to do about it." I hated our connection sometimes. Actually, most of the time. We didn't use it to work together, so it was always in the way. Sparky rarely surfaced anymore unless I specifically called for him, which I didn't do often. I left him with Kellen, knowing our connection was more than just a little spark.

"Did he say where he was going? Kellen asked.

I shook my head. "I didn't ask."

He pushed away from the counter and pulled two boxes from the fridge, transferring them to the microwave. "I planned to take a night off, so let's do that. No training, no history lessons, and no talk of the supernatural community."

I forced a smile I didn't feel. "Deal."

Chapter 28

The next morning started the same as any other, with a knock on my door at eight in the morning.

"Do you not remember how late we stayed up?" I yelled, knowing Kellen could hear me through the door. He didn't answer, so I didn't get out of bed. Four hours of sleep wasn't enough.

"Get up, sleepyhead!" Kate's voice brought a smile to my face. I heard the door open and close, and I rubbed the sleep from my eyes.

"Finally. Do you know how hard it is to live without another woman in the house?" I asked, sitting up in bed as she wandered in with a plate of pancakes. Her straight, dark hair was pulled back in a ponytail, and her brown eyes shined with excitement.

"I do," she replied. "Raul and Sammy are a pain in the ass."

Her smile removed any criticism from the comment, and I chuckled. I rolled out of bed and headed for the bathroom, while she set my plate on the dresser.

"I'll be right back," I said. "Don't go anywhere."

"No worries about that," she replied. "I wanted to chat without my nosy brother."

A few minutes later, we both sat on my bed. I struggled not to drip maple syrup on my favorite quilt. "Tell me what's happening with your mages and the palace," I said.

"No way! I want to hear what's up with you and Kellen," she countered. "I can tell something happened. Are you two really partners?"

I stuffed a forkful of pancakes in my mouth and pointed at her. I needed to know how much Kellen shared with her. Our last conversation about Kate included warnings about not getting her involved.

"Fine. Not having the portal here is really inconvenient. I expected Kellen to have it fixed already. It's been over three weeks, and it's still broken." She turned and folded her legs beneath her. "We rescued two more groups of mages, one in Vermont and one in Denver." Her smile faded quickly, and she looked at my closed door. "Raul thinks there are more; we just haven't been able to find them. It's kind of scary."

"How are things at the palace?" I asked between bites.

"Tense." Her full lips drew into a thin line. "Our group can't go back. The Magister has forbidden us to continue looking for the others."

I nearly choked on the thick pancake, but forced it down. "Does Kellen know?"

"Yeah, I talked to him a few minutes ago. He's with Raul and Sammy now."

"Did she say why you couldn't keep looking?" I asked, forgetting about the half stack of pancakes.

"Some stupid excuse about using resources we didn't have." She paused, and I squirmed under her gaze. "There are some crazy rumors flying around, AJ. Are you really a dual mage and Kellen's partner?"

"What did he tell you?" I asked.

"He avoided the question."

Of course, he would. He did it to me all the time. I couldn't think of any reason to hide it from her. "Yes, for both questions."

"I knew it!" She jumped off the bed and started pacing. "You already have a strong following at the palace. The Magister's supporters continue to dwindle, especially when we found out about the bounty on your head. It makes sense now. That's why Kellen hasn't fixed the portal."

"Why hasn't the Magister come after me here?" I asked.

"Our guardians are well known at the palace. She cannot fight them alone."

"But she can send others to do it for her," I added, thinking of the guardians we had to heal.

"I heard about the vampires that attacked." She stopped pacing and looked at me. "I'm glad you weren't here for it."

I slid off the bed and put my plate on the dresser. How much had she heard? Did the shifters tell them about our battle at Victor's? "We should probably join the boys," I said, pulling clothes from one the many drawers.

"Probably, but I have one more question." Her grin returned, and I knew what she was going to ask.

"No, we're not sleeping together," I said, feeling my face flush.

"Liar." She skipped out of my room, closing the door behind her.

I wouldn't convince her, but Kellen and I had not had sex. My rigorous schedule and exhausted body never allowed the time for the two of us to be close; we barely even had time to talk. But somehow, Logan found the time to talk and answer my questions. I shook the thought from my head and got dressed.

I joined the others a few minutes later. They huddled around a low coffee table in the sitting area and looked towards me as I entered.

"My shocking little friend," Raul said with a smile. "Long time, no see."

"It's good to see you too," I said, joining their little circle.

"I like the blue highlights," Sammy said.

I couldn't tell if he was serious or being sarcastic, so I let it go. "Thanks."

"We were discussing our mutual allies and potential enemies," Kellen said, drawing my attention. "Over a dozen mages have been thrown out of the palace because they refused to stop looking for the others."

"Do they have someplace to go?" I asked.

I thought about mine and Logan's shared space. I didn't think there were any other available rooms here. While I didn't mind adding some sleeping bags or cots to my room, I was sure no one wanted to share with Logan.

"We can make room for a few here, and some of the others have family outside of the palace who will take them in," Kellen replied. His look of apprehension made me worry. "We'll talk about sleeping arrangements later."

"Have we heard from Victor or Mr. Smith recently?" I asked.

"As you know, Matt keeps in touch regularly," Kellen said. "I met with Mr. Smith yesterday. His resources are astounding. He's the only reason you and I have had time to train for the last two weeks."

"Who's Mr. Smith?" Raul asked.

"He leads a group of hybrids who are currently keeping the vampires busy fighting amongst each other," Kellen explained. "I still don't trust him completely, but for now, he has our best interest in mind. I'm hoping his distraction will allow us a silent entrance into the palace."

Everyone looked at me, and I sunk into my chair. They expected me to take my mother's place, but I still wasn't sure if I was ready.

"I'm not ready," I mumbled.

"Yes, you are," Kellen argued. He'd told me that several times in the last few days.

"It's only been two weeks. How can I possibly be ready?"

"Your elements know what's at stake," he replied. "You learn very quickly, and you're no longer the bony little girl you were two weeks ago."

"Besides, it's not like you're going to meet a lot of resistance," Sammy added. "I'd bet the only one who objects is the Magister herself."

"There are others who would challenge AJ once the Magister is out of the picture," Kellen said. "The Magister has sown the seed of doubt into the royal family's garden."

"Is there a reason the mages don't rule by democracy?" I asked. "It works pretty well for normal humans. Even the vampires have council rule."

Everyone looked at me like I'd grown another head.

"Really?" I asked. "You all live in the United States of America and can't see your mages ruled by a democracy?" Their blank stares astounded me. "Don't you vote in your local elections? Please tell me you vote for the president."

"That's different," Raul said. "The elements decide who is worthy of ruling our magical community, and we accept that. Humans have proven they can't be trusted with magic, so we rely on the elements to do it for us."

"Yet, my mother is trying to sacrifice all of you," I said, not hiding my bitterness.

"Which is why she was rejected by the elements," Kate added. "Bad people exist everywhere, but our elements have proven time and again that they are much better at seeing it than we are."

I folded my arms over my chest, shaking my head. "If I have to take my mother's place, I want a council with me." If the mages weren't open to council rule, having advisors would at least take some of the pressure off me while I figured out what I was doing.

"We'll make sure that happens," Kellen said. His pride and admiration made me blush. He'd mentioned the possibility a couple times, but it was good to hear it confirmed.

"So, when do we crash the Magister's party?" Raul asked, grinning.

"Soon," Kellen replied. "I need to talk to a few people first."

"I can't wait to see the look on her cold, bitter face when her people turn against her," Sammy added.

"The vampires will probably react immediately," Kellen said. "They won't be happy about losing their direct line to us."

"Something doesn't make sense to me," I interrupted. "Why would the vampires be okay with making super vampires? The mages-turned-vampires seemed to be so much stronger. Wouldn't they eventually overthrow the council?"

"I hadn't thought of that," Raul replied. "Why would the vampires do that?"

I was grateful not to be the only one confused by it.

"Because they intend to use our brothers and sisters as fodder for their war," Kellen said. "They'll be strong enough to help defeat almost any opposition, but their numbers will be too small to be a threat to the vampire council."

"That's just wrong," Sammy said.

"All the more reason to make sure we do this right." Kellen stood and looked at Raul. "Now for sleeping arrangements. You have seven others that need a place to stay, right?"

"Yep."

"I have two rooms that share a bathroom. We'll have to round up a couple cots and sleeping bags, but they're welcome to stay. Hopefully, it will only be a week or so, and then everyone can have their own space back."

I eyed Kellen, knowing he just gave away my room.

"Kate, show the boys where our camping gear is in the garage," Kellen said. Then, he turned to me. "Come with me, and help me get the rooms ready."

Everyone filed out of the room to complete their tasks. I followed Kellen down the hall, and he stopped at Logan's room first.

"Does Logan know we're kicking him out?" I asked.

"I texted him this morning. He said it wasn't a problem."

"Really? Where will he stay?" I asked.

"He said he'll be gone longer than he expected." Kellen picked up a trunk similar to mine and turned to face me. "He wouldn't give me details, but apparently his first source didn't tell him what he wanted to hear about your connection."

I gave him a blank stare, waiting for him to elaborate, but he didn't. What did that mean, and why wouldn't he tell me more about Logan?

"Make sure he doesn't have anything in the bathroom, then pack up your stuff."

Kellen left me in Logan's room before I could come up with an intelligent reply. I stomped into the bathroom and collected everything, mine and Logan's, then dropped it in the trunk at the end of my bed. Kellen came back by the time I finished emptying my dresser.

He picked up my trunk, and I pulled my favorite quilt from the bed. His eyebrows rose, but he didn't say anything. He walked past Kate's room and turned the corner to the next hall. The only thing down that corridor was the training room and Kellen's room. I jogged to catch up to him.

"What are you doing?" I asked. "I thought I would be sharing Kate's room."

"Get the door for me," he said, ignoring my question.

I didn't move, and he rolled his eyes.

"Kate will likely have Raul's company most of the time, which also means Sam. Your room will be shared by three other men, and Logan's will have four men. You're welcome to plant your ass anywhere you like," he snapped. "I just assumed you would prefer me over them, but I suppose I could be wrong."

Of course, he was right, but he didn't have to be an ass about it. We hadn't slept together, not that I didn't want to, or at least I used to. I was afraid he would think I was easy or loose or whatever people called it. We'd only known each other for a month. Regardless of everything else between us, I didn't want to rush that part. His insistence not to push me only reinforced my decision about it.

I stuck my tongue out at him and pushed open the door, motioning for him to go in.

~~~~~~~~~~~
~~~~~~~~~~~

Packing, unpacking, and greeting new people took up the rest of my morning. By lunch, my stomach was pissed. Lucky for me, two of our new folks loved to cook. I couldn't remember their names, so I called them Chef One and Chef Two as they prepared sandwiches and pasta salad for lunch.

Chef Two, a tall, lanky redhead, stirred a large pitcher of punch. He smiled when he caught me watching him from my favorite barstool.

"You don't mind a little whiskey in your drink, do ya?" he asked.

"I guess not," I replied.

Sharon introduced me to rum a couple years ago, but that was the first and last time I had any alcohol. Thoughts of my old life made me somber. I longed to talk to my friend, but I understood why I couldn't. If the vampire council knew of her connection to me, she wouldn't be safe. And safe was more important than my need to talk to her.

"You alright?" the redhead asked.

"Yep, just a little tired. I'm running on four hours of sleep," I replied.

"Well, that'll do it. You should nap after lunch."

"That's a great idea." I hoped Kellen would be busy with everything else and give me the opportunity. The red-head poured a generous amount of amber-colored whiskey into the pitcher and continued stirring.

He grinned and poured me a cup. "This will help."

I took a tentative sip, feeling it tingle all the way down my throat.

"Too much whiskey?" he asked.

"I don't think so," I replied, taking another swallow. "This is really good."

"Thanks."

Chef One crossed the narrow kitchen with an empty cup. "I've already been replaced as the official tester?"

Chef Two winked at me. "She's cuter than you."

"But does she know anything about mixing a drink?"

I smiled at their banter. It was a refreshing distraction from what I knew was coming.

"AJ can't have alcohol today, gentlemen," Kellen said, entering the kitchen from the garage.

"Is that so?" I asked, titling back my glass of whiskey goodness.

He leaned over the pitcher and smelled. "Definitely no more of that. How much alcohol did you put in there?"

"A little," the redhead replied.

"Come on, little girl. We have stuff to do." Kellen took my glass and finished my drink.

I frowned, my stomach growling. "But what about lunch?"

"Sandwiches are portable." He turned to Chef One. "She likes everything."

"Except mustard," I added. "No mustard for me."

Within moments, I followed Kellen down the hall, my sandwich wrapped in a paper towel. "What's so important that I can't eat in the kitchen?"

"Logan's meeting us in my room," Kellen said, his voice quiet.

"Oh." If they were risking Logan's presence, then it must be serious.

Kellen closed and locked the door, then marched across the small sitting area. I felt Logan racing across the desert towards us. I almost said something but held my tongue as Kellen opened the glass door leading to the desert. The vampire appeared moments later.

"Is this room secure?" Logan asked. "Can anyone hear us?"

Kellen's eyes widened, then he shook his head. "Follow me."

We went into the next room. A queen-sized bed and two night tables filled the opposite wall. A tall wardrobe and another door were to my right and a panel of windows to my left. A large writing desk took up the space beneath the high windows.

"What's wrong, Logan?" Kellen asked, standing in the middle of the room.

Logan glanced at me. "Her life is tied to mine," he whispered.

My partner's anger and possession washed over me as he took a step towards my vampire. "What do you mean?"

"If she dies, so do I," Logan replied.

"And if you die?" Kellen asked.

Logan nodded.

"What the hell?" Kellen hissed, his face contorted in anger. "How could you do this to her?"

"I didn't know," Logan said defensively, his voice rising.

"But you suspected. I can see it in your eyes."

"It was that or death, Kellen, and I couldn't let her die any more than you could! She's too important."

My partner turned his back on Logan and pulled out the chair at his desk. He dropped into the wooden seat, rubbing his temples. "Who else knows?"

"No one."

"Not even the one who explained this to you?"

"No."

An uneasy silence filled the room. I fidgeted with the paper towel wrapped around my sandwich; my appetite evaporated with Logan's news. How was this possible? Drinking a little of his blood shouldn't do that, should it?

"What does this mean going forward?" I asked. "Other than the obvious: avoid dying."

"I don't know," Kellen replied, his voice grating in the silence. The wall that had been growing between us since the incident at Victor's lodge grew again.

I looked at Logan, who avoided my gaze. "What else did your buddy say?"

"Nothing. Just don't die," he replied.

I could feel the deception. He was holding something back. I closed the space between us and looked into his hazel eyes. "Tell me."

He flinched, and I realized I commanded him without trying to.

"There is nothing to tell," he whispered, his gaze meeting mine and drawing me in.

Again, I knew he was lying. Was he lying to protect me or himself? Was there even a difference anymore? "Is there any way to undo this connection?"

"I haven't found that out yet," he replied. "That's my next stop."

"Don't you think you should stay with us?" Kellen asked, rising from his chair.

Logan's gaze flicked from Kellen back to me. "I can't."

"What if something happens to you? Her life will also be in danger," Kellen persisted. "There's safety in numbers."

"You think I don't know that?" Logan asked, his voice rising again as he turned towards my partner. "I need answers, and I won't get them by staying here."

Again, he lied. Guilt and anger flooded our connection, but I wasn't sure which emotion belonged to which man.

"I will not risk her life, but I can't stay here either," Logan said. He reached into his front pocket and pulled out an old-style flip phone. "Take this," he said, handing it to me. "In case something stupid happens. Mine and Kellen's numbers are already programmed in it."

I took the phone and looked up at him. "Why does this feel like goodbye?" I asked, a lump forming in my throat.

"It's not," he replied softly. "I'll be back with answers."

An overwhelming urge to hug him made me step forward, but he was gone. The bedroom door stood open, and a warm desert breeze fluttered through the patio door.

"What the hell was that?" I asked, tracking Logan across the desert until he faded in the distance.

"I'm going to do some of my own research," Kellen replied.

"Do you know what happened that night?"

"Only that he had to give you some of his blood to keep you alive." He moved past me into the sitting room, pushing the glass doors closed. "That in itself would not create a bond. There had to be more he isn't telling."

I knew Logan was hiding something. Could Kellen feel it through me? Why didn't Logan want to tell Kellen? They were friends and trusted allies in this mess. What could be so bad that he wouldn't share it?

"What creates that kind of bond?"

My partner remained silent, staring across the desert. His rigid posture and motionless stance kept me from approaching him.

"Kellen?"

"I only know rumors about vampire's magic, not facts. But I think I know someone who can tell me," he finally replied.

"Mr. Smith?"

"Yep."

"Do we really want him to know that Logan and I have this thing?" I asked. I knew I didn't want anyone else knowing; it would be so easy to use it against us. Logan wouldn't be that easy to kill, but I was an easy target.

"No, I don't trust him not to sell the information," Kellen replied, turning around to face me. I could see the questions in his eyes and feel them through our connection.

"No, Kellen. I don't remember what he did to me."

"He's been my friend for years. I've trusted him with everything dear to me." He crossed the space between us and ran his fingers through my hair. "I have to believe he wouldn't hurt you."

I leaned against his hand and let him draw me into his stiff embrace. "The alternative is pretty unpleasant."

Chapter 29

"Explain the plan again." I stared at a swirling portal, the one that was supposed to be broken. Everyone else was sleeping and assumed we were, too. I still didn't understand why we had to go tonight. What changed to make this so urgent? Even after the arrival of our guests, Kellen hadn't planned to make this visit for a few more days. The only change was my connection to Logan.

"As I said earlier, I would very much like to go in unannounced," he said. "The Magister hasn't always been unreasonable. It's possible we can talk to her, convince her to step down."

"Obviously, you know her better than I do," I said with a snort. "The woman I met will never back down."

He held his hand out to me, and I took it.

"What time is it at the Palace?" I asked.

"They're in the same time zone as us."

"Will anyone be awake?"

"Possibly, but very few. And I know how to get around the palace without being seen."

I looked down at my all-black ensemble. "Hence our dark clothes?"

"You got it."

"Let's get this over with." I took a breath and let him pull me through the portal.

I stumbled through the other side, but Kellen kept me from falling. We quickly side-stepped to the right into a nearby shadow. The open courtyard appeared empty. Faint moonlight filtered through the tree tops, and a cold breeze pulled against my long sleeve shirt. I shivered, and Kellen squeezed my fingers. I could barely see his outline in the shadows.

He pulled me along a stone wall to the right, moving slowly and methodically. He paused several times to point out stone benches and thorny shrubs. I tried to be quiet but knew I failed miserably. Luckily, we met no one on our trek to the palace doors.

Rather than go through the large wooden doors at the front, we entered a narrow corridor on the right side that ended at a metal gate. To my surprise, it wasn't locked. Kellen pushed it open, the metal whispering a moan. We darted through.

Wall-mounted lamps barely brightened the narrow hall in front us. Kellen led the way, passing by numerous doors. After several minutes, I noticed the floor sloped upwards in a long, winding spiral. I tried to picture the outside of the palace and where this might be, but I couldn't. My single visit didn't give me a good layout of the building.

I blindly followed my partner until the hallway ended at yet another door. He paused with his hand on the doorknob.

"This opens into a foyer in front of the Magister's chambers," he whispered. "There should be two guards posted at her door. I'll immobilize them, then we'll have a chat with the woman."

I nodded. It sounded like a good plan to me, but I wasn't a planner.

The door opened soundlessly, and Kellen peered into the next room. He grunted and pushed the door open, revealing an empty chamber.

"I thought there were supposed to be guards?" I whispered.

"Her room shouldn't be unprotected."

"So, where did they go?"

He shook his head and crossed the space. Two doors engulfed the other side. A large, gold circle crossed both doors. Symbols for the four elements stood out against the dark wood, evenly spaced inside the circle. A strange shape that reminded me of bells with wings or maybe intertwined, wispy clouds, centered the art. I stared at the wisps, trying to decide what they were, when the doors opened.

A tall, pale woman with long hair and icy blue eyes stood in the doorway. My mother. Instead of the fitted black dress she wore the last time I saw her, a deep, red fabric covered her body. It almost looked like a bathrobe, but not quite.

"It's rude to linger, Kellen," the Magister said. "Come in and chat. We have a great deal to discuss."

Something didn't feel right to me, and I was certain Kellen felt it too. Somehow, she knew we were coming.

"Don't make me ask again."

The Magister disappeared into the room, and I looked at my partner.

"We should leave," I said. "This feels like a trap."

"Or it's her unorthodox way of conceding. She hates to be wrong and will never admit it. Without the guards here to witness us, she can have an honest discussion without losing face."

"But how did she know we'd be here?" I asked. "We didn't even know."

"I don't know, but we won't get this chance again."

He started towards the open doors, and I shook my head, knowing this was a bad idea. Kellen was normally the smart, level-headed one. How did he not see the trap?

I followed him into the room, and my mouth dropped open. Dark pink wallpaper dotted with tiny white cherubs covered the walls. The Magister sat across the room in a narrow chair upholstered in purple striped fabric. A matching loveseat sat opposite her with a low table in between. Tall, slender windows covered in thick, ivory drapes framed the seating area.

My shoes squeaked across the glossy, white tiled floor, and a sneer formed on my face. I expected something more elegant and refined, not tiny cherubs and colors meant for five-year-old little girls. A bitter aroma hung in air like recently burned incense. I sat on the edge of the sofa and stifled a snort. It must have been fabric stretched over wood for all the comfort it provided.

"What brings my second-in-command back to the fold?" the Magister asked.

My head snapped to Kellen, not bothering to hide my surprise.

"I see my little girl has not been informed of your place here." The woman leaned back in her chair, drawing a deep breath. The rings around her eyes darkened, and I swallowed hard. "I brought Kellen into my care after his parents died. He and his sister needed someone to look after their affairs. His talents won him a place at my side."

I looked over at my partner who avoided my gaze, but he didn't look at my mother either. Another secret kept from me. How many more were there? This was something I really needed to know before we walked in here.

"He still refuses to look at me," she said, clicking her tongue. "He used to admire me a great deal."

"I used to trust and respect my leader," Kellen said between gritted teeth, "both of which you threw away."

"We didn't come here to talk about Kellen," I said, drawing another deep breath filled with the bitter stench I suspected came from my mother. Had she allowed herself to be turned into a vampire?

"And why did you come, *daughter*?" she spat out the last word, a snarl on her lips as her attention turned to me.

"Will you step down as Magister?"

The ring around her irises darkened again, confirming my suspicions. We walked into a trap, but I feared it wasn't one we'd survive. She wouldn't be the only vampire here, and the others would surely be the new mages-turned-vampires.

"Why would I do that?" she asked with disbelief. "The mages are in a place of power and control."

"Even I know a mage without her partner will become unstable," I replied. "I hoped you would prevent your people from seeing you that way."

"They will never see me that way, silly girl." She tilted her head back and laughed over-dramatically, her platinum hair billowing out behind her.

I glanced at Kellen, who still refused to look at her. He couldn't see her blue eyes changing to red. His stupid arrogance was going to get us killed. "Kellen, do you not see what she's doing?" I asked, forcing my anger and frustration towards him.

His sharp intake of breath fueled my rage. He finally looked at the damn woman. Fury flared through our connection, and he jumped to his feet, towering over her. It was about damn time.

"What have you done?" he demanded.

"What needed to be done," the Magister replied. "Single mages without partners can now be strong, without fear of losing themselves. I've given them a future, which is more than my parents ever did." A deep red now replaced her icy blues, and the tips of her fangs peeked out from her upper lip.

"No, you have ensured their death," Kellen replied. "How can you not see that? The vampires will throw them on the front line for cannon fodder. They will use our people to win their war, then throw us away so we aren't a threat."

The Magister stood as well, and I rose with her as she closed the space between herself and my partner.

"You have no vision," she hissed. "We will win the war for the vampires, and then destroy their council. I will lead them into the new dawn that will rise with us!"

I didn't have to feel Kellen's disgust. It was written all over his face in his narrowed eyes and curled lips. Unfortunately, I could understand my mother's reasoning. I didn't necessarily agree, but I understood.

"You're batshit crazy," I said, stepping closer to my partner. "The vampire venom enhanced your instability, making you stupid." I knew I was poking the bear. I just hoped she would react before her help arrived. We might be able to defeat one super vampire, but I wasn't sure about more than that. Despite my efforts, I still couldn't catch Logan. These people would be no different.

Before I could blink, her hands wrapped around my neck.

"Back off, Kellen, or I *will* kill her," she growled.

"Your death is guaranteed regardless," he said. "Release her, and I'll make it quick."

Did he just seal my death or hers? I wondered, clawing at the iron fingers around my neck.

"You'll be too busy fighting for your own life to worry about my precious daughter."

A myriad of smells assaulted my senses, and I cut my eyes to the side. Six people appeared in the open entry, all of them with red eyes. Pain and regret flared through my connection with Kellen. He must have known some or all of them. A line of fire raced across their path, preventing them from getting any farther into the room.

Niyol, I could really use your help right now. I struggled to draw air into my lungs as my mother's grip tightened. No amount of clawing on her arms would loosen it.

It would be my pleasure, he whispered back.

"Don't make me kill them," Kellen said in a low voice, unaware of my conversation with Niyol.

"You have to, or they'll return the favor."

A strong wind whipped through the room, consuming Kellen's line of fire and creating a fiery tornado. Kellen tackled the Magister, forcing all of us to the floor. Niyol rampaged through the other vampires, but even he wasn't quick enough to prevent them from charging into the room. Two of the six collapsed in a smoldering death, but the other four evaded it.

I jumped to my feet and whipped my hands into the air, tossing the men into the farthest wall just before they reached the fight between my mother and partner. Niyol picked up another of the mage-vampires in his fiery cyclone while I struggled to hold the last three against the wall. One of them stayed, but the other two broke free, heading back towards the Magister. A man with bleach-blond hair and blood-red eyes focused solely on me, and my resolve faltered. I couldn't release the monster on the wall, or I'd have all three within seconds. Proving my fear, blondie's strong fingers were suddenly gripping my bony arms, and his hot breath lingered on my neck.

"You smell delicious, little girl," he whispered in my ear.

I froze, remembering the last time one of them was this close to me. "Niyol," I whimpered, feeling my grasp on the other vampire weakening. I wasn't made to battle these things. Why was I here? My elemental spat out a charred husk, its body shattering the low table and loveseat beside me. Wind and fire separated from one another, taking on their humanoid forms. Fire pressed the farthest vampire back against the wall, and a piercing scream shattered what remained of my pitiful courage. I closed my tear-filled eyes as the vampire's fangs scraped across my skin. His grip on my arms suddenly vanished, and I stumbled forward. My eyes popped open, and I choked back a hysterical laugh. My attacker floated in a whirling tornado, his rage-filled eyes still directed at me. If looks could kill. Luckily, Niyol had saved me again. What would I do without him? Die a horrible death at the hands of every vampire who wanted to kill me, probably.

A low rumble shook the floor, and I turned to the opposite side of the room to find the Magister wrapped in a large stone hand. Kellen dangled inches off the ground with the last vampire's hands clawed around my partner's neck.

"No!" The harsh scream erupted from my throat, and I pulled my pointed spear from the heated air around me. Without thinking, I charged the vampire, sinking my weapon into his wide back. He howled, dropping Kellen to the floor. The vampire reached back over his shoulder and grabbed my wrist. I tumbled over his head and crashed to floor, my head smacking against the hard tiles. Pain exploded through my skull, and my vision clouded with bright flickering lights. I rolled to my stomach and forced myself to my hands and knees, struggling to keep the room from spinning around me.

My head snapped up as a large hand landed gently on my back. Kellen knelt in front of me with a haunted look. His fear subsided into relief, confusion, and wariness.

"Are you okay?" he asked, his voice as raw as his emotions.

"I think so," I replied.

He nodded and pushed himself to feet, then held his hand out to me. I let him pull me off my knees, and that's when I finally noticed the last vampire. My eyes widened. Ropes of fire circled his body, pinning his arms to the side as he lay on the white tiles. The smell of burning flesh brought bile to my throat. Niyol's tornado still contained blondie, and the Magister remained in the earth's tight grasp.

Had we really done it? Had we fought against all those vampires and won? Yes, but only because of our elements. I never would've done it on my own. Without Niyol and Kellen's fire, I'd be lying dead on the floor.

"You're a fool, Kellen. My new army will destroy everything you care for, starting with my daughter." The Magister's voice broke my revelry, and I turned to face her.

"Do you even hear yourself?" Kellen asked. "You wish for the death of your daughter, the one you gave life to."

My elation that came with our victory deflated with their words. I held my breath, hoping she would show some sign of remorse or compassion for me.

"If I don't kill her now, she will only kill me later," she hissed. "There cannot be two magisters, and I'll not take a back seat to *that* half-breed."

I should've known she'd let me suffocate. I didn't hold back my sadness, but I wouldn't let it consume me, either. Whatever happened to this woman, she was not my mother, and I was done grieving for her.

"You don't have to die today," Kellen argued. "Surrender, and we'll let you live."

A hollow laugh escaped her lips. “Yes, because life in prison is exactly what I want.”

“It’s better than death,” he said, his lips drawing into a thin line.

“What about the other two?” I asked, pointing at our elementals and the remaining vampires.

“They can join their Magister in a prison cell,” he replied. “I’ll be sure there’s plenty of sunlight to keep them company.”

Chapter 30

Kellen and the three elementals escorted their prisoners from the horrible, pink room. My legs gave out, and I slid to the ground, fighting back the tears threatening to spill down my face.

"She would've killed me with no remorse whatsoever," I whispered to the empty room. "What did I do to make her hate me like that?"

"You did nothing, child," Water's voice whispered to me. "I've already told you she is broken. The vampire's curse merely amplified her evil heart."

"I just wanted..."

I hugged my knees and cried, unable to voice the emotions raging through me. I didn't want to be Magister. I sucked at being responsible and dreaded the thought of having an entire community depending on me. Because of my ineptitude, I would expect Kellen to bail me out and make all the decisions I wasn't capable of making. My element wrapped its arms around my shoulders, flooding me with warmth and kindness, yet somehow keeping me dry.

"I can't do this."

"Yes, you can," Water said. "Remember you are not alone."

I looked up at its fluid form, its eyes shifting like tiny waves. "How?"

"The idea for a council is sound. Your great-grandfather had one that served him well." It shifted around in front me. "You will need to be the one to make the final decisions, but taking advice from others makes you strong. Your mother wanted full control and would listen to no one. In the beginning, she made good decisions, but the draw of power overtook her desire to serve her people."

"How will I know who to trust?" I asked, my thoughts immediately turning to Logan. "And what can I do about my connection to Logan?"

Water's form shimmered, and I thought it would leave. It slid across the room, stopping in front of the windows. It stood there, its translucent form shifting back and forth methodically.

"I'm undecided about the one who is dead to me," it said. "It appears you can benefit from the connection. Your ability to see people's intentions will grow as your bond to him grows. This will help you know who to trust, but it comes at a price."

I swallowed hard, unsure if I wanted to know the price. Who was I kidding? Not knowing would kill me.

"Tell me, please."

It glided back to my side and lowered itself so we were eye-to-eye. "I cannot tell you," it said. "He has taken that memory from you. If he chooses to give it back, you will have your answer."

"You know what he did to me, don't you? You and Niyol are both keeping it from me." My fragile heart felt like it might snap in two. How could they do that to me?

"There is no benefit in telling you," it replied. "I fear it will create a rift that cannot be healed."

"Not telling her will also create a rift." Niyol appeared next me, nearly blowing me over.

"We've already discussed this, brother," Water said, rising in one fluid motion.

"Yes, and I think your caution will be her undoing. Kellen's actions towards her are insincere." Niyol's flickering eyes glanced down at me. "While I share your distaste for the dead one, his concern for the princess is genuine."

I raised my eyebrows. "What do you mean Kellen's actions are insincere?"

"Kellen's motives are to protect the mages," Water argued, ignoring my question. "He will do what is necessary to restore their balance, but he will not hurt our princess."

"You are blinded by your hatred for the Magister," Niyol hissed, stepping in front of Water.

"I have good reason to hate her. She destroyed him, ripping him from me with total disregard for the damage it would do to us both."

I remained motionless on the floor, entranced by the revelations playing out before me. Was my water elemental once connected to Logan? Did Kellen really care more about his mission to oust my mother than he did about me? The wind picked up around me as Niyol put distance between himself and Water.

"We should be protecting our princess and ensuring her place of power, not allowing some imposter to take her place," he said.

"He also carries royal blood, you fool," Water hissed. "His passion is for his people, which will ensure Alisandra's future."

The air around me grew heavy, and small droplets of water pelted my skin.

"Stop." I stood, and both elements turned to me. "Both of your arguments make sense. I understand the importance of removing my mother, especially now. While I lack the skills to lead anyone, I'll try to be what is needed to keep our people safe." I looked at my water element. "I have to trust your decision to connect me and Kellen. You..." I waved my hands at both of them. "You're the ones who said he and I had to be together to do this. As a matter of fact, I remember you saying he could not do it without me."

"No, our stone brother said he *would* do it without you," Water corrected. "Even Kellen knew he could not. These mages will not accept a foreign family to rule them. It must be you, or a council with you leading it."

"Wait." I shook my head as its words sank in. "So, you guys weren't in agreement about our partnership?"

Niyol and Water looked at one another. How were they not in agreement?

"No," Niyol replied. "Kellen's fire was completely against it."

I remembered the raging battle between the two. "Which is why you fought the way you did."

"He surrendered only because of Water's intervention," Niyol confirmed.

My thoughts whirled once again. All this time I trusted their decision, but they lied to me, too. Was there no one I could trust? "Why? Why did he not want us together?" I asked. "Don't give me some bullshit answer. I want the truth!"

Niyol sighed dramatically, stirring the curtains across the room. "His fire, and to some extent, earth, believe Kellen does not need you. He refused to accept that the mages need the stability of your family, not an outsider."

As much as I didn't want it to, Fire's argument made sense. Kellen was a much better leader than me, but I could see the people here protesting, regardless of Kellen's dedication to them.

"And what about Logan and this bond? How does that change my standing with the mages? And don't tell me it doesn't," I asked.

"We need more time to find out," Niyol replied. "I will continue to press my brothers for information."

"As I said before, I think you should use your connection to him to determine the loyalty of those around you," Water added.

"But how could I possibly trust someone who deliberately lies to me and steals my memory?" I asked.

"Because you can tell when he's lying," Water replied. I thought I heard it chuckle. "Don't be afraid to confront him in a lie, child. I don't believe he can hurt you, no matter how angry you make him."

"Because of our life bond?"

"Exactly."

I rolled back on my butt and folded my legs in front of me, thinking about what I'd just learned. So much had just been revealed to me. Why couldn't they tell me all this sooner?

"Are you two done fighting?"

"We were not fighting," Niyol said. "We were merely voicing differences of opinion."

"Oh, sure. It sounded like a fight to me," I said, rolling my eyes. "Thank you for sharing with me. I feel like everything is happening around me, and I have no control over any of it. Yet, I'm supposed to be the glue in this great big puzzle."

The two elements looked at each other, then turned to me.

"We are dedicated to you first and foremost, but every decision we make must be for the good of your world," Water replied. "We cannot exist, our world cannot exist, if we are not balanced."

"I guess that makes sense." My gaze flicked between the two of them, grateful for their presence.

"Be careful, princess, and call if you need me," Niyol said.

"Don't wait for me to call, Niyol. I may not be in a position to chat the next time I need you."

His translucent form shifted slightly as he knelt closer to me. "I have to have your blessing to act against another," he said. "I cannot strike out against a human without it."

"You have my blessing to save my ass anytime," I replied.

His wispy chuckle ruffled my hair. "Thank you, princess. That will make my job much easier." He turned to Water. "I'll be spying on our brothers if you need me." He disappeared, leaving behind a pile of dust.

"Can I know your name?" I asked, looking up at the flowing form in front of me.

"I am Göksu," he replied, sinking to the floor so he was eye level with me.

"That's cool. Göksu..." I repeated. "What does it mean?"

"Ah, humans and your need to have meaning." It chuckled fully this time, its body wavering with the movement. "I prefer the Turkish language that interprets it as sky and water."

"I like it. So, were you responsible for the thunderstorm during my confrontation with Victor?"

"No, that was Niyol's doing. Well, mostly. The rain was mine, but you asked for my healing waters."

"I think I asked for the thunder and lightning, too, on a subconscious level. Victor is really irritating."

"He has endured much since the passing of your grandfather," Göksu replied.

I frowned, picturing Victor's arrogant stance and chocolate eyes. "Have the shifters always been our allies, or was he lying about that?"

"He spoke the truth. They have been your protectors for centuries. They understand and share our connection to the earth." Göksu's form shifted again, and its face turned to the door. "Your bonded-one nears." It disintegrated into thousands of tiny droplets and disappeared.

I sighed. It felt good to talk to them. They brought clarity to so many things, except for Kellen's motives. Were his feelings for me genuine? Niyol implied they weren't, and Göksu didn't correct his assessment. Even if I asked my partner, would he be honest with me?

A shiver ran through my body, and I felt Logan's presence very close. I thought Göksu meant Kellen, but apparently not. How did Logan get here? How did any of the vampires get here? Obviously, the portals were not the only way.

I jumped to my feet and ran from the room, following my connection to him. Unfortunately for me, he ran faster than I did. We collided at the bottom of the stairs. Rather than stopping to make sure I was okay after running face-first into his solid chest, he quickly picked me up and raced back to the Magister's rooms. He passed through the awful pink sitting room and into her bedroom. He closed the door and locked it, then pushed a chair in front of it, bracing the edge under the door handle.

"What the hell, Logan?" I asked, feeling his panic.

He closed the space between us and looked down at me. His hazel eyes stared, and I struggled to follow his whirling emotions. "I cannot undo the bond between us, not without killing us both," he whispered.

"I sort of assumed that," I said. "That doesn't explain the panic I feel from you."

He glanced at the door, then back to me. "I need to tell you something..." He bit his bottom lip and sighed. His shoulders slumped, and my hands trembled. He was going to reveal what he did to me. I could see it in his eyes. "Kellen will discover how the bond was created. I would prefer you find out from me. That's not true. I'd prefer you didn't know at all, but that isn't a choice."

He knelt in front of me and a lump formed in my throat. He was sad and angry, but most of all guilt-ridden.

"What happened?" I asked.

He took a deep breath and the corners of his lips turned up. "You smell like jasmine, in case you were wondering." The smile disappeared. "I need to give you the memory of that night. My words will not explain what happened."

~~~~~~~~~~~~~~~~

I sat in the middle of the floor, hugging my knees, unable to see past the scenes still floating in my vision. Logan gave me my memories back, kissed my forehead, and left. He just disappeared, leaving me alone to deal with the shock of what happened between us. He promised he would never leave me, but he had. Again.
~~~~~~~~~~~~~~~~

A trembling sigh escaped my lips. It explained so much. No wonder I felt so comfortable around him. It never made sense to me how I could so easily abandon my fear of him. I assumed it was because of his impeccable listening skills and willingness to answer questions that Kellen avoided. It wasn't that at all. Okay, maybe some of that. My opinions and concerns mattered to him. He didn't belittle me because of my ignorance or lack of understanding. He never answered my question with, 'Because that's how it is.' And he knew what it felt like to be abandoned and unwanted.

But it also created more uncertainty. Kellen was supposed to be my partner, the one I turned to for my strength and understanding of our magic. So why was Logan in charge of my combat training and not Kellen? My partner should've been teaching me how to fight with him. Wasn't that the whole point? Didn't he say we were stronger together? We hadn't even tried to practice anything that involved our elements working together. Maybe we didn't need to, though. Niyol seemed to know exactly what to do with Kellen's fire.

My thoughts moved to my conversation with Göksu. Could I trust my element to lead me in the right direction? He said I could use Logan's connection, but there would be a price. Was Kellen the cost of embracing my bond with the vampire?

My body shook at the thought of losing Kellen. Nope, there was no way I could give that up… or could I? Kellen had always been so supportive, but he'd changed after that night at the shifters' lodge, the wall between us becoming more substantial every day. I didn't think I could ignore the pull of my heart towards Logan, either. And how in the world would I tell Kellen what happened? Logan was right; my partner would find someone to explain the bonding. Would it be better to spill the beans now, before he found out on his own? I knew that answer. Kellen needed to hear it from us.

The phone in my pocket buzzed, scaring me. I pulled it out and flipped it open. Logan's name flashed on the small screen with a message.

Logan: I'm sorry

Me: whatever

Logan: I couldnt be caught in the palace. we'll talk at kellens soon

Me: whatever

I flipped the phone closed and stuffed it back in my pocket. It buzzed again, and I ignored it, wrapping my arms around my knees once again. I couldn't think of any way to tell my partner I'd had sex with his friend and thoroughly enjoyed it. What the hell was happening to me? I longed to go back to my tiny, one-room apartment and hide from the world.

The door to the Magister's room opened with a scrape against the white tiles. Kellen's head poked through the gap, and my lip quivered. Why did I feel so guilty if Kellen didn't even care about me that way? Niyol and Göksu had confirmed that much.

He hurried into the room, and the tears flooded down my face.

"I'm so sorry, AJ. I shouldn't have left you alone."

He reached down and scooped me up. I buried my face in his chest, but I knew he felt my guilt. How could he not?

"Are you hurt?" he asked, carrying me through the pink room and down the dimly lit hallway.

I shook my head, unable to speak past the lump in my throat. Another door opened, and the room we entered smelled faintly of Kellen. He sat me down on a soft chair and pulled the one across from me closer.

"The hardest part is over," he said quietly.

I took a deep breath. He thought I was upset about my mother. Maybe I had too many emotions to sort through, even for a bonded partner.

"That was likely the easy part," I whispered, staring at my hands in my lap. "I have no idea how to take her place."

"Those plans have been in the works for almost two years," he said. "You won't be alone."

"Can we go back to the estate?"

"Now?"

I nodded. I couldn't stay here, but I wasn't sure I could stay at Kellen's either. Logan wouldn't be there right now, not with a pile of mages sleeping in his room.

"We snuck out, remember. The others will be expecting us for breakfast in a few hours."

He frowned and nodded. "You're right. I'd forgotten about that."

"Are they secured?" I asked, knowing he would understand I meant my mother and the other two vampires.

"Yes. I found several people loyal to me who are willing to make sure they don't escape," he replied.

I didn't miss the 'loyal to me.' Not loyal to AJ, loyal to Kellen. His brown eyes stared back at me with compassion and understanding. How could I doubt him? He'd been nothing but supportive to me. Then again, he would be. He needed me to overthrow the Magister, after all.

I squeezed my eyes shut for a moment and rubbed my temples, then pushed myself to my feet.

"We should go," I said, attempting a smile. I had too much to figure out, and staying in the palace wasn't going to help.

Chapter 31

Morning came too quickly. Despite my lack of sleep the night before and only four hours just now, I lay awake, staring at the ceiling. Exhaustion took me when we arrived back at the estate, but now my mind felt like it had enough rest to jump back into overdrive. I heard Kellen leave the room a few minutes before, despite his efforts to be quiet.

I pushed the covers back and rolled out of bed, stumbling to Kellen's bathroom. The mirror lied to me about my appearance. No one could look as tired as the person staring back at me. Deep circles hung beneath my blood-shot eyes, and no amount of cold water was going to fix it.

I brushed my teeth, changed my clothes, and prepared to face the million and one questions I knew were coming. Maybe I could stay in bed and let Kellen do it. The thought faded as quickly as it surfaced. I already had guilt over Logan. I didn't need to add selfish laziness to the list.

I opened the door to Kellen's room and nearly ran into Kate. Her glare turned into concern.

"You look like shit, girl."

"Thanks, I feel even worse." I tried to go around her, but she pushed me back into the room and handed me a cup of coffee. A small smile crept across my face. "Thank you."

"I need information," she said. "Bribery is a thing. So, tell me Kellen's lying. Did you really sneak into the palace last night?"

"Nope, and yep." I took a sip of coffee and closed my eyes. It was hot and strong, just what I needed.

"Holy shit. Is she really a vampire?"

"Yep."

"Can I get more than that?"

I heard the exasperation in her voice and relented. "She and two others are imprisoned at the palace. I suppose we'll need to go back and make an announcement." I took another sip of coffee. "Can we get breakfast now?"

"I can't believe you're acting so calm about this," she exclaimed. "We've worked so hard to get to this point."

I lowered my cup and eyed her suspiciously. Kellen said he'd kept most of his traitorous activities from her. "I wasn't very calm when we got home this morning," I said. "I think I'm too tired right now to provide an appropriate reaction."

I skirted around her and made my way to the kitchen. What was wrong with me? Was it just exhaustion causing me to doubt the people who saved me? Or would the vampires have done the same when they discovered who I was? I guess the real question was did I want the vampires as allies or the mages? I didn't think my elements would have approved of the vampires, which answered that question.

I shook my head, trying to clear my thoughts as loud, agitated voices drifted towards me through the open door to the kitchen. I sighed. Maybe I would let Kellen deal with it.

Silence filled the room as I entered and ten sets of eyes landed on me. Wonderful. Just when I looked my best. I made a beeline for the coffee pot and ignored their stares.

"Good morning, Magister," Raul said.

I turned around and glared at him, unsure why the moniker made me angry. Maybe because it was my mother's.

"There will no longer be a magister," I said. "The previous one has ruined that title, and all who hear it will only remember the harm she did to her people. You're in my spot."

Raul slid from my favorite barstool with a smile. How did he find that amusing? I wasn't trying to be amusing.

"So, what do we have the pleasure of calling you?" Sammy asked.

"AJ," I replied, sipping my coffee.

"We need time to discuss the details," Kellen intervened. "In the meantime, you guys need to get back to the palace and make sure there aren't any more vampires lurking about."

"Can you tell if someone's a vampire?" I asked, looking over my cup at Kellen. "I mean, I can't unless their eyes happen to turn red or they show their fangs." I was certain my partner recognized the lie, but the others couldn't know of my connection to Logan.

"Most of the time," Raul replied. "They move really quick, even when they try not to. They also give off a weird vibe."

"But the ones at the palace will likely be former mages and people you know," I countered.

A soft mumbling surrounded me. No one wanted to suspect their friends.

"We'll be right behind you," Kellen added. "We need to announce the Magister's capture and her new status as a vampire."

The others drifted from the room, leaving my partner and I alone. I looked at the coffee cooling in my cup. I hated that I was so grumpy when there was so much to do.

"Do you think you could sleep for a few more hours before we go?" he asked.

"No, I tried to stay in bed, but it didn't work out so well."

"I tried to keep Kate from bugging you." He didn't hide the apology in his voice or the annoyance.

"I was already up and dressed when she showed up." I took another sip of coffee.

Kellen leaned on the counter, bringing his face within inches of mine. "Tell me what's wrong," he said. "I can feel the turmoil rumbling through you."

I wanted to tell him everything, but I settled on the most immediate. "Our next step will set the stage for the future of your people," I said. "It has to be the right step. I feel like you've already got a plan outlining my future, and I don't know what it is." I tried to hide my resentment about not knowing the plan, but failed.

"My plan is to create a council to rule the mages," he said. "It would be best if you are at the helm, but it isn't something I'll force on you."

"And if I decide to let the council rule, what happens to me?" I asked. Even through my fatigue, I could feel the ambition Kellen was trying to suppress. Now that his plot was complete, what would happen to me?

"Whatever you want," he replied. "The important thing was to remove your mother. I believe your destiny is to take her place, but that decision is yours."

"And one I have to make today." I snarled, trying to suppress my grumpy.

"Not necessarily." He slid around the counter and sat in the stool next to me. "For stability sake, you can accept the role as leader, call it whatever you like, then hand it over to the council when you're satisfied with their ability to take over."

I raised my eyebrows at him. "You know how ridiculous that sounds, right? I have no authority to determine whether or not they're doing it right."

"You may not think so, but we need to convince everyone else otherwise."

"Leaders aren't born, Kellen, they're made. And I've spent my entire life in poverty looking after no one but myself."

"I believe you can do this," he said, his look of sincerity almost making me believe him if it weren't for the other emotions pushing through our bond.

"Let's convene a council." I gulped down the rest of my coffee and left him in the kitchen. Would he really let me just walk away? Shouldn't he be fighting to keep me with him, as his partner if nothing else? Or did he really not care now that my mother was out of the picture?

~~~~~~~~~~~~~~~~~~~~

Two hours later, I sat at the head of a table large enough to accommodate twenty people. Only twelve filled the stiff-backed chairs. Portraits of previous rulers lined the stucco walls. The empty frame where my mother's had been glared at me.

Kellen sat to my immediate left, while an old man sat on my right. My partner had already introduced everyone, but my foggy brain didn't retain anyone's name. The group consisted of six men and six women, including Kellen. My attendance would break an even vote according to the council rules that had already been established. Again, my thoughts wandered to my predetermined future.

Everyone looked at me expectantly. Had someone asked a question? Kellen must have noticed my dazed expression.

"The Magister is being held in confinement along with two of the mages-turned-vampires." He looked at me for confirmation he didn't need. I nodded, and he continued. "They will have the trial that is afforded all mages."

"But they are no longer mages, if what you say is true," the older man on my left said in a low, gravelly voice.
~~~~~~~~~~~~~~~~~~~~

"No, but we would be no better if we just executed them," I said. "We cannot start a new council under less than ethical circumstances."

They all stared at me with wide eyes, as if seeing me for the first time.

"I believe my dislike for her is equal to your own," I continued. "But I won't see our new leadership fall into the same power-hungry selfishness that ruined my mother."

"Yes, Magister," the older man said, dropping his eyes to the table.

Had I commanded them? I didn't think so.

"There is no longer a Magister. The mages of North America will be ruled by this council." I looked at each of them. "I believe my mother has proven that singular rule in the wrong hands doesn't work, not that we didn't already learn that in history class." Their sullen silence continued. "This council will be responsible for making the best decisions for our people. Hopefully, twelve heads are better than one."

"What will the people call you, if not magister?" a heavy woman at the end of the table asked.

"AJ..." I paused. "Alisandra is my name and all that is necessary. If the council members wish to create official titles for themselves, I have no objections."

Several members nodded their heads in agreement.

"When will we have the Magister's trial?" the same woman asked.

I turned to Kellen.

"As soon as possible. I'd rather not keep the vampires any longer than necessary," he replied.

"Are there more among us?" a young man with blond hair and green eyes asked from the left side of the table. "How do we know who's been turned?"

"We have a plan in place to identify any remaining vampires," my partner replied. "The scanning process will begin as soon as we finish here. Any more questions?"

"When is our next meeting?" the older man asked.

"We should meet once a week until everything is settled," Kellen responded and looked around the table. "If there's nothing else, let's introduce our new council to the people."

When no one moved, I rose from my chair. They immediately did the same and filed towards the door.

"Can I eat before we do this?" I asked my partner. "I assume I'm your plan for sniffing them out."

"I'll definitely feed you first," he replied with a nod.

He led me to a small dining room and directed a middle-aged woman to feed me. "I'm going to coordinate our meeting. See you in half an hour."

He kissed my forehead and quickly walked away. I felt the distance between us growing by the minute. The wall I tried to ignore reared its ugly head again. I needed to decide if I cared who ran the council. Kellen was definitely more qualified and actually wanted it. I was just a tool, a way for him to get what he wanted. I really needed to set aside my exhaustion and think with a level head.

Chapter 32

Hundreds of people pushed their way into the crowded hall as I stifled a yawn. Their low murmuring vibrated with anticipation as the council filed onto the raised platform in the front of the room. My nose wrinkled at the smell of body odor, perfumes, colognes, wide varieties of foods, and shampoos. There was no way to tell who was human and who wasn't; I would've had to meet them all individually.

Kellen called for order, and the crowd settled. "I'm sure the rumor mill has circulated rapidly, so let's get the important one out of the way first," he began. "Your Magister has given herself to the vampire's curse."

Voices rose in astonishment, and he raised his hands.

"As such, she is no longer our Magister. Even before her fall into darkness, she secluded us from our allies and painted a target on our backs. For those who didn't know, our allies in Reno were attacked by vampires just over two weeks ago. The Magister was not there to aid in their defense. As a result, they lost eight members of their pack, with dozens more injured. If the Magister's daughter had not been at Victor's lodge, the shifters would have seen defeat. Alisandra and her wind elemental forced the vampires' retreat and ensured our victory."

The crowd reacted with shouts of approval, and Kellen's satisfaction drifted through our bond. He was a good liar and an even better speaker.

"Alisandra and I spent that time evading the Magister's bounty hunters and discussing a way to free us from her clutches. Not just the mages, but our circle of allies created long ago, a circle that was broken by our fallen queen." He paused as the throng of people leaned forward in anticipation. "We will embrace our past while creating a new future, one that promises inclusion, hope, and prosperity."

Cheers filled the hall, but I noticed more than a few looks of doubt.

"You're not here to listen to me," he yelled over the gathering. They quieted, and he turned to me with a smile. "I humbly introduce Alisandra Rosewynn."

Cheers erupted as I stood and smiled, clasping my shaking hands behind my back. Kellen and I had already discussed my very short speech, but the words left my mind as I looked out at hundreds of faces. My partner came to my rescue once again, tracing his hand down my back and intertwining his fingers in mine. He gently squeezed my hand, and some of my tension released.

"Thank you. These first few weeks will be challenging for me, but thankfully I won't be alone. I believe it's best to have the voice of many making our decisions, rather than the voice of one." Silence greeted me, and I swallowed hard. "Many of you have suffered because of the decisions made by my mother. She allowed no one to interfere with her plans, nor did she listen to anyone else's advice or council. All of these things led to the abduction and loss of dozens of our mages. We can't allow that to happen again."

Murmurs of agreement drifted across the large, open space, but I didn't wait for their voices to rise.

"From this point forward, we'll be governed by a council of our peers. They'll vote on the decisions that need to be made. We'll establish time in service requirements and hold elections for new council members based on those time limitations."

Cheers rose from the congregation of mages, cutting off the end of my speech. I smiled and tried not to fall into my chair. Kellen released my hand and quieted the crowd, then fielded the numerous questions that followed.

Even as Kellen answered the crowd's questions, I failed to listen. Logan was down there somewhere, but even searching the sea of faces, I didn't see his. Were there other vampires present? How many knew how to infiltrate the palace? Why didn't Logan tell me he could get in? He was obviously no stranger here. Kellen's hand on my shoulder brought my attention back to our meeting.

"It's time to go," he whispered.

"I'm sorry," I said, rising from my chair. "I'm so tired."

"It's okay. We're almost done."

I shuffled my way across the platform, following Kellen's lead. I tripped on the edge of a step I didn't see and stumbled, falling on my hands and knees. My face flushed as I pushed myself to my feet, wiping my hands on my pants. They left a fine, gray dust across my jeans, and I mumbled several curses trying to wipe it back off.

"What the hell?" I whispered, curling my lip.

A trail of dusty footprints lined the steps and disappeared through the doorway Kellen just entered. I huffed and jogged to catch up with him.

He and two other men stood just inside the door, having a heated conversation.

"What do you mean they're gone?" Kellen asked.

"I believe someone killed the two men and helped the Magister escape," said a tall man with short hair and a thick beard. "We found what looks like the remains of the two vampires in their cells, but the Magister's is empty."

Had I heard them correctly? Someone killed the vampires and released the Magister?

"Were the cells open or the locks tampered with?" Kellen asked.

"No." The man's eyebrows narrowed, his face darkening. "Are you suggesting one of us let her out, Kellen?"

"No, I trust the two of you more than anyone else here," he replied. "I'm just trying to understand how she escaped."

I felt the lie in his voice. Did he not trust them, or did he already know what happened? I searched for my connection with Logan. He was still here in the palace and not very far away. Was Logan responsible for releasing her? Were they sneaking away as we spoke?

I poked Kellen's elbow, and he looked down at me with surprise, almost as if he'd forgotten I was there.

"You need to get some sleep," he said, his face softening. "David can take you to my room if you like or back to the portal, whichever you prefer."

"I'd rather sleep in my own bed."

He nodded at the tall, bearded man who I assumed was David. My escort looked at me with a smile reserved for a child. Next to him, I probably looked like one. I followed him back to the portal.

"I've got it from here," I said. "I'll learn my way around soon. Promise."

"I'll escort you anytime." He gave me a shallow bow and left me staring at the familiar swirling fog that would take me home.

Spearmint assaulted my nostrils, and Logan crashed into me, dragging me through the portal. The world lurched painfully and we fell in a tangle of limbs.

"I thought you couldn't use the portal!" I yelled when we landed on the other side.

"Be silent," he whispered, standing perfectly still and holding me tight.

Tension and fear radiated off him. What could he possibly be afraid of?

"What are you doing?" I snapped.

"Trying to save your life, princess," he replied. "I believe the house is empty, but we need to hurry."

"What are you talking about?" I asked again as he pulled me down the hall and into Kellen's room. He locked the doors to both the hallway and the garden, then went into the bedroom. Why all the fear and caution? He knew what happened to the Magister. That had to be it.

"You need to tell me something, Logan. You're scaring the shit outta me."

"Get in here," he called from the other room.

I reluctantly obeyed, and he locked the door as soon as I entered.

"Are your things still packed in your trunk?" he asked, disappearing from my side and reappearing next to our boxes on the opposite side of the room.

"Yeah, why? What's going on?"

He pushed the lid on both and started throwing my things into his. "Kellen killed the vampires in their cells—all of them. He buried the Magister's ashes in the stone floor so it would look like she escaped."

"That's ridiculous," I hissed. "This is Kellen you're talking about. You know, your best friend, my partner." I refused to believe it, but my mind drifted back to the trail of fine dust I'd fallen into. Was that the remains of a vampire? I looked at my hands and bile rose in my throat. I rushed to Kellen's private bathroom.

"Do you have any other clothes besides the ones you're wearing?" he called to me.

"Why does it matter? I'm not leaving. I'm exhausted and going to bed." I turned on the water and scrubbed my hands with more soap than was necessary.

"You have to leave," he said, appearing in front of me. "If my information is correct, you're next." His eyes softened. "I can't let that happen."

"Because my life is tied to yours." I immediately felt guilty for the comment, no matter how true it was. Self-preservation was important.

He laughed, and I glared at him. None of this was funny.

"Come on, we're leaving." He reached for my arm, but I stepped back avoiding him.

"I don't understand why. Kellen won't hurt me. I'm pretty certain he cares for me."

Logan's smile vanished. "Does he *care* for you, or does he *need* you?"

I thought about his question. Couldn't it be both? A dull thud startled me. Three more followed in quick succession, then muffled voices came from the sitting room. Logan quietly closed the lid on his trunk and grabbed the handle with one hand.

"Check the closets while I look in here," a man's voice said from the other side of the door. The handle shook. "Over here!" he yelled.

"We have to go, princess," Logan whispered in my ear. "They aren't here to chat."

Fear and confusion froze me in place. Who were they, and why were they here? It wasn't David's voice.

"Just bust it down," another male voice said. "I want to be back before dinner."

"This doesn't feel right. It's like we're doing the Magister, man."

"Yeah, whatever." The door shuddered, and its frame splintered against the impact.

Logan's arm wrapped around my waist again. "Sleep, princess, and let me save you."

"No," I mumbled. "We aren't doing this again."

My eyelids drooped, and I felt him toss me over his shoulder. Sleep took me as the desert rolled by in a sandy blur.

Chapter 33

I woke to complete darkness and immediately panicked, kicking away the heavy quilt covering me. I sat up, blinking several times, but nothing changed. Cold air surrounded my body, and I shivered. Where the hell was I?

"Don't panic. Take a deep breath and stay calm," I told myself.

I remembered my phone and pulled it from my pocket, flipping it open. The faint blue light from the screen lit up a small space around me but did nothing to tell me where I was. I held it out at arm's length and waved it around. The quilt laid at my feet in a pile. I ran my hand over the covered mattress. It was still warm and smelled like spearmint.

"Dammit, Logan. You could've left a light on," I muttered. The bastard put me to sleep again. If he stole my memory, I was going to be really pissed. Would I even know if he did? I would ask and make him lie to me.

I dropped my bare feet over the bed and landed on soft carpeting. I creeped across the room, waving my phone in front of me, trying to locate a wall. Who put the bed in the middle of the room?

"At least he left my clothes on," I mumbled, immediately regretting the thought as my memory took me back to Victor's house several weeks earlier.

I took a few more steps before finding the wall. I followed it to a door and pushed it open. Low lights from a hallway spilled into the room, only illuminating the first few feet. I continued my trek along the wall until I found a light switch.

The sudden brightness forced my eyes closed. I leaned against the wall until I could open them with relative comfort. As I suspected, the bed *was* in the middle of the room, but I understood why. Bookshelves lined three of the four walls, and they were all filled with books.

I stared in amazement and disbelief. Did Logan live here, or were we borrowing someone else's house? I reached for my connection and found him easily. Two doors occupied the wall I leaned against: one to my left opening into the hall and one to my right leading to Logan.

I pressed my ear against the wooden door and heard a shower running. "Not going there."

I padded to the nearest book shelf, stuffing my phone back in my pocket. My fingers trailed the spines of dozens of books as I read their titles. He had everything from history to romance. Surely this was someone else's house; Logan never struck me as the intellectual type.

"Did you find what you're looking for?" he asked, surprising me.

He stood next to me in a pair of shorts. Water dripped down his bare chest from his wet hair. I scowled at him and opened my mouth to reply, but his lips met mine and stifled my response. Against my better judgement, I kissed him back, threading my fingers into his hair. Memories of our night together flooded my mind, not just the lust and passion, but the oneness we shared. He understood my fear of rejection, my need to be loved and accepted, and he willingly gave me all those things. He responded immediately, picking me up and carrying me back to bed. I wanted every part of him, but I also wanted answers.

"No, you don't," I said, scooting away from him. "We have stuff to talk about. I won't be distracted so easily."

"We can talk later," he said, crawling across the bed towards me in full predator mode. I could feel his fierce desire, laced with anger and resentment. "No one knows where we are. We have plenty of time to discuss whatever you want. I've suppressed my feelings for you because of a man who only wanted one thing."

I reached the other side of the bed and stopped. He hovered over me, his black hair hanging around his face. "He used both of us to remove the Magister," he said.

I placed one hand against his bare chest, my heart pounding against my ribs. I couldn't tell if it was fear or lust; maybe it was both. "You both used me to get what you wanted," I whispered. "I've been lied to, manipulated, and seduced all to overthrow the Magister."

He rolled onto his back next to me with a huff. "I thought I knew his motives," he said. "I trusted him to restore the mages' place of power."

"Isn't that what he did?" I asked, glancing over at his profile.

"Yes, but he wasn't supposed to hurt you."

"Were those his people at the house looking for me?"

He nodded. "Their only reason to be there was to silence you. Kellen had already told you to get some rest. He knew where you'd be."

"But why did he need me silent?" I asked. "I would've stayed by his side and help him lead." I bit my lower lip, contemplating my words. "Is he like my mother, looking for power of his own? No, that isn't right. He wouldn't have suggested a ruling council if he intended to keep everything for himself. Besides, that's not the Kellen I know."

Logan rolled onto his side to face me. "How long have you known him?"

"Whatever. It's only been a month, but he's my partner. I can feel his emotion."

Logan raised an eyebrow at me and frowned. "Can you? Or do you feel what he wants you to feel?"

I looked away from him, thinking about my conversations with Kellen. When I first felt the connection between us, he was able to suppress his feelings. Did I catch him off guard that one time, and he hid them ever since? I didn't think so, but I had no way of truly knowing.

"He told me he couldn't live without me," I replied. "I felt his hopelessness and sense of loss when he thought that vampire's bite would kill me."

"Was it a sense of loss for you or his cause? He's been planning this ever since his parents' death. Your arrival merely shortened his timeline."

"I thought I knew, but you've planted these seeds of doubt. He saved me, Logan." I rolled off the bed, glaring at him. "He saved me from a lifetime of living in that veil or dying because of my binding. He saved me from the wolves and vampires, and even my own mother. How I can doubt his loyalty? How do I know you aren't lying to me?"

He propped himself on his elbow and returned my stare. "You already know that answer."

"How can I possibly know that?" I braced my hands on my hips, scowling.

"Because I hate you with every part of my being and would kill you myself to see you die with me."

Pain surged through my connection with him, and tears stung my eyes. I fell to my knees on the floor and cradled my head in my hands. The lie was so blatant it physically hurt.

"That doesn't explain why he would want me dead," I whispered.

"Because of me." Logan was at my side within seconds, his fingers tracing my spine. "His partner cannot be bound to a vampire. How would their new council react to that? The people would abandon him, and his world would return to chaos."

My argument died on my lips. Regardless of Logan's loyalty and sacrifice, the mages would never see him as anything more than a vampire.

"What do we do now?" I asked.

"I need your phone."

"Why?"

I pulled it from my pocket and handed it to him. He flipped it open and pushed several buttons, then crushed it in his palm. "I don't think he can track a phone I gave you, but I need to be sure."

I stared at him. "You suspected him when you gave me that phone, didn't you?"

"I knew something wasn't right, I just couldn't put my finger on it."

"Tell me," I commanded, not feeling bad about it. I wanted to know what I missed, *how* I missed so much.

He rose to his feet and held out his hand. I looked at his long fingers and sighed. I'd been thrown into another situation I had no control over. I placed my hand in his, letting him pull me to my feet.

"When I realized I could feel your emotions, it didn't take long to also recognize Kellen's," he said, sitting on the edge of the bed. "He would say what you wanted to hear, but he didn't mean it. He patronized you constantly the last two weeks."

"He did not," I argued, standing a few feet from him. "I know what it feels like to be patronized."

"Only from those people who were trying to get away from you," he said softly. "Kellen wanted to keep you with him. His method was a little different, but the result was the same. He said what you needed to hear, to keep you close."

His words hurt, no matter how true they were. I wanted to believe that Kellen and I would have more than our partnership. I didn't want to accept that he used me. I thought back to all the time I spent with him. We shared a genuine friendship, if nothing else. I couldn't believe he really wanted to kill me. Logan was convinced, but I wasn't. Wouldn't my elements have told me if they thought my life were in danger? I was certain Kellen and I would see each other again, and I'd force him to prove himself to me.

I bit my lower lip and frowned. My future was in turmoil once more, and the only certainty was the strengthening bond with the man in front of me. The security of knowing the truth from him brought more reassurance than I thought possible. My obvious desire scared me. I'd already placed my life in one man's hands, and look where it got me. Could I really do it again? Did I even have a choice? I met Logan's gaze, knowing he could feel my indecision. There was no judgement or hostility, just patience and understanding.

I closed the space between us and sat on the bed next to him. Could I get him to take me back to Vegas? Was it safe for me to go? Was it safe for me anywhere other than here with a vampire?

"Where are we?" I asked, looking around the room. "And that reminds me, I thought you couldn't use the portal."

"I cannot use it by myself," he replied, flopping back onto the mattress.

"So, you used me as a shield to get through it?"

"Do you really think I would risk you just so I could use the portal?"

I felt the twist in his words, and the realization dawned on me.

"Yes." I turned sideways on the edge of the mattress so I could see his face. "You believed they were killing me anyway. It was the quickest way to get both of us out of the palace. Whatever means you normally use to get in and out obviously takes longer. If they really did intend to kill me, you wouldn't have gotten there in time, and your life would've been forfeit as well. Taking the risk with the portal ensured we died together, or survived and escaped." It was devious, but had I been in his place, I might have done the same thing. Or not. I wasn't sure I had the courage to do it. That was something else I needed to consider. It wasn't just my life, but his as well.

He frowned and threaded one hand behind his head. "This is mine," he said, waving the other hand above him and ignoring my comment. His quick change of subject had me confused, and it took me a minute to realize he referred to the home we were in. I would play his game, for now.

"Seriously?" I asked. He really didn't strike me as the binge reading type.

"Just because I don't dress like a professor doesn't mean I can't read."

He looked away from me, but not before I caught his frown deepening. Did I offend him? Surely not.

"Have you read all of them?" I asked.

"Mostly," he replied.

"You're not pouting, are you?"

He rolled over, turning his back to me.

"Really? A sensitive vampire?" He didn't reply. What a baby. I sighed and crawled towards him. "I'm not good at playing games, Logan. They usually just piss me off."

Before I could react, he flipped over and pulled me to him. "Only because you lose," he said, his face within inches of mine. His hazel eyes delved into my own, forcing his desire and longing through me. My own yearning bubbled through my core, my heart racing with it.

"You're impossible," I hissed.

"No, it's called persistence."

His lips pressed against mine, and I melted against him. I didn't stop his hands as they inched closer to my ass, and I willingly allowed his tongue to explore mine.

Was he somehow making me want him? Was he manipulating my primal urges?

"Wait," I said breathlessly, pushing myself a few inches from him.

The green in his eyes overtook the brown as he smiled.

"What are you doing to me?" I asked.

"I thought it was fairly obvious," he replied. "Maybe I need to try something different if you haven't figured it out."

I couldn't stop the corners of my lips from rising. "That's not what I meant, and you know it." I rolled off him, putting a little space between us. "My hormones don't behave this way, ever," I said. "Are you doing some magical-vampire-thing that makes me..." I paused feeling my face flush.

"Makes you what?" He looked at me with not-so-innocent eyes and a lop-sided grin.

"I think it's pretty fricking obvious," I replied.

"Yes, it is, and no, I'm not doing anything to you to make you want this," he said. "I've never manipulated someone's emotions like that and would never do that to you."

I squinted at him, trying to detect the lie that wasn't there.

"Are you done second guessing me?" he asked, raising an eyebrow at me.

"No. Well, maybe." I took a deep breath, trying to quell the fire burning in places it shouldn't. Or maybe it should.

"You know there's an easy way to take care of that," he said.

"Yes, I know, but I'm trying not to get distracted," I replied.

"And I told you, we have plenty of time."

"But I'll forget my questions, if I don't ask them now."

He rolled his eyes and laced his fingers behind his head, stretching the lean muscles in his chest and arms. "Then let's get on with the questions."

Chapter 34

"What will Kellen do now that I'm gone?" I asked.

"I may have left a message for him," Logan replied, glancing at me.

"And what did that message say?" I asked warily.

"Kellen and I have shared a lot of information over the years. I just made sure he doesn't implicate either of us in the Magister's death." Humor danced in his eyes. "I might have even suggested that you left on a mission with his secret team of vampire hunters to locate any rogue mages."

I couldn't stop the bark of laughter that escaped my lips. "No one will ever believe that."

"They have no idea what you were doing for the last few weeks," Logan replied as he sat up. "There are also tons of stories about your grandfather's connections to his elements. It would be too easy for Kellen to suggest you have the same abilities."

I tore my gaze from his, thinking of my conversation with Niyol and Göksu. I did have that connection, and my elements had already explained why.

"What is it?" Logan asked, suddenly in my space again.

"Did your element ever speak to you?"

He gave me a strange look. "Only once. Yours?"

"All the time, but you already knew that about Niyol."

Apprehension flooded our connection. "And the other? Has it revealed its name to you?"

I nodded.

"It's my element, isn't it?" he asked, looking away from me.

"I believe so," I replied. How long had he suspected it?

"What did he say to you?" he asked, still avoiding my gaze.

"Let me ask him if I can share it," I replied.

He looked at me with hope, but I could feel his fear of rejection.

Göksu?

I'm uncertain, princess.

How can you be uncertain? You're a damn elemental, protector of the world. You aren't allowed to be uncertain.

His chuckle rumbled through me.

Is that a yes, Göksu?

When he didn't respond, I assumed it was. Logan still stared at me.

"Why are you smiling?" he asked.

"Because your damn element drives me crazy," I replied, my smile fading. "He was outraged that the Magister stole you from him. He suffered physical and mental pain from the separation."

Logan's eyes widened, and he sat completely still. "Really? I assumed he abandoned me."

"I got the impression your death ripped the two of you apart," I explained. "You guys should talk. That way, none of the questions get confused by the stupid messenger."

"You are far from stupid," Logan said, "and I would love to talk with him." He reached out and took my hand. I laced my fingers in his.

"I'll let you know when he gets over his emotional constipation."

A nervous laughter escaped his lips, and I smiled with him.

"So, what's next?" I asked.

"Training, and then we'll assume the role of vampire hunters," he replied.

"You're not serious, are you?" There was no way I was hunting vampires.

"You need training. Why wouldn't I be serious?"

"You're an ass. You know what I meant." I reached out to smack his arm, and he grabbed my wrist.

"I'm very serious," he said. "We can't allow the vampires to keep the mages they turned."

"You do realize you're a vampire, right?" I asked, instantly regretting it. Of course he knew. He didn't need me throwing it in his face.

He rubbed my palm with his thumb and released my hand. "Yes, but I was a mage first."

"And what are we doing with the mage-vampires we find?" I tucked my feet beneath me, grabbing the quilt I piled at the end of the bed. "I'm not ready to kill a bunch of people, even if they are vampires. You've jaded the legends of vampires for me."

"They aren't all like me," he replied. "Actually, most of them are exactly what you believe them to be. We'll be trying to convince as many as we can to leave the vampire council."

"Can we do that? I thought there was some kind of command, some possession thing with a vampire and its creator. Can they just leave?"

"It depends on who created them."

He looked away from me to the wall of books. I waited for him to continue as he debated what to tell me. I wrapped the blanket over my shoulders and hugged my knees. Would he be just like Kellen and reveal information bits at a time? I knew he had secrets, probably tons of them, but I didn't want to find out something relevant when it was too late. My partner did that to me so many times.

"The vampires learned the hard way that if they wanted to keep me, my creator should've been strong enough to kill me," he finally said, still staring across the room. "It was difficult for me to believe they didn't know that. It's not like our supernatural families haven't been around for centuries." His gaze drifted back to mine. "Now, only the strongest vampires are allowed to sire a mage. The only downside for them is that a sire can only effectively control so many. Their connection becomes overwhelmed, which is beneficial to us."

"I can't fight a bunch of vampires, Logan," I argued. "I can't even get away from you, and I always know you're there."

"I watched you fight off six vampires while Kellen wrestled with the Magister," he said.

"I didn't do that. Niyol did, with Kellen's fire. And what do you mean you watched? You were there?" He was there and didn't help. What the hell?

Logan laughed and edged closer to me. "You think Kellen's fire willingly allowed Niyol to consume it? And yes, I was there, but you had it well under control."

"Well, obviously I thought Kellen's fire cooperated," I replied. "I can't believe you didn't help."

"If I suddenly appeared in the Magister's room, what would you have thought?"

I didn't like the question, because I'd already thought he released her.

"Exactly." He shook his head and chuckled. "Besides, Niyol bitch-slapped that little flame and used it like a... well you get the idea." His smile faded as his gaze bore into me. "You're stronger than Kellen."

"That can't possibly be true," I said, pulling the blanket tighter around my shoulders. I'd watched Kellen fight. He knew exactly how to use his elements.

"It is true, and looking back at it now, Kellen knows it, too. He wasn't training you the way he needed. Don't get me wrong, the skills you've gained will help you, but it isn't what you need. You don't use your elements; you allow them to work with you to accomplish what you want. Most mages are taught to control the element and make it do their bidding."

"I can't see Niyol allowing that and definitely not Göksu. I think they'd both tell me to piss off."

A strange expression crossed his face. "And I think that's why they talk to you the way they do. You've made them a partner. We'll build on that relationship."

I looked down at the soft quilt covering me. Kellen had spent a great deal of time in history lessons about the mages. I didn't mind because I needed to know, and it was interesting. But now that Logan mentioned it, Kellen was trying to teach me to command my elements. I was so stupid not to see it. Göksu even told me to call him with love and compassion, and he would come. I couldn't expect him to help when I treated him as a slave under my control.

But I was still just a human. Why would the mage-vampires listen to me? And what would we do with a group of them? I looked at Logan, who continued to watch me think. His patience seemed unending.

"What will we do with the vampires who are able to reject their masters?" I asked.

He frowned and indecision rolled across his face. We weren't starting this way. He would tell me everything, or I was finding a way to leave.

"If you're not going to tell me everything, I'm done," I said. "Kellen infuriates me with his little breadcrumbs of information. I need to know what I'm getting into. I hate finding out stuff the hard way."

He sighed, resignation bleeding through our bond. "I've spent a great deal of time working with Jonathan," he began.

"Are you talking about Mr. Smith?" I asked, interrupting him. Anger swelled in my gut. He lied about not knowing Jonathan, which meant that Kellen had no idea.

"Yes." He looked away from me again, and I scowled. "Jonathan provides a place for those who have nowhere to go. I helped Kellen rescue the mages who have not been changed and took the others to Jonathan."

"How long has this been happening?" I asked, realizing the enormity of the situation. The vampires could have a vast army right now.

"I've been helping the mage-vampires for about a decade or so," he replied.

The pieces of the puzzle started clicking together. I unfolded myself and rolled off the bed, pacing across the room. "That clears up a lot," I said. "Kellen doesn't know about your association with Mr. Smith, does he?"

He shook his head. "No. Kellen didn't know I was helping the turned mages. He accepted anything I could give him about the ones who were kidnapped, but he abandoned the others."

I stared at him, and he held my gaze. I understood. Logan was one of the mages Kellen would've left behind.

"I think it would have made the rest of the mages embrace your cause, to know that their brothers and sisters were not lost to the vampires," I said. "If you're typical of the other mage-vampires, you'd be amazing allies. All the books I've read show vampires with no compassion, but you've proved me wrong."

"Weren't you listening a few minutes ago?" he argued, his dark eyebrows meeting in the middle. "Vampires don't feel compassion. They aren't going to ally with you because they share your hope for the future. They'll do it to keep their lives from being exposed to the humans. The ones who want this war will destroy or enslave humanity so they don't have to hide anymore."

"So, where does your compassion come from?" I asked, daring him to lie to me.

In a half a breath, he was standing in front of me. Red swirled in his eyes, mixing with the brown and green. "What makes you think I have any?" he asked.

I tapped his chest with my finger and smiled. "I can feel it, right here."

"Maybe you're just feeling my desire," he suggested, closing the small space between us and wrapping his arms around my waist.

"I'm pretty sure I can tell the difference," I said. "Besides you've already admitted your feelings, and I'm really liking that I know when you're lying."

His lips twitched and his eyes returned to normal. "I'm glad you no longer fear me," he whispered, pressing his body against mine.

I let him pull me closer, feeling my body respond to his obvious attraction. *I will not let myself be seduced. Not right now. I have questions, dammit.*

His left hand traced a trail up and down my spine, and his gaze drifted to my lips. I stuck my tongue out, and he smiled.

"I'm trying to refrain from being crude," he said. "But you're making it difficult."

"Haven't I always been difficult?" I countered.

"Yes."

In one smooth motion, he swept me back on the bed and hovered over me.

"Are you sure no one else knows where we are?" I asked.

"I like to keep my secrets a secret," he replied.

"But once you tell one person, it's no longer a secret," I teased, placing both hands against his chest. "And now I know."

"I guess I'll have to make sure you don't tell," he said, a smile spreading across his face. "What is the price for your silence?"

"Steak, mashed potatoes, and green beans." I laughed at his rising eyebrows. "Oh, you thought you could bribe me with sex."

"You could bribe me with sex," he said.

"I'll think about it, after steak."

Epilogue

Jack glared at the six men sucking up the space in his office. Each one had a task to complete and half of them failed. The failures avoided his gaze, finding even the most minute speck of dust interesting. The other three portrayed a careful indifference. They knew him well enough to know he wouldn't tolerate losing the fight they'd spent decades preparing for.

"Sergey," Jack's voice drew the Russian's attention. "You are my biggest disappointment. How is the Magister's whelp still alive?"

"I have no excuses," Sergey replied, not dropping his gaze but unable to hide the sliver of fear Jack detected.

Irritation at Sergey's lack of explanation bled into Jack's next question. He could make the large man talk. He wanted to make him talk, but he still needed Sergey and his army. It would do no good to unleash his anger and destroy one of his prime military leaders.

"What of you, Simon? I gave you six of your own mages to sire and bolstered your army with seventy of the council's. How did you fail to destroy the dogs?" Jack's voice rose with each word, his anger unhinging his tight control. The shifters should have been easy to eliminate, and with them, the final alliance in the North American continent.

"We were not expecting the mages and their elements," Simon glanced at Sergey with unease. "They were supposed to be dead."

Jack's lips pulled into a thin line, and his fangs pushed them apart. "Yutaka." His most faithful and trustworthy companion looked at him with wide, unwavering eyes. "How did we not know that Kellen and that little witch would be at the palace last night?"

"No one knew, master," Yutaka's soft voice answered. "I have to assume that Kellen suspected a spy and acted on that knowledge."

"How many of our mages remain in the palace?" Jack asked.

Yutaka frowned and looked away. "None, that I'm aware of. He killed all but the one who reported back to me."

"Did Kellen kill them or the witch?" Silence filled the room, and Jack's anger boiled over. He lunged across his desk, fangs in full view, claws digging into the dark wood and bloody rage in his eyes. "Where is she now?" he demanded, scanning the council members who cowered before him. A red haze clouded his vision when it settled on the blond Englishman with his irritating smirk, unfazed by his master's outburst.

"I will find her," the Englishman stated. "Unlike the others, I will not fail."

Jack snarled at the man's casual posture. "Don't make promises you cannot keep, Braden."

"Have I ever failed you, Jack?" he asked, brushing his blond hair off his forehead and draping his arm over the back of his chair.

"No, but neither has Yutaka, and here we are." He dropped back into his chair and rolled his shoulders, retracting his claws and breathing deeply. "If we do not kill her, she will be the reason we fail. We've already had this discussion. She cannot be allowed to unite the others."

"The only place for her to hide is with that filthy half-breed," the large Brazilian growled. "Let me take my army into his lair and kill them all."

Jack agreed with his enthusiasm, but shook his head. "I need you to continue building our army, Ernesto. Braden is an irritating ass, but he has always come through for us. Maybe I should've given him the task from the beginning." He leveled his gaze at Sergey, and the man flinched. Did the Russian betray them all? Surely not. He was a formidable leader of a difficult clan. Sergey had never backed away from his responsibility even when the humans in his territory waged war against each other.

"We'll reconvene in a month," Jack said. "Our timetable has not changed. Within six months, we will reveal our armies and annihilate all who oppose us. We are done hiding in the shadows. We will rule the lesser species or they will die."

Thank you for reading *Magister's Bane*, the first book in *Call of the Elements* series. You can continue the series with *Vampire's Crucible*.

Please leave a review on Amazon or Goodreads.com. Reviews are very important for both readers and authors.

Feel free to contact me on Facebook.com, Twitter @YvetteBostic or my website (www.yvettebostic.com), where I post updates for new releases, along with non-essential information about my books.

Join my newsletter to receive fantastic opportunities for free books and prizes. Go to my website and wait for the lovely popup asking you to join.

Made in United States
Orlando, FL
09 July 2022

19570886R10200